THE FIRST LIGHT
OF DAWN

PRAISE FOR THE FIRST LIGHT
OF DAWN

"Like a bracing wind of morning, *The First Light of Dawn* slaps you awake and widens your eyes. Jefferson Glass's debut of the Conor Armenta mystery series is truly something to look forward to any time of day."

— CRAIG JOHNSON, *NEW YORK TIMES*
BESTSELLING AUTHOR OF THE WALT LONGMIRE
MYSTERIES

"The First Light of Dawn is Sheriff Conor Armenta's debut, and a beguiling one it is. Glass has a talent for crisp and well-rounded characters."

— W. MICHAEL GEAR, *NEW YORK TIMES*
BESTSELLING AUTHOR

"...offers enough red herrings to intrigue mystery aficionados and enough plausible plot twists to keep the reader turning pages."

— PRESTON LEWIS, SPUR AWARD-WINNING
AUTHOR

"Glass's Conor Armenta novel is an action-packed thriller with memorable characters that rival any of those featured in the works of Johnson, Box or Hillerman. Exceptional writing and unforgettable plot twists."

THE FIRST LIGHT OF DAWN

A CONOR ARMENTA MYSTERY
BOOK ONE

JEFFERSON GLASS

WOLFPACK
PUBLISHING
— EST 2013 —

The First Light of Dawn
Paperback Edition
Copyright © 2024 (As Revised) Jefferson Glass

Wolfpack Publishing
1707 E. Diana Street
Tampa, FL 33610

wolfpackpublishing.com

Paperback ISBN 978-1-63977-543-9
eBook ISBN 978-1-63977-542-2
LCCN 2024941622

To my loving wife, Debbie.
Without her encouragement, intuition, and inspiration this novel
would not have come to fruition.

THE FIRST LIGHT OF DAWN

1

WEDNESDAY, APRIL 2, 1930

Sheriff Conor Armenta stared through the dusty windshield at the distant lights of Las Vegas. In daylight, the town of 4,500 looked like a tiny green dot in the center of an expansive desert with a single railroad line that disappeared in the distance to both left and right. At night, it might be mistaken for a sprawling oasis. The stale air in the truck's cab did not diminish his drowsiness. The dusty road deterred fully opening the windows to allow in the cool night air.

Someone had shot a half-dozen sheep on Luis Garza's ranch southeast of town. It took a few days for the owner to get word to the sheriff from the remote locale. Being an old family friend, Conor chose to investigate the incident personally. As he mulled over the details of his day, the roar of an Auburn Speedster racing past his door jolted the startled sheriff alert. Not quick enough to identify the tag, the taillight disappeared into a cloud of dust in the desert night.

In a reflex reaction, he mashed down hard on the accelerator of his pickup, then backed off almost immediately, abandoning the notion of pursuit.

"No point trying to catch him," he grumbled to himself. "I couldn't keep up from an even start, let alone make up for the head of steam he has built."

As he redirected his train of thought, he muttered, "Where in the hell did he come from anyway? And what's his damned hurry?"

"Bootleggers," he replied to his own one-sided conversation. Ten years of prohibition had done little to defeat the sale of liquor. The car's top had been up, completely concealing the identity of the driver.

Con continued straight home. He had no desire to get sucked into some longwinded conversation at the office with a nightshift deputy trying to kill time on a slow weeknight. The clock on the mantel chimed two o'clock as he walked in the door. He left the back door open and slid up a window in the hot, stuffy house before he collapsed into his favorite chair. He picked up the telephone and called the office.

"Clark County Sheriff's Department," a pleasant female voice answered.

"Evening, Dottie. Anything going on?"

"All is pretty quiet, Sheriff."

"Okay. I'm at home. Oh, and let the boys know to keep a lookout for a light-colored Auburn Speedster with dark fenders. I think Nevada tags, but not for sure. Bootleggers, maybe."

"Will do, Sheriff."

"Good night, Dottie."

"Good night, Sheriff."

A slight breeze entered the back door as Con dragged himself from his chair and into the bedroom. He didn't remember lying down.

* * *

THURSDAY, APRIL 3, 1930

The ringing telephone woke him what seemed like only moments later, but the sun peeking into his bedroom suggested at least a few hours had passed. The early morning air refreshed the house as he made his way to the living room.

"Con," he answered.

"Sorry to wake you, Sheriff," Dottie replied. "I think you need to come in right away. It looks like we have a suicide outside of town."

"Anyone we know?"

"Brice Campbell."

"What? I'll be right in! Is Jesse there?"

"He just walked in."

"Send him out there and tell him to wait at the gate. I don't want anything disturbed. And call Hal!"

Con quickly washed his face and put on a clean uniform shirt. He grabbed his jacket and holstered 1911 Colt on his way out the back door. Minutes later he walked into the sheriff's office while strapping the belt around his waist. The smell of fresh coffee filled Con's nostrils and activated his taste buds.

Dottie handed him a steaming cup. "Leanora Campbell called about twenty minutes ago. She seemed relatively calm. She said Brice had been in his study when she went to bed last night and had not been to bed when she awakened this morning. She woke with the gardener pounding the front door, yelling Brice had shot and killed himself in the garden."

"Did she go to the garden?"

"The gardener assured her Brice was dead and she didn't want to look."

"Did she hear the shot?"

"No."

"Hal?"

"He said he'd be there shortly."

Con gulped down the scalding coffee as he headed for the door. "Write it all down."

"I already did."

"Good girl," Con answered as the door closed behind him.

As he drove to the Campbell hacienda, Con ran through his mind what he knew of Brice Campbell. He owned the largest construction company in the county and had made millions building roads and leveling drilling locations for the oilfields at Circle Cliffs in Utah. When the frenzy subsided there a decade ago, he spent another year preparing locations for oil tank batteries, pipelines, and pumping stations. Since coming to Las Vegas, Campbell's Fremont Construction Company had grown large enough to participate in the Boulder Dam project, but Campbell did not have the capacity or engineering background needed to manage an endeavor of its size. Con pondered why a man like Campbell would commit suicide in his garden at the first light of dawn? It was almost too cliché.

On the right-hand side of the road ahead stood the gate into the Wagner estate, a small rancho of one hundred acres or so, Con recalled. The Wagner Trucking Company had also done well at Circle Cliffs. He had heard the Campbells moved their company here at Gary Wagner's suggestion after business slowed down in Utah. Sheriff Armenta didn't move in the same circles as these wealthy families, but he knew who they were and heard gossip of their business dealings. They lived in a small town in a sparsely populated county. It was important to understand the background of its residents.

As he passed the Wagners' wooden gate, fresh tire tracks down the driveway caught Con's attention. Gary Wagner had died in some sort of accident in Europe several years ago. Strangely, his widow, Katherine Wagner disappeared without a trace six months ago. No one had lived there since.

* * *

Calmness in the air belied the foreboding circumstances of the morning. When the sheriff entered the garden, a hint of deer scent hung in the air. He thought it odd the musky odor should linger. It was usually not overly prevalent except during the rut. And dust…why would the smell remain on the air in the damp garden? The roses were just beginning their blooming cycle, but their smell was remarkably masked by other aromas.

"…if that's alright with you, Con?" brought the sheriff from his reverie as he squatted on his haunches near the body.

"Sure. Uh, just a minute. What did you say?"

"Is it alright to take the…corpse to town now?" Dr. Martin replied.

At scarcely seven o'clock, the sun already warmed the desert floor. Another scorcher, he surmised. Sheriff Conor Armenta looked back at the body of Brice Campbell. He lifted the blanket the elderly coroner had placed over it—tall, athletic, and handsome, graying hair at his temples only added to his distinguished looks.

The scents of sagebrush and dust emanated from Campbell's clothing. Where could he have been so recently before the fatal end to the night? The man lay face down, headed away from the residence. He wore khaki trousers and a coat. His body lay twisted. While his left leg rested nearly straight, his right leg bent at the hip. The knee held his right hip up slightly off the path where he fell. His left arm also bent at the elbow, hiding the hand beneath his torso. His right arm stretched almost fully extended at an upward angle and away. His head turned to the right. Had his eyes been open, it almost looked as though he reached for the pistol laying less than a foot from his right hand.

The bullet had penetrated his right temple precisely in the center. Little blood shown around the injury. Had it not been for the surrounding powder burn, it could have been a simple puncture wound. The pool of drying blood on the path beneath his head suggested the most likely cause of death.

"Help me turn him over, Hal. You got pictures of all this?"

"Yep, two rolls of film."

"Roll him over easy. I don't want to miss anything."

Brice Campbell's face appeared serene. No grimace of pain, no anguish, no sorrow, no regret. If not for the immense exit wound on the left side of his head, it could have been the face of someone who died peacefully in his sleep. Coagulated blood, however, glued small round pebbles from the pathway to Campbell's face, coat, and pale blue shirt. A scrape on the palm of Campbell's left hand, other small lacerations, and the swollen knuckles and fingers were recent, but not from the stones of the path where he lay. Neither had the tear in the right knee of his trousers nor the scuff on the round toe of his right boot happened here. He had fallen somewhere else, earlier. His boots were black and highly polished beneath a heavy coating of dust. There were other remnants of dust on his clothing.

His wallet rode in an inside pocket of his coat. It contained seventy-seven dollars in cash, his identification, a photograph of his wife Leanora, and a laundry receipt from Service Cleaners dated March twenty-seventh. Sheriff Armenta placed the wallet in the pocket of his own denim jacket.

Con stood and turned to the coroner. "Grab your stretcher, Hal. I'll help you load him into your car."

As the coroner walked to his sedan delivery, Con carefully picked up the pistol with his bandanna. A fiveshot Smith & Wesson revolver, .32 caliber. Odd a man of Brice Campbell's stature would carry what most men considered a lady's gun. The small pearl grips would barely fit two of his own fingers. One shot fired, one empty chamber, and three loaded cartridges remaining. The gun showed wear, but was clean and in good condition. As Hal returned with the stretcher, the sheriff carefully tied the pistol up in his bandanna and placed the bundle in his other jacket pocket.

With experienced hands from unwanted practice, the two men picked the body up by the blanket in one quick movement, placing it on the stretcher. Deputy Jesse Slater appeared from the front of the house just as Con and Hal slid the stretcher into the back of Hal's delivery.

"Fine time for the youngster to show up," the old coroner prodded. "Right when the heavy work is done."

"Sheriff Armenta told me to question Mrs. Campbell. Just doin' my job, Dr. Martin," Jesse replied with a grin.

He turned to Con and said more seriously, "Not much to add beyond what Mrs. Campbell already told Dottie. Her daughter, Amelia, arrived from town a little while ago. I told them you'd be in to see them when you finished out here."

Con nodded. "Is Lorenzo Montoya still their gardener?"

"That's the name she gave me," Jesse answered after checking his notes. "He lives in a room above the garage."

"You can go on back to town," Con told him. "If Dottie is waiting to talk to me, tell her to go home and get some sleep. I'll see her when she comes on shift this evening, if I need to."

"Got it," Jesse answered as he started toward his car.

Hal had secured the corpse in the back of his car and prepared to leave. "Anything else, Con?"

"Get the film developed and do a preliminary on the body. Call in another doctor to assist if there's anything out of the ordinary. Anything," he repeated.

Con watched the coroner's delivery and his deputy's sedan turn onto the county road and disappear over the first rise. He turned to survey the surroundings. The grounds were immaculate. The recently built Spanish-style home had all the character of those constructed over a century ago, but with luxurious extras. In addition to the central courtyard, the Campbells had added a second adobe and stucco wall, which enclosed several acres of pristine gardens with a variety of both imported and regional flora. Leaving the garden by the house, Con soon spotted Lorenzo raking the ground beneath a smoke tree. They had known each other from school days, when Lorenzo and Con's younger brother Patrick had been good friends. They still were, though life's paths had led them further apart.

"*Buenos días,* my friend," Con greeted, mocking their common Hispanic ancestry in a slightly elevated voice to catch Lorenzo's attention.

"*Si, buenos días,* Sheriff," Lorenzo replied in kind. "How is my compadre Patrick's big brother today?"

"Oh, pretty good, Lorenzo. The county has grown too fast

with this Boulder Dam project firing up. A lot of new faces. Good folks come in to look for work, hundreds, maybe thousands of them, and bad ones follow them to steal their money, if any of them have any. Politicians are afraid to step on some racketeer's toes for fear of losing votes, or possibly worse, depending on who they're dealing with. But I'll manage." He paused. "How about you?"

"Mrs. Campbell is a nice lady." Lorenzo's face gave away no expression. "I think I'll be okay for a while, too."

"What happened?" Con asked.

"I go to bed early every day. Everything is very quiet out here in the desert, so I leave my windows open to enjoy the fresh evening air." He waited.

"And?" Con nudged.

"When it's hot I get up about 1 or 2 o'clock and water until just before dawn. Then I go back for a nap before I start my day."

"Today?"

"Yes. When I went back in my room, I closed the windows to keep the cool air inside. Just after I laid down, I heard *Pop*. Not loud. Like a firecracker in the distance. It was just getting light out. I thought maybe someone had a flat tire out on the road or something. It didn't bother me, and I went to sleep."

"When did you find Mr. Campbell?"

"An hour or so later, I got up, made some coffee, and went to work. When I walked around the house, I scared a deer eating the roses. They know I shoot them with my BB-gun. It ran away and jumped the back wall. That's pretty high, you know!" he said with a mock look of astonishment on his face.

"Uh-huh."

"When the deer ran, it scared a crow up from the path. That's *curioso*, you know, peculiar, I thought." He hesitated.

"So I looked closer and saw someone lying in the path. When I got near enough, I saw it was Mr. Campbell, and the blood in the gravel. I thought, how did he fall and hit his head? Then I saw the pistol, and the hole. I didn't want to, but I knelt down and felt his neck. It was pretty cold, and there wasn't a pulse." Lorenzo turned pale, remembering the ghastly scene. "Then I ran around to the front door and banged the big clapper and yelled until Mrs. Campbell came to the door. When I told her what I saw, she started to run to the garden. I grabbed her and held her tight. I told her not to look. She only had on her nightgown." Lorenzo blushed through his swarthy complexion when telling he had wrapped his arms around his sparsely clad *matrón*.

Con waited, allowing Lorenzo to regain his composure. "Is there another way into this garden?"

"Yes. The door to the kitchen is right over there," he pointed, "and there is a side gate and a back gate through the wall. Through the back gate is a stable where they kept some horses when their daughter still lived at home. Not since I came here."

"I'm going to look around a little. Then I'll go talk to Mrs. Campbell. Let me know if you think of anything else." Obviously shaken by the whole affair, Lorenzo forced a smile and nodded.

Con returned to the rose garden. He found where the deer had grazed on rose blossoms and bolted from the scene when Lorenzo approached. *That explains the scent*, he thought. There were other tracks on the damp ground, Lorenzo's from his early morning watering. He could not imagine Lorenzo Montoya as a suspect. A scrapper with his fists maybe, if defending a friend or loved one, but not a murderer. *Why am I so suspicious?* Con thought. *All the evidence so far points to an obvious suicide. I could tie up a few loose ends, maybe find a note in the victim's study, case closed. Then go figure out who shot Luis Garza's sheep.*

From the spot Brice Campbell's body had fallen in the garden, Con scanned the scene, following a branch of the path with his gaze to the side gate. The loose pea-gravel of the path made it impossible to distinguish any tracks. Con worked his way toward the gate, sweeping the area with a keen eye for any sign of a clue. When he reached the gate, he found it latched. And locked with a padlock from the inside. He had already lifted the lock to inspect the keyhole, when he realized he may have just smudged a critical fingerprint. "Rookie!" he said aloud, then quickly looked to see if Lorenzo had heard him. Lorenzo continued to toil with the same small patch of dirt he had been raking for half an hour. It seemed he was puttering in the garden today more as a distraction than a necessity.

Recovering his composure, Con carefully examined the lock. Other than a slight coating of surface rust, it seemed relatively new. On closer examination, the surface rust had the smallest of scrapes at the edge of the keyhole. Someone had opened the lock—or at least inserted a key into it—recently. Last night, or this morning? Maybe, but Con had just about eliminated the possibility of lifting a usable fingerprint from the lock. And in any case, it may have been Lorenzo, going about his meticulous care of the grounds. Lorenzo must have a key, but Con did not want to draw attention to the gate at this point in his investigation.

He returned to where Campbell had been found. One last look around. Flies were already buzzing around the remnants of blood on the path. To spare Lorenzo any more trauma, Con grabbed the nearby garden hose and washed away the last of the blood into the pebbles. Just as he turned to return the hose, something glimmered in the sunlight. A wedding band. Right where Brice Campbell's left hand had been beneath his body. How could the ring have possibly fallen from his finger? Con kneeled, staring momentarily. It couldn't have. He wondered how this piece would fit into the jigsaw puzzle. He pulled Campbell's wallet from his pocket. Carefully, he picked up the ring on his pencil and placed it among the bills in the wallet.

Con stood and returned the wallet to his jacket. He turned and walked to his truck where he gathered a well-worn tally book from the glove box and deposited the pistol in the bandanna and wallet in its place. He pulled off his jacket and laid it on the seat, then stood momentarily by the truck. From habit, he removed his Stetson, wiped the sweat from his brow onto the sleeve of his shirt, and glanced at the sun. With hat in hand, he turned and strode to the front door.

2

THURSDAY, APRIL 3, 1930

Amelia Westcott answered the door almost before Con finished knocking, as if she had been standing there with her hand on the knob. Even with reddened eyes, he thought her an attractive woman. Tall and athletic like her father. While family responsibilities had cultivated Con through his adolescence, Amelia Campbell had attended a sophisticated school for young ladies in New England. The experience had left her well-educated, aggressive, self-important, and prejudiced. Soon after returning from her studies, she married Robert Westcott, a bright and promising young attorney from Los Angeles who had set up shop in Las Vegas. Amelia wore her long chestnut hair pulled back in a loose ponytail. Dressed casually in a fashionable riding skirt and simple blouse, her slight smile seemed strained.

"Come in, Sheriff," she quietly invited as she waved him in the door. "Mother is in the sitting room."

"I'm sorry to bother you, ma'am," Con replied as he entered.

"Understood," she responded briskly as she showed the sheriff into a room just off the foyer. The cool, airy room felt pleasant and not overbearing.

"Mother," she said, "this is Sheriff Armenta."

Leanora Campbell was strikingly beautiful, Con thought. At fifty-eight she carried an aura of sophistication and poise about her. He had never seen her this close in person. She and Brice must have made a stunning couple.

Mrs. Campbell rose to greet him and offered her hand. She wore a conservative sundress, and Con noticed a mild flowery perfume about her when he accepted the firm, yet gentle handshake.

"Good morning, Sheriff," she welcomed, though her face remained somber. "Please, sit down." She motioned to a comfortable-looking brown leather chair. "Would you like some coffee?"

"If it's no trouble."

"None at all," Mrs. Westcott answered for her mother and left the room.

"I hope not to repeat too many questions Deputy Slater asked earlier," Con began.

"Please go ahead, Sheriff."

"Thank you, ma'am. Can you tell me, has Mr. Campbell seemed troubled or depressed recently?"

"Not that I have noticed. He is"—she paused, swallowing the lump in her throat—"*was* a very busy businessman." She took a deep breath to compose herself. "Some business trans-action or another always troubled him. The progress on a construction project or finding materials for it, you know," she remarked as if he would, in fact, know. "It was his nature. He worried over details." She paused in thought for a moment. "I cannot recall anything particularly unusual."

"No sign of being melancholy or morose?"

"None I am aware of," she answered as her daughter reentered the room carrying a tray that contained a sterling silver coffee service and one China cup and saucer.

Setting the tray on the coffee table, Amelia filled the cup and offered it to Con. "Cream or sugar, Sheriff?" she asked.

"No, just black, thank you."

Con took a long sip of the hot coffee. His stomach growled. He hadn't eaten since lunch yesterday. He looked guiltily at his hostesses and hoped they hadn't heard it. If they had, they ignored it. Con placed the half-empty cup and saucer on the tray and returned his attention to the ladies and his tally book.

"Have there been any financial or marital difficulties?"

"Sheriff!" Amelia Westcott blurted out. "That is uncalled for!"

"It is alright, Amelia," Mrs. Campbell interrupted calmly. "I understand."

"I am sorry, ma'am."

"No need to apologize for doing your job, Sheriff. Brice and I have been married forty-one years. Like any other couple, we have had our differences and occasionally some pretty heated…discussions."

Con watched this lovely woman as she obviously recalled some past occasion. Her pleasant expression showed no sign of regret.

"Please excuse my digression, Sheriff," she muttered as she returned her attention. "Brice and I have not significantly disagreed on anything I can recall for quite some time." She hesitated a moment, thinking. "Months anyway, perhaps over a year."

"How about money issues? Finances? Is the construction company solvent?" he queried.

"I certainly believe so," she answered. "I have really not dealt in the operation of the business in recent years. I worked in the office for a long time, but it was several years ago. You will have to ask Mr. Goldstein those kinds of questions. He is in the office downtown. I do know Brice recently ordered quite a lot of new equipment for contracts with the dam. I am sure Mr. Goldstein will have the details."

"Thank you," Con replied. "You told Deputy Slater Mr. Campbell was working in his study when you went to bed last night."

"Yes, that is correct."

"Do you recall what time?"

"Oh, early. Nine o'clock, or perhaps nine thirty."

"And Mr. Campbell did not retire soon afterward?"

"No," she answered simply.

"Is that typical for Mr. Campbell?"

"Brice often worked very late in his study."

Her answers were getting shorter and less conversational. Changing the subject, Con asked, "Did Mr. Campbell own a revolver? A .32 caliber Smith & Wesson?"

"Yes, his *pocket pistol* he called it. Well, actually, it is mine. Brice bought it for me for self-defense when we lived in a construction camp in Utah. We lived in a shack in the middle of a wild and booming oil field. There were roughnecks from all over the country and many had dubious reputations. There certainly was no law around. Brice worked all hours of the day and night. He hated me being alone in the shack. Especially at night. He taught me how to shoot it and told me to keep it close at hand. I never felt threatened by any of the men there, but Brice felt better knowing I had it."

Suddenly, she quit talking and her face turned ghostly pale. Con thought she might faint and started to rise. Leanora Campbell looked straight into the sheriff's eyes. "That's the gun, isn't it." She momentarily lost her perfect diction, perhaps slipping back in time along with her recollections. The statement was a statement. Just that. Not a question.

Her stare never left Con's eyes. He tried to look away, but he couldn't. "Yes," he finally agreed as consolingly as possible.

Her gaze lasted a second longer. It felt like an hour to Con. Then she looked down at the hands in her lap.

"A few years ago," she continued calmly and quietly, "Brice discovered a foreman in our company had been stealing materials from us and selling them to a competitor. Brice thought the man, a ruffian and a big man, might be dangerous. And some of his subordinates may have been accomplices. Brice was no coward, but he stopped at home and retrieved the little pistol. He placed it in the pocket of his trousers. His suit coat covered the slight bulge. Then he drove to the jobsite, confronted the man, and fired him. The story I was told, while he escorted the man from the site, an obvious conspirator challenged them. Brice told him he could join his partner, but the cohort kept advancing. The foreman had not moved, but Brice sidestepped anyway and reached his hand into the pocket. The accomplice could see the bulge of the pistol and froze. The duo then left the property. Brice carried the little gun with him for a while afterward. Eventually it ended up in his desk drawer in the study."

Her gaze never left her lap as she sat entranced in thought, toying with the rings on her left hand.

"Would you like more coffee?" Amelia Westcott broke the silence somewhat hoarsely.

"No, thank you," Con replied. "May I see the study?"

"Of course, Sheriff," Leanora Campbell answered in the same subdued yet steady voice. "You can show him, Amelia."

Sheriff Conor Armenta recovered his Stetson from the floor by his chair and stood. With hat in hand, he stepped toward Leanora Campbell, still seated a few feet away. "Thank you very much, Mrs. Campbell," he said softly. "I know this is difficult for you. I am very sorry for your loss."

She looked up at him with a faint smile. Tears were again welling up in her eyes. The quiver of her lower lip gave her answer.

Con turned and followed Amelia Westcott across the foyer to the study. She held the door for him as he entered, then closed it behind them. Her mother may tolerate the coarse nature of this disrespectful sheriff, but she was not afraid of any man and could put him in his place.

"Sheriff Armenta," she began in a firm, steady tone. "This is an extremely emotional time for us. We have just lost from our lives a father and husband in a most tragic way. A wonderful and compassionate man. You can plainly see how distraught my mother is, yet you strive to deepen her wounds with your inappropriate questions." Her volume gradually increased to a crescendo as she lost her cordiality. "I should ask you to finish your *investigation*," she hissed the word emphatically, "as quickly as possible and not return!"

"Well then," Con replied in a calm yet firm manner, "perhaps you can assist me in allowing this procedure to continue as quickly and painlessly as possible."

She crossed her arms and glared.

"May I?" Con motioned toward Brice Campbell's desk.

"Please do!" she snapped.

As he gradually rounded the desk, Con's careful eye methodically scanned the room. A comfortable-looking, well-upholstered chair sat behind the large ornate desk. The study smelled slightly of pipe tobacco, but not smoke. Con guessed the humidor on the sideboard as the source of the aroma. Three crystal decanters with varied levels of amber liquid occupied a tray near the humidor. Prohibition had little effect on the wealthy, Con mused. The desk was cleared. A small inkwell sat beside a decorative stand holding two pens. A late-model telephone sat to the right of the desk pad. A desk lamp loomed over the pad, as might be expected for someone who worked there late into the night. Only a pencil laying haphazardly on the desk pad and a business card tucked beneath one corner showed any sign of the desk being recently used.

"Has anyone been in here today?" Con asked.

"No one I am aware of," Amelia answered in a much more cordial tenor than earlier.

"Did your father smoke?" he asked.

"Yes," she answered, thinking the question a bit odd. "But never in the house. Mother does not allow it."

"So, if your father wanted to have a smoke while working, he would take a break and step outside."

"Yes," she replied again, puzzled by his line of questioning.

"Perhaps, stroll around the rose garden while enjoying his smoke, if there were ample light from the moon?"

"Yes, of course." Now she began connecting the dots, yet she thought his presumption shallow.

"May I look in the desk?" Con asked.

"Certainly, Sheriff," The ice in her voice had melted slightly.

Laying his hat on the corner of the desk, Con sat down in the large chair, and for a split-second, thought of the small, hard oak chair in his own office. A small doily sat to the left of the desk pad. Probably to sit a crystal glass of bourbon or scotch on, he thought to himself. Con picked it up and used it to open the center drawer. Nothing unusual—a brand-new notepad, a well-used ink blotter, two more pencils, and an eraser. The top right drawer held a Las Vegas telephone book and business directory. The larger drawer below held business directories from Los Angeles and Salt Lake City.

Con moved his attention to the left side of the desk. The top drawer contained only a box of .32 caliber cartridges. Con picked up the box. About half full, he guessed, judging by the weight. A dark wear-mark in the bottom of the drawer likely signified the usual residence of the little pistol. He found the bottom drawer empty. Brice Campbell's study mystified him. This man reportedly spent many late-nights working at this desk. If it weren't for the pistol drawer and the ink blotter, it would look as if no one had ever used this desk. Especially not last night.

Con placed the doily back in the proximity of where he found it. He pulled his tally book from his pocket. Picking up the pencil from the desk pad, he wrote down the name and telephone number from the business card. Capital Equipment Company—Salt Lake City, Utah—R.C. Doyle: General Manager.

Con rose to his feet. "May I see the garage?"

The question surprised Amelia. "Well, yes."

When Mrs. Westcott opened the door, her mother stood at the entry to the sitting room. Mostly recomposed, she offered a slight smile when Con appeared.

"I apologize for the intrusion, ma'am. Again, thank you," Con said pleasantly.

"You are welcome, Sheriff." She forced a larger smile.

Con donned his Stetson as they left the house, and Amelia

Westcott escorted him to the garage. She unlatched the large wooden doors of the first stall and swung them open. The hinges groaned loudly at the intrusion. "This is father's car," Amelia commented as Con evaluated the nearly new light blue LaSalle sedan in front of them. Even with a light coating of dust from the gravel road from town and darkness in the garage, it was a beautiful automobile. The smell of oil, grease, or gasoline did not exist in this garage. Only the slight fragrance of car wax.

On the front passenger seat of the LaSalle sat a brown leather briefcase.

"May I?" Con asked, indicating the briefcase.

"Yes, of course."

Con picked up a soft rag from the adjacent workbench and opened the door. The case contained only one folder. Inside were a dozen receipts for various machinery parts. Nothing outstanding, he thought as he replaced them. Closing the door, Con peered at the car in the next stall. A Buick touring car a few years old, with the top down.

"Mother's car," Amelia stated. "She doesn't drive much, but likes the fresh air when she does."

The spotless car had obviously been washed since the last time it had been to town, Con observed. He helped Amelia close the heavy, noisy doors on the garage. He doubted anyone could open or close them in the night without waking Lorenzo in his room above. As they walked toward Con's pickup truck, he could not help but notice Amelia Westcott's flashy red Buick roadster parked in the driveway. The Whiskey Six, bootleggers dubbed the model. The big engine made it a favorite of smugglers for its ample horsepower to outrun most law enforcement.

"Thank you for your cooperation, Mrs. Westcott," Con

offered when they reached his pickup. "I'm sorry to have burdened you and your mother."

"I hope we have answered your questions satisfactorily for your report, Sheriff," she said, presenting her hand to his surprise.

"Thank you, again," he replied, accepting the exceptionally firm handshake. He turned and climbed in.

"You're an old tin-can compared to the machinery around this place," Con said aloud to his pickup truck as he fired it up.

* * *

The Campbell hacienda sat about center of a section of desert they owned there. Brice had planned to start a small ranch where he hoped to raise a few cattle in his leisure. The occasion never materialized, and it remained unfenced except for a paddock beside the stable. Just over the first hill of the driveway, Con steered his pickup to the side of the road. Gathering a pair of field glasses from under the seat, he left the truck out of view from the house. He skirted the hill and worked his way back into a position to look things over. With the sun behind him so as not to reveal his position by a reflection from the lenses of his field glasses, Con carefully scanned the estate. From his location, he could just see over the outer wall. To his right lay a low, dry wash running toward the hacienda near the side gate. The route should assure him access without detection. Con began to maneuver his way toward the gate.

Twenty minutes later, he stood outside the wall of the hacienda. As he suspected, there were fresh footprints outside the gate. Two sets. The set going toward the gate covered those coming from it. Both the same, and as he recalled, similar to the boots Brice Campbell had on when he died. Questions piled up faster than Con could answer them. Where had Brice Campbell gone to smoke his pipe last night? Taking care not to expose himself from the house, Con followed the tracks. Thirty yards out, the trails split. He followed the outbound tracks. Eighty yards further, he looked back and could clearly see the windows of the house over the wall. He hit the dirt. Keeping his head below the level of the brush, he crawled to lower ground at his left. Able to again stand without being seen, he circled around a low hill and headed back to his right, scouting for tracks.

He found them, but they were headed toward the hacienda. He backtracked them, and twenty yards later, the two sets of tracks crossed. Con paused for a minute to scan the countryside. He saw nothing but desert near and far. He removed his hat, mopped his brow with his sleeve, looked up at the sun, and followed the outbound set of tracks.

The tracks had crossed once more by the time Con topped a low hill a quarter-mile away. He estimated to be a half mile from the Campbell's hacienda as the crow flies. Another quarter-mile ahead lay another house. Not as elaborate as the Campbell estate, but no sheepherder's shack. The low stucco house sprawled under its red tile roof. No courtyard. No yard at all Con could see through the field glasses. "Wait a minute," he whispered to himself. "I haven't seen you from this side before, but I'll bet a Washington you're the Wagner's place. Gary Wagner named it the Muleskinner's Rest." Con continued to scan the landscape. Nothing. "Nobody's lived here for months."

He again removed his hat and performed the little ritual without realizing it. *Must be noon* he thought to himself, as he looked at the sun. His stomach growled. He hadn't eaten in twenty-four hours and had only had the two cups of coffee to drink today. The sun baked the desert floor, and the rocks and pebbles absorbed the heat to completely eclipse a man in its snare. He turned and walked in the approximate direction of his pickup. He needed to have some food and time to think.

Conor Armenta only missed his estimation by a hundred yards of where his pickup should have been parked. When he topped the little knoll, bringing it into view, a bright red Buick roadster sat at its rear bumper. He did not have to search for the driver. Amelia Westcott leaned casually against the spare tire mounted in the left front fender well. She looked directly at him from beneath her floppy straw hat as if she expected him to appear at this precise instant from the very direction he came.

Not missing a step, Con continued on a straight line toward the two vehicles.

"Are you lost, Sheriff?" Amelia Westcott asked sarcastically as he came nearer.

"No," he answered with a grin and a chuckle. "I thought I saw a lobo crossing the road. I wanted to be sure before I told the government hunter about it. He gave me a long walk before I could get a good enough look with my field glasses. Just a big coyote."

"Well," she replied skeptically, "I surely would not want to have some tenderfoot dying of heat stroke so close to my parents' home." She kept her gaze on the sheriff and made no move to leave.

"Not me, ma'am. My Irish mother gave birth to me in a sheep camp not far from here, while my Mexican father hunted the lobo who killed four of their flock the night before. I know this country pretty well."

"Oh, I know your family history fairly well also, Sheriff

Armenta," she retorted as she climbed into the roadster. "The newspaper reported it in your bid for election. Pretty good run for a second-generation sheepherder turned deputy."

Con could feel her appraisal and attitude. Amelia Westcott considered people of his race and background incapable of positions above servitude. The newspaper had lavishly boasted Con's birth in the Las Vegas valley, a rarity since most residents had arrived after the railroad ten years later. He had gone to work in the gypsum mines at an early age. They quickly recognized his natural leadership skills and promoted him to foreman. When laid off three years ago, he became a well-liked deputy sheriff. A year later, the aged Sheriff Baker suffered a stroke and Con was appointed interim sheriff until a special election could be held, which, to Amelia's disgust, he won by a landslide.

"*Buenos días, Señora*," Con bade her farewell with a wry grin as he tipped his hat.

She had already started the engine. "Good day to you, too, Sheriff." Slamming the car into gear, she raced around Con's pickup in a cloud of dust.

"Well, Conor," he said to himself as he waited for the dust to drift away in the slightest bit of a breeze. "I believe you may have lost that round."

3

THURSDAY, APRIL 3, 1930

C limbing behind the wheel, he wished he had brought water with him. As he lay the field glasses atop his jacket on the seat beside him, a glint of red cloth protruding from the glove box caught his attention. His bandanna. He opened the glove box and examined the contents. The pistol in the bandanna was where he had placed them. Under them still lay the wallet. He breathed a small sigh of relief, but Amelia Westcott had, at the very least, opened his glove box. At most, she may have tampered with evidence, but why? Well, she certainly didn't trust him. He supposed that might be fair, since he didn't trust her either.

Conor Armenta had difficulty comprehending people like Amelia Campbell Westcott, who had not grown up in the environs of Las Vegas. Before the railroad came, there were only a handful of ranchers sprinkled around the random springs in a thirty-mile radius, with the Stewart ranch at the Big Spring in the middle of it. Mineral deposits brought prospectors, but most of their efforts centered much further away. When the railroad came through, they needed a large supply of clean water to fill their steam-powered locomotives. They subsequently purchased the Stewart ranch and thus secured the largest source of the precious commodity within a hundred miles.

Those who could endure the environment and the rolling tide of prosperity in the new town that sprung up, were of many nationalities and backgrounds. Italians and Hispanics made up a large percentage of the populace. A sprinkling of Native Americans, Asians, and African Americans added to the mix. His mother's Irish family was a rarity. They all worked hard, learned to adapt, and depended on those who were worthy, regardless of ethnicity, or else moved on in search of another rainbow.

Starting the engine, Con continued down the road at a leisurely pace. He slowed as he neared the drive into the Wagner place. Rolling to a stop across the road, he eyed the padlock hanging from the chain around the gate. Here, the low hills concealed the house from view. From the seat of his pickup, he contemplated the tire tracks disappearing down the dusty drive. Fresh since last week's rain, he thought. He climbed out and crossed the road for a closer look. His stomach growled again.

Examining the ground at the gate revealed two sets of tire tracks. From this vantage point, they were clearly more recent than last week. Probably last night. One set coming out, partially covered by another going in. A pair of boot tracks of the person unlocking the gate showed exiting from the driver's side of the vehicle. They matched the tracks Con followed from the Campbell hacienda. The driver apparently left the gate open while gone and had reached over the gate to both remove and replace the padlock on the outside.

Con's curiosity nearly overtook him. He desperately wanted to further investigate the Wagner place, but he also needed to get back to the office. There were too many rabbit trails of questions that led to too many directions at once to follow. Despite first appearances, the circumstances were far too complicated to suggest a typical suicide. If any suicide could be considered typical.

He needed to study the Wagner estate, but did not want to draw further suspicion from his actions. He wished he had prepared for a longer day away from town. Con climbed back into his pickup truck and drove toward Las Vegas. The situation required him to devise a way to scrutinize the Wagner place without being detected.

By the time he arrived at the sheriff's department shortly before two o'clock, rumors surrounding Brice Campbell's death already swarmed the county.

Hazel Corbyn, the matronly clerk, secretary, dispatcher, and primary overseer of business for the office, greeted Con on his arrival with a myriad of messages. Calls from Hal Martin and Robert Westcott topped the list. The young reporter from the *Evening-Review* had been in repeatedly. As per Con's strictly enforced policy, Hazel told the man he would have to talk to the sheriff. "Keep an eye peeled," she warned Con, "he's getting pretty anxious for a scoop."

"Never mind him, and Bob Westcott can wait, too," Con told Hazel as he dialed the coroner on the telephone.

"What did you find?" he asked Hal when he answered the telephone.

"Couple of things you might want to look at. His left wrist

is freshly broken for one thing," Hal began, "probably three or four hours before his death. I called in Joe Anderson to assist."

"I'm going to stop at the Mesquite to grab some lunch, then I'll be over to see you. Give me an hour."

Con placed the pistol and wallet in separate large sealed envelopes, which he marked and locked in the office safe. "I'm getting lunch at the café, then going to the morgue," he told Hazel. "If Westcott calls back, tell him I will be stopping by to see him later today." Con then drove the two blocks to his parents' Mesquite Café on Fremont Street. They had owned and operated the eatery since Con's father shattered his leg over twenty years ago. As his grinning father limped from behind the grill to greet him, he could not help remembering the accident that ended Juan Armenta's ranching career when Con was thirteen.

As the eldest of three children, responsibilities to his family had weighed heavily upon his young shoulders that summer.

4

TUESDAY, JULY 2, 1907

"Keep watch on the sheep," Juan Armenta told Con as he prepared to continue pursuit of the puma they spotted on the rim of a nearby bluff. The gangly teen stood shoulder to shoulder with his stocky father as they surveyed the jumble of stone in the distance. They had lost several lambs in recent nights, and the tracks they followed for a couple of miles from their herd led into the rocks. "She's teaching her cubs to hunt and kill. We cannot afford to lose more lambs."

An hour later, Juan carried his Model '92 Winchester as he climbed between the boulders of the outcropping where they had seen the big cat from below. As he scaled a projecting pillar, keeping a firm grip on his rifle, Juan caught a fleeting glimpse of tawny gold in the corner of his eye a split-second before the lunging predator struck him shoulder high. As adrenaline surged through his veins, Juan's world distorted into slow motion. When he tried to turn to shoot the animal, his rifle struck the puma's ribs midway down the long octagon barrel, sending the .38-40 slug into the deep blue sky above. The impact of the puma and recoil of the rifle caused Juan to lose his footing on the precarious perch. As he began to fall, the agile lion released Juan with her right forepaw, grabbing hold of the jagged rock. Claws of her left paw penetrated Armenta's jacket. The big cat reconfigured from lunging in flight to a complete stop in a millisecond that spun Juan around, hurled his rifle away over the cliff, and sent his hat sailing over the precipice like a hawk riding an updraft.

Her claws, penetrating his clothing, hooked the flesh of his back. Then suddenly, the motion thrust him beyond the rim, tore him from the grip of his nemesis, and sent him plum-meting over the edge. Almost gliding like a bird, he fell, but lacked wings or tail to guide himself or keep aloft. A gnarled, stunted tree protruded from the face twenty feet below. He squirmed midflight. If he could catch the tree with his left leg, it might slow his momentum before crashing into the boulders and brush at the foot of the cliff another twenty feet beyond. It looked like he might succeed as he tried to aim himself for the twisted snare. It worked. His leg slid behind the misshapen trunk. But suddenly, it stopped. His torso continued to fall. It felt as if his leg had been ripped from his body. Whipped like a rag-doll, his upper body, arms, and face slapped into the rock wall.

* * *

In midafternoon, the teenage Conor Armenta, along with two herd dogs, tended the family's flock. An hour after his father had left that morning, Con heard a single rifle shot. The sound came from the direction of the rim where they had seen the puma. Predators rarely attacked in the heat of the day, so Con left the band of sheep grazing with Skip and Ranger while he hiked a half mile to the camp he and his father set up a week earlier. They had peaches, bacon, bread, cheese, and beans along with mutton jerky, coffee, and a few sundries.

Con moved the horse's picket to fresh grass. Orphaned at birth a decade ago, his father had bottle-fed the well-built sorrel mare. He named her Trueno, Spanish for Thunder, the daughter of Lightning. Con prepared a lunch of cold beans from the dutch oven under the wagon, a piece of bread, and a peach. He sat in a scant bit of shade at the rear of the wagon. As he ate, he worried over his father's absence. It bothered him. Juan was a good shot, and Con felt certain he must have killed the cat. He should have been back by now. Perhaps he continued to hunt the cubs.

After filling his stomach, Con refilled his canteen and slung it over his shoulder. The water was low in the keg strapped to the side of the wagon. Seeing dark clouds forming to the west, he gathered his jacket from the wagon. With two pieces of jerky in his pocket, he returned to the sheep.

The flock had scarcely moved since his departure. Ranger let out a single yip, letting Con know he was still on duty. Con had never moved the band by himself before, but he thought he should try to bed them down in a small valley just over the hill from where they were. It seemed likely to offer some protection if the ominous clouds turned into a storm and it was a little closer to their camp. He slowly began to push them that way. He didn't want to drive them, just urge them to graze their way in that direction. With very little instruction, the dogs soon understood the plan and helped Con to ease the flock along.

As the band of sheep settled into the valley and began bedding down, dusk fell early beneath blackening clouds. Con was afraid, not of the darkness or even an impending storm… he feared for his father. He laid down among the sheep with Skip and Ranger. Resting his head on the canteen, he covered himself with his jacket for a blanket. He stared into the total darkness. The dense clouds veiled the moon and stars completely. His father should have returned long ago. He might have ventured far beyond the bluff pursuing the lioness. Perhaps she and her cubs had killed him, or even eaten him. Con shivered at the thought and fought back self-pity as he lay there alone. Evaluating the situation, he needed to plan. His father's last words to him were concern for the sheep.

Con's family depended on them for their livelihood. They had no other source of income. They were in his care, and for now, were solely his responsibility. He felt driven to feed and protect them to the best of his abilities. He and his father were not expected to return for supplies for several more days. No one would come looking for them for at least a week, he calculated. There was enough grass in the area for the sheep to graze for two or three days, and then he must plan to move them and the camp to a new range. He was wondering where that should be as he finally fell asleep.

* * *

Juan Armenta awoke in total darkness. He lay wedged between two massive rocks, his right side down. His right arm extended above his head and ached intensely. His right cheek pressed hard against the rock in front of him, and he could not move his head. The darkness nearly overwhelmed him, but the rocks were warm and somehow felt comforting. Had he lost his sight in the fall? He could open his left eye. He tried to look around. Nothing. *It should be cooler at night,* he thought. *I must be blind.*

One member at a time, Juan Armenta gradually assessed the damage to his body. His hips and legs rested higher than his shoulders in the crevice. He could move his right foot and leg below the knee. It didn't hurt too badly. His left arm seemed to be totally free. Other than abrasions he could feel on the fingers, there seemed to be no injury. His left leg had no feeling at all. Total numbness. When he reached as far below his waist as possible, Juan could feel the cloth of his chinos stiff from dried blood and stuck to his skin. The fabric stretched tightly from his swollen thigh. He had to figure out a way to extricate himself from this trap. He knew his left leg and possibly his right arm were seriously injured. And he could not see.

Juan carefully felt the surface of the rock in front of him. He worked his way up with his left hand. Just short of his maximum reach he found a crack barely wide enough to insert his fingers to the first knuckle. Pulling with all of his strength and moving his head back and forth a quarter of an inch at a time, he managed to raise his upper body about an inch before an excruciating sharp pain shot through his left leg. Flexing his right leg as much as he could, he succeeded in keeping from falling back the inch that he gained as he held himself in place, waiting for the pain to subside. A half hour later, he tried again. This time, he gained three more inches before succumbing to the pain in his left leg. As he held himself in place again, he discovered he could slightly move his right arm. It eventually began to tingle, giving hope that lack of circulation might be the greatest cause of the ache in the appendage. He could also move his head almost a quarter turn now and decided he probably had not broken his neck.

It took longer this time for the pain in his left leg to subside. Juan spent the period clenching and unclenching his right fist until he gradually regained most of the feeling in the limb. Nearly an hour later, the pain in his left leg remained intense, but Armenta's will to survive prevailed. Now able to help push with his right arm, in an extreme effort, he hoisted himself nearly a foot before he practically lost consciousness to the pain. His head finally free, he now held it against the rock behind him as he gasped for air in agony. His head and shoulders were now at the approximate height of his legs. No longer elevated, his left leg throbbed without mercy. *At least,* he thought, *there must be some circulation.*

Two hours passed with little change in the level of pain, but Juan could not bear to be idle any longer. Both arms were free and he had gained substantial mobility in his right leg. Exploring the surroundings by feel, he thought if he could gain another foot out of the crevice, he could turn and sit on the rock behind him. The trick would be to extract his right foot from the crevice so he could use it to push with. The fingerhold he had used with his left arm now lacked the leverage needed to pull himself further, but if he could push himself up with his right arm, he might find another spot to utilize his left. As he pushed with all of his might with his right arm, he groped desperately with his left hand in search of a fingerhold. At his furthest reach, his fingers crossed a crevice just large enough for two fingers. He accessed it just as his right arm failed. Ignoring the pain, he pulled himself just far enough to free his right leg and begin pushing. With all of his concentration he pulled and pushed until he had turned and seated himself on the boulder behind him. Tortured and exhausted, Juan leaned back against the rock and succumbed to unconsciousness.

* * *

WEDNESDAY, JULY 3, 1907

Juan Armenta awoke to dull, gray light. Birds chattered to each other nearby. "I can see!" he said aloud excitedly. The revelation brought a flood of new energy to him. He could barely open his right eye, but he could see the dark gray sky through the slit also. Cautiously, he touched the right side of his face, feeling the scrapes and swelling of his cheek and forehead. "Quite a shiner, I'll bet," he mumbled. Carefully propping himself up on his right elbow, he hoped to look over his surroundings. The motion brought attention to a new area of discomfort. With the shirt adhered to his back, his present movement pulled against the gashes left by the puma's claws in the melee. Keeping his left leg motionless, it throbbed but could be tolerated. Looking down, he could see the swelling stretched the fabric of his pants taut, and the bulge a few inches above his knee could only be the result of a displaced fracture. The ends of the bone cutting into muscle explained the excruciating pain when he moved it.

Guarding his movement, Juan surveyed the boulder field he found himself in. The shredded remains of the scrubby tree that broke his fall lay strewn around him. The little tree probably saved his life, but he sure paid the toll for the sudden stop. He could reach two branches about three feet long. They were the diameter of hefty sticks and marginally straight. He needed to set his broken leg without severing an artery and bleeding to death in the process. Scattered boulders ranging from the size of his head to a small house dissipated away from the base of the rim. Two boulders the size of bushel baskets were only a few feet away. The gap between them formed a vee facing away from him. Juan prepared to move himself into position.

Using the two sticks as props and levers, he began lifting and sliding his leg toward the notch. The slightest movement brought piercing pain as he gradually scooted himself toward the boulders. Every few inches forced him to stop to catch his breath and recover from the unbearable anguish. An hour later, he arrived at his destination, four or five feet away. Clouds had dispersed, and the sun rode high in the sky. The temperature climbed steadily, and there would be no shade where he sat for several hours. The motion had loosened his shirt from the wounds on his back. Juan removed his jacket. The slashes below the shoulders were caked with dried blood. Señora Puma had left her calling card. The gashes in his flesh were painful, but nothing compared to his leg.

Sitting up in the rock pile, he searched his pants pockets for his jackknife. Unfolding the blade, Juan cut the arms from his jacket, then split each sleeve into two long, wide strips. With his left ankle positioned in the notch between the boulders, he carefully slid the strips beneath his leg. Two above, and two below the break. They would barely reach around his swollen thigh. He laid the two sticks on each side of his leg. The sun was getting very hot. He tried to mentally prepare for the torture he planned to inflict upon himself. His left leg needed to be relaxed so the muscle would stretch into its normal position.

Juan wrapped his left arm around a large boulder and positioned his right foot against another. With his left ankle held in place by the notch in the two boulders, he prepared himself. As quickly as possible, he pulled with his left arm and pushed with his right leg in a swift and powerful jerk against the stationary ankle. The bone in his leg moved, and a scream escaped his lungs as the blinding rush of pain flooded through him. As he collapsed on the stones, a halo surrounded the sun, glaring into his left eye, and an odd dimness overcame him, and he slipped into oblivion.

* * *

A drop of rain on his face returned Juan to reality. The rain's approach brought the deep, earthy aroma of ozone with it. He could see the storm in the distance to the west. It did not appear to be approaching very quickly. The sun, hidden from view, made him wonder how much time had passed. He carefully sat up and examined his leg. It looked straight. His pant leg seemed looser. The swelling had begun to subside. It may have been hours he had lain there. His materials for a splint remained in position. Juan began to bind the branches to his leg with the strips of cloth from his jacket. He was not sure how tight to tie them, so he pulled them just a bit tighter than comfortable. He wanted them tied firmly, yet not restrict circulation. He could barely reach the lowest one which hit him about the middle of his calf. If the splint worked, he should be able to move with much less pain.

Only a light spatter had reached him thus far, but heavier rainfall approached. Juan slipped on the remains of his jacket, which had become a vest, and plotted a route to his nearest shelter from the coming storm. Some thirty feet away and slightly downhill stood a boulder the size of a small house. It leaned rather eastward, thus offering a scant form of protection. Most importantly, there were few obstacles to prevent him achieving the destination. Juan half crawled, half dragged himself in that direction as hurriedly as possible. He could tolerate the discomfort from his fractured leg if he could slide and keep from jarring it. He reached his refuge just as the heavier rain had and propped his injured leg on a stone. Leaning back against the boulder, he rested and listened to the rain fall as it steadily increased.

Water dripped from the overhang above him and gradually became a rivulet. Holding his hand beneath it, he could gather a palmful at a time, of cool rainwater to drink. He had neither eaten nor drank since yesterday morning. Now evening, Juan spent the next hour repeating the process continually until the rain ended. The water refreshed him immensely, but his ordeal had robbed him of strength and energy. As the water he drank slowly penetrated his parched body, Juan fell asleep beneath the boulder.

* * *

THURSDAY, JULY 4, 1907—INDEPENDENCE DAY

He awoke to a golden line of light on the eastern horizon. Juan was stiff and sore, but the throb of his broken leg had ebbed significantly. The gashes from the puma's claws frightened him. He could feel the heat radiating from infection setting in. The tough sheepherder needed help, and he knew it—the nearest of which was his son, Conor. In the gray predawn light, Juan evaluated his circumstances. He did not consider his weakness. The sheep camp was about a mile away, maybe two. He felt certain, even with his injuries, he could easily make it in a day. The wounds brought back thoughts of the puma. He had lain helpless at the foot of her lair for two days. Why had she not come for him?

The thought did not persuade him to stay. In the light he could see the swelling in his thigh continued to abate. So had his face, to the point he could almost open his right eye completely. He retied the upper bands on his splint and set off crawling in the direction of the camp, dragging his useless leg as gently as he could.

Almost miraculously, within the first twenty yards, Juan spotted his Winchester lying in the rocks. He crawled to it. Sitting up, he grabbed the rifle and examined it. The rear sight was missing and the stock cracked, but at a glance, it appeared still operable. The thought boosted his morale, given the possibility of the puma still lurking nearby. When he tried to lever a fresh cartridge into the chamber, however, he discovered the lever bent and the action jammed. Disappointed that he remained unarmed, he reevaluated the use of the gun. Useless as a crutch, the long-barreled rifle could still serve as a walking stick. With a spent cartridge stuck in the chamber, he did not fear an accidental discharge. He crossed his hands over the muzzle with the butt on the ground, and pulled himself to his feet for the first time in two days.

Reenergized by the accomplishment, Juan smiled. Lifting his bad leg forward, he hopped ahead on his right leg almost as effectively as if he had had a crutch. As the jumble of rocks dispersed, he progressed another thirty yards to a mesquite tree. He stopped to collect a half-dozen bean pods to chew on. He had no idea how nourishing they might be, but knew local natives ate them. The pods tasted sweet to him, making him think that in his hunger his mind played tricks on him. Not knowing how his body might react to the foreign food, he chose to eat sparingly and continued on.

* * *

It had been two days since young Conor Armenta's father left in pursuit of the puma. Midmorning yesterday, he heard a faint and odd sound from the direction of the bluff. It may have been the call of the big cat he now believed had killed his father. It rained quite hard for a while last night. The sheep huddled together through the storm and bedded down afterward without any mishaps. He fed the dogs the last of the cold beans and some moldy bacon fat trimmed from the slab. Not building a fire, he instead ate bread, cheese, and peaches. Con loved his mother's cheese, created by a secret process from an old Irish family recipe which resulted in a pungent cheddar made from their sheep's milk. He watered Trueno and moved her picket twice yesterday.

The sheep had nearly grazed out the little valley he'd moved them to after his father failed to return. He knew he needed to move them again, but was apprehensive about making the decision as to where that might be. The question had troubled him for two nights and a day. He had to choose. He recalled a spring, about two miles west. It would make a good camp. He started the sheep in that direction, moving them slowly to allow time for them to graze along the way. Ranger and Skip kept them together. By midday, the flock had covered about half the distance, and Con allowed them to stop. They were in a good area to feed through the evening and bed down for the night. Leaving them under the dogs' watchful care, Con returned to the camp.

He gathered the few belongings displaced around the light spring-wagon, placing everything inside. He covered it all with the light-colored canvas they sometimes used for a lean-to. He brought the mare to the wagon and gave her a handful of oats and water as he harnessed her. In spite of her fiery name, she had matured to a gentle disposition. It made the old routine a simple task. As an afterthought, Con placed rows of stones in the shape of an arrow in his direction of travel. If anyone came looking for him, they might discover the marker. Climbing onto the seat, he picked up the reins, and at the slight cluck of his tongue, they were underway toward the grazing herd of sheep. He had picked a route through the brush worthy of the small wagon as he had walked over the terrain the past two days. The broad-shouldered horse pulled the wagon easily over the rolling landscape.

Ranger barked momentarily when the creak of the wagon reached his ears, and Skip joined in chorus. Their barks changed to yips as they wagged their tails in anticipation when Con came into view. He skirted the herd with the wagon, positioning it in a location that would suffice for a temporary campsite. Unhitching the mare, he unharnessed her, then gave her water and drove her picket nearby. Con rewarded the dogs with some coarse rubbing and petting, followed by a treat of mutton jerky. Checking the water keg on the wagon, he found it was nearly empty, and what was left was warm and musty. The fortunate rain had left ample puddles to water the herd for a couple of days. The afternoon had nearly passed and there would not be time enough to finish moving the camp today. He grabbed the spare canteen from their gear and left to scout for the spring he recalled and to reconnoiter a track to drive the wagon there the next day.

He found the spring fairly easily about a mile and a half from the wagon. Con filled the canteens and began his return. There were a couple of spots along his way to the spring where he hoped to find a better course for the wagon. He found a detour for the first obstacle without much trouble. The other proved a more daunting ordeal. The arroyo seco was not terribly wide nor deep, but the banks were steep. Too steep, Con thought, to maneuver Trueno and the wagon through. It took nearly an hour to find a suitable alternative.

At dusk, Con arrived back at the wagon. He quickly checked on the sheep. To his relief, they had all lain down for the night and the two dogs with them. Always on a lookout for burnable materials, he had a collection of dry twigs and branches in the wagon. He soon had a small fire burning and heated the cast-iron skillet beside the blaze while he cut slabs of bacon with the big butcher knife. As the flames subsided, he placed the pan over the embers and began cooking his first hot meal in three days. The first time he really felt like eating. As he let the sizzling bacon cool in the pan on a nearby rock, Con tore a couple of large chunks from the round loaf of bread. While eating his bacon straight from the pan, he mopped up the extra grease with his bread. By the time he had finished eating, the fire burned down to the lowest of coals. It had been a long and tiring three days. He missed his dad. Laying back against the wheel of the wagon, he fell instantly asleep.

* * *

Juan Armenta hobbled and hopped short distances, resting often and gradually making his way toward the camp he shared with his son. Anticipation of water and food drove him on into the hot desert afternoon. He wrapped the remnants of his jacket around his head to stave off the intense sun. By midafternoon he could no longer tolerate the penetrating heat. When he halted to siesta in the shade of a large clump of brush, he found the space occupied by a rattlesnake. The familiar buzz of its rattles brought a fresh rush of adrenaline

through Juan's veins. A fist-sized rock injured the snake sufficiently to immobilize it. Supporting himself on his right knee,
he pinned the snake's head in place beneath a larger rock
while he separated it from its writhing body with his
jackknife.

Armenta made quick work of stripping the skin from this
latest adversary and eating the raw meat from its spindly
carcass. Though it would have made a tastier meal roasted on
a stick over a campfire, the nourishment of the raw meat
served well enough to the ravenous man. Nevertheless, he
devoured the meat too hurriedly and soon his stomach twisted
in pain, but Juan managed to keep it down. Taking care to not
disturb the still venomous head beneath the rock, he reclined
under the bush. As his digestive system began to settle, he fell
into an easy slumber.

When Juan awoke, the sun lay low in the sky. A slight
breeze lessened the harshness of the temperature. The scant
moisture infused from his meal had little effect on his state of
dehydration. His mental faculties, decayed by his physical
condition, distorted his ability to think clearly. The wounds on
his back were on fire from infection, but he was unable to
discern the cause. No longer sweating and suffering an intense
headache, Juan neared the threshold of heatstroke. He had
another quarter-mile to the campsite, he thought, and a half
hour of daylight left to cover the distance.

Pulling himself up with his rifle, he pressed onward. He
paused to rest, standing after twenty yards. As the sun began
to set, he continued on. After two more similar breaks, it was
nearly dark when he came across an arrow made on the
ground with lines of small rocks pointing to his right. Nearer
than he thought, it looked like the spot where they had
camped, but the wagon and their gear were gone. Moving

ahead a few more yards, he found a spot where Trueno had been picketed. Clumps of grass were cropped short, and a pile of manure marked her absence. His foggy mind methodically processed the information. Con had moved their camp. He hobbled back to where the camp had been. Finding a spot in the dark, he lay down. He tried to make sense of the situation, but reasoning escaped him. Both physically and mentally, he was far beyond enervation.

* * *

FRIDAY, JULY 5, 1907

In the morning, Con woke to the sun, trying to peek through a few distant clouds. A brief thunderstorm overnight had sent him seeking shelter beneath the wagon. The sheep were moving around grazing, their woolly outer coats glistening from last night's rain. The dogs were busy momentarily with a rabbit or lizard cornered in a tangle of brush. A noisy choir of wrens sang an unknown medley to each other across the small valley. The mare lifted her head and nickered at the sight of him moving around in the camp. For some reason unidentifiable to Con, the dawn seemed to carry an unusual sense of joyfulness. Finding the sack of pinto beans among their supplies, he poured some into the dutch oven and covered them with water from the spare canteen. Placing the lid over the pot, he sat them on the seat of the wagon to soak.

Looking across the small valley where the sheep grazed, the dogs' quarry appeared to have escaped them, though Skip was slow to give up the chase. Con carved a couple of chunks of fat from the slab of bacon and put them in his pocket. Then he grabbed a handful of oats and turned the opposite direction to the sorrel mare, switching a fly with her tail as she grazed peacefully. Con took care to assess Trueno's surroundings as she ate the grain from his hand. There were several bunches of grass within her easy reach and three puddles of water left from last night's rain that would last for a little while. He petted and rubbed her tenderly, not forgetting her favorite spot to scratch beneath her halter, where it rode behind her ears.

From there, he circled the grazing sheep. They also were in good terrain with plenty to eat and sufficient water for perhaps two days. They had been getting plenty to eat and drink recently, and the ewes' udders were full of milk for their energetic lambs. Looking ahead, Ranger and Skip wagged their tails emphatically in anticipation, but waited his arrival to their position. Con sat down on their viewpoint with them and gave each their morsel of bacon fat, which they swallowed almost without tasting. When finished, they each took their place on either side of him, nuzzling and licking at his face. With an arm around each of them, he avoided showing partiality to the jealous duo. Skip always insisted on a larger share of the attention, while Ranger accepted what was offered and seldom begged for more. Con petted and played with them until both sat beside him, watching over the flock.

* * *

Juan Armenta stirred awake at the first light of dawn. He lay on his side with his tattered jacket for a pillow. He had rolled beneath the slight shelter of a scraggly bush during the storm last night. He felt the dampness of his clothing from the rain. As he gradually became aware of his surroundings, he remembered a flat area of bedrock just a few feet away. As he rose up on an elbow, he saw his memory had not deceived him. There was the rock. And as he had suspected, the surface formed a slight basin. And it contained a pool of clear water. Not wasting the time or energy to stand, he crawled to the basin.

He first submerged his burned, dry, and chapped face into the water. The sensation was refreshing beyond belief. The water was cool, but not cold. What a simple pleasure to have gone without for so long. Returning, he sucked a careful drink into his mouth and held it there for a long time. Then swallowed. Slowly and carefully, he repeated the process for an hour. Soaking his face for every few drinks he took.

Then, crawling back to his jacket and rifle, he laid again beneath the scraggly bush. He still lay there as the sun gradually rose higher, listening to the birds thanking the Lord with anxious chatter for last night's replenishing gift. Juan, too, thanked Him as he napped intermittently while allowing his body time to absorb the moisture it so desperately needed from the drink of water.

At midmorning, Juan returned to the basin to repeat the ritual. By now, he had begun to regain his mental faculties. He watched bees skipping about the pool in a ceremony of their own, buzzing loudly as they passed nearby. The rain had awakened the flora of the desert and opened flowers that had closed themselves in self-preservation from the heat. The burn from his inflamed back regained its intensity, or Juan regained his awareness of it. When he finished this session, he rolled over and submerged his back in the water. It was no longer cool, but cooler than the inferno beneath his skin. He laid there a long time and the heat nearly left the wounds briefly.

As the sun rose high, Juan refilled himself one more time. He removed his torn shirt and soaked it in water before putting it back on. Then did the same with his jacket before

covering his head. Sitting by the pool, he last adjusted the
splint on his leg. Greatly refreshed, though still very hungry,
he pulled himself to his feet. The rain had obliterated much of
the trail left by the wagon, but not beyond Juan's ability to
follow in the direction of his son's arrow.

* * *

Conor spent the morning watching the flock and gathering
sticks to bolster his cache of valuable firewood. Considering
the circumstances, he revised his plan to move the camp to the
spring. He and his livestock had plenty of water for at least
two days and the present vicinity had abundant ricegrass for
them to graze on. He chose to maintain his camp here for a
couple more days before resuming his relocation plan. With
that in mind, he constructed a better firepit to cook over in an
area clear of vegetation near the wagon. After excavating a
slight depression in the soft soil, he located two angular rocks.
He positioned them strategically so as to rest the dutch oven
over the fire.

With his cooking area in shape, Con returned his attention
to the sheep. A half-dozen of them had wandered a short
distance down the valley, and the dogs were urging them back
among their comrades. The hottest part of the day
approached, and they were not inclined to meander far.
Comfortable with the conditions, he built a hot fire of small
sticks. As the blaze began to decline, he placed his two largest
pieces of wood atop the fire, knowing they would burn down
to sufficient coals to hold good heat for a lengthy time. As the
logs disintegrated into embers, he positioned the dutch oven
full of beans over the fire.

The afternoon progressed, and Con scouted the region

more thoroughly. He located the remains of a dead tree about a hundred yards from the wagon, and from it, salvaged several good branches, larger than any he previously collected. He spent the next hour transporting them to the campsite. Checking the pot of beans, he found they simmered nicely and gave off a pleasing aroma. He added more water to the pot and a newly acquired log to the fire. As a slight breeze lent negligible relief to the fervid afternoon, Con took refuge in the shade beneath the wagon. The only sound to be heard was Trueno occasionally swatting a fly with her tail. Even the noisy wrens were subdued. Hypnotized by the random patterns of heatwaves rising above the fire around the dutch oven, he dozed in the heat. As the afternoon waned, Con rose and checked his supper. Temperatures were beginning to drop, but heat still radiated from the soil.

Suddenly, Ranger began barking fiercely. He feared the puma may be near, though it seemed too early for one to be on the prowl. He quickly looked through the wagon for a weapon. Locating a small axe among the belongings, it seemed the best armament he could find. He ran in the direction of the dogs as they disappeared over the far hill. Before he reached the spot where he had last seen them, their barking stopped abruptly. His heart racing, Con slowed his pace. A score of possible tragedies ran through his imagination as he continued on.

Cresting the hill, he saw a man in the distance. He hopped along toward him with some sort of crutch and had a strange hat on his head. Skip and Ranger wagged their tails profusely as they ran circles around the man. They obviously knew him. Con continued walking toward him as the man stopped and waved his right arm in the air. He knew the man also. As he ran to him, tears of combined joy and disbelief overtook him. Con could scarcely see when he reached him.

Holding dearly to his father in a long embrace, he finally blurted out, "What happened? I thought I'd never see you again."

"It's a long story, son," Juan replied through tears of his own. "An adventure I'd not care to repeat."

"Camp is just over the hill," Con finally said. "There are beans cooking on the fire."

Juan gave his son a brief synopsis of his injuries as they prepared to make the short hike to the wagon. The water he drank throughout the morning had significantly invigorated him. Enough so that he greatly increased his pace through the afternoon compared to what he had managed the previous day. Seeing Con and knowing he survived the worst of this tribulation further reenergized him.

Con looped the rawhide tether on the short handle of the axe around his left wrist. Taking Juan's rifle in his left hand, he supported his father with his right arm wrapped around his waist. Juan, in turn, held onto his son with his left arm over Con's shoulders. In this manner, they made their way the three hundred yards to camp, looking much like two men in a very slow three-legged race.

The sun had nearly set when they reached the wagon. Con seated his father on the side facing the campfire, then dished up beans on a tin plate. He handed him jerky and bread along with a cup filled with water. Juan ate as slowly as he could force himself to. The famished man knew his shriveled stomach could not withstand the introduction of too much food too quickly.

While Juan ate, he narrated the story of all that had happened the past four days. It helped him eat less hurriedly.

At his father's request, Con bolstered the fire and filled the blackened old coffeepot, sitting it over the flames. Then he rolled out his father's bedroll and fashioned a lean-to with the canvas from the side of the wagon as his father ate and talked.

Con filled another plate for himself and sat down near his father. "She never came back after you?" he asked. "The lioness?"

"No," Juan replied. "I think maybe the rifle shot singed her, or possibly the sound frightened her away." He thought for a moment. "I would have made an easy kill for her cubs."

When Con finished his beans, he reached in the wagon and grabbed the sack of coffee to add to the pot of then boiling water.

"No," his father said. "Not tonight."

"Sure?" Con asked curiously.

"In the morning," Juan answered. "Tonight, you need to find the whiskey."

The statement caught Con by total surprise. His father rarely drank alcohol. When he did drink, he preferred tequila, but the saloon did not have any when they supplied for the trip. He had seen his father's flask while preparing the beans and knew where to look. He quickly produced it and handed it to him. Juan took a swallow from the flask and winced as the alcohol burned its way to his weakened belly.

"The cuts on my back from the puma are infected," he told Con plainly. "You need to treat them for me. It will not be pleasant for either of us, but I will tell you what to do."

"I understand," Con answered. He became very serious, and his face paled at the thought of the job at hand. He truly did understand the gravity of his duty.

"Find a clean rag," Juan began as he scooted the few feet to the bedroll Con had laid out. "Probably the flour sack will work."

Con found the empty sack in the wagon and held it up to show him.

"Cut it in half," Juan told him.

Digging deep in his pocket, Con found his jackknife and began sawing at the cloth with the dull blade. Juan shook his head knowingly and located his own knife.

Handing it to his son, he tried to make light of it, grinning, "Here, use mine. You need to take better care of yours."

His face flushed in embarrassment. "Yes, sir," Con answered as he easily split the sack sufficiently to tear it into two pieces.

"Now soak the cloth in the boiling water," he said as he removed his tattered shirt. Taking another swallow of the whiskey, Juan sat the flask aside and laid himself face down on his blankets. As Con approached the bed with dripping rag and steaming coffee pot, the sight of his father's back nauseated him. He wished he had not eaten so much supper. He sat the pot near the flask and knelt at Juan's side.

Even with his dark complexion, the bright red inflammation and swelling nearly consumed Juan's entire back. Four distinct gashes from the lion's rake began at his left shoulder blade and crossed his back at an angle, departing from his right rib cage. They were evenly spaced almost two inches apart. Unlike the smooth cuts of a knife, the fissures were jagged with tags of skin protruding randomly where the muscled body had contested entry of the predator's weapons. They were deep, and yellowish puss of infection oozed from each arbitrarily.

Trying to keep his voice from cracking, Con asked what to do through the lump in his throat.

"Scrub the infection out of the cuts. Lots of hot water. Scrub hard. Get it all out. Scrub hard," he repeated. "When you are done, pour whiskey over them. We don't have any dressings, so spread the cloth over my back to keep the flies off." Juan paused his instruction. "I might pass out. Do you know what to do?"

"Yes," Con answered shakily. "It looks bad. I think they should be sewn closed."

"It is too late. They have quit bleeding and begun to knit. I am ready."

Con began to gently wash his father's back.

"Scrub hard!" Juan growled. "You must! Scrub hard!"

As tears began to streak his face, Conor started to wash the wounds more aggressively. When Juan moaned in pain, he stopped.

"Don't quit!" Juan gasped. "Scrub hard! Finish! Do not prolong it!"

Con could not bear hurting his father more. His tears flowed freely in sorrow and helplessness.

"You are a man! You must do this!" Juan yelled at his sobbing son. "You have to clean the wounds! You have to get the infection out or I will die from fever! You must! Scrub! You must finish!" he demanded.

The young man took several deep breaths and regained some control of his weeping. Pouring more scalding water over the cloth, he resumed.

"Yes," Juan said, trying to reassure his son. Every time the pain evoked a moan or a cry, he muttered, "Yes!" The repetitive encouragement gradually bolstered Con's confidence and nerve. Darkness had overtaken them by the time he had finished scrubbing the lesions. Dim light from the dwindling fire gave a rosy amber glow to the lean-to. Juan drifted in and out of consciousness. When Conor carefully dribbled whiskey down the slashes across his father's back, he shuddered but did not speak. A dense cloud cover held the day's heat in the desert night, but neither lightning nor rain accompanied it.

Con carefully laid the damp cloth across his father's injury. Even in the dim light, he could see the bright redness of the skin. He could feel the heat rising from the tissue. He feared for his father. Upon adding another small log to the fire, new flames leaped to life, bringing a comforting light to the camp. Con settled himself where he could watch both his father and the campfire. Trueno nickered in acknowledgment of his presence in the glow. The noise silenced the sounds of the night. He listened intently as the varied sounds of insects attracted by the light, scurrying lizards, rabbits, and kangaroo rats all gradually returned. He leaned back against the wagon wheel, staring blankly at the glowing embers. A nighthawk voiced its strange nasal call in the darkness as he drifted wearily to sleep.

5

Two enormous fans hung from the ceiling over the eating area, and a small oscillating fan sat on the serving counter above the back bar, pointing toward the kitchen. All of them circulated the same hot air throughout the café and blended the wonderful aromas of Juan's cooking with the smell of the wilting flowers in vases adorning two tables and the lingering odor of sweaty patrons who had packed the place for lunch a couple of hours earlier. The sagging screen door somehow managed to prohibit the entrance of most insects and admit a little fresh air into the building.

"How is Sheriff Conor Armenta this fine afternoon?" Juan asked his son as he sat a Coca-Cola on the lunch counter in front of him.

"I'm as starved as an old sheepherder who didn't get much

sleep last night and hasn't eaten since noon yesterday," Con answered.

"Well, sir, I don't want to get arrested for bribing an officer, but I've got a pan full of enchiladas, with rice and beans. The kind of food a starving sheepherder would wrestle a coyote for."

"That would be wonderful, Papa. And where would your beautiful wife and her ugly daughter be?"

"Oh, they ran over to J.C. Penney, big sale on fabric," Juan answered as he dished up a hearty plateful of enchiladas for his son. "I told them I had plenty of flour sacks every week, but they'd have nothing to do with them. I'm just getting things ready to close up," he added as he sat the plate in front of Con. "And you shouldn't be so mean to your sister. At least she has given me grandchildren. You don't even have a girl-friend anymore," he teased.

"Ah, women," Con moaned. "I'm too busy." For some reason, the suggestion brought Amelia Westcott to mind. "Besides, they're too suspicious and hateful. And expensive!"

"How is the Brice Campbell case coming?" Juan asked as he refilled the Coca-Cola.

"Oh, so you've heard?"

"Everyone has heard. It's the talk of the town. Big shot millionaire blows his brains out in his front yard. Pretty big news."

"Side yard," Con corrected. "Now you know more about it than almost anyone else in town."

"What else?" Juan prodded. "There must be more!"

"Yep," Con replied. "I'm going over to see Hal when I leave here."

"Dr. Martin is a nice man. How can you eat your dinner

then go over there and play with a dead body? That's disgusting."

"My father taught me how to deal with disgusting things when I was a teenager," Con answered with a wink as he stood up from his empty plate. "I almost forgot. I saw Luis Garza yesterday. He wished you and Mama well."

"How is he?"

"He seemed fine and healthy. Some of his sheep? Not so much."

"What is it? Scabies?"

"Lead poisoning. Someone shot 'em."

"Who would do such a thing?"

"Drunken workers from the dam blowing off steam, I would guess. No one around here, I think. We'll figure it out." With that, Con dropped some money on the counter and took his Stetson from a hook by the door. "Gotta go." And stepped out into the blazing heat, the screen door slamming behind him.

Con climbed behind the wheel of his pickup truck and drove to the morgue. The strong smell of disinfectants erased any sense of appeal when entering the cool hallway. Bold lettering on the window of the door to the right read Clark County Coroner followed below in smaller letters with Dr. Harold Martin, M.D. No one sat at the desk. The same bold lettering adorned the solid door to the left which read PRIVATE. Con entered it.

The two men hovering over the cadaver on the table wore lab coats and looked up at Con. They acknowledge each other in single-word greetings.

"Con."

"Hal."

"Sheriff Armenta."

"Dr. Anderson."

"A couple of bullet fragments from the skull in the petri dish over there, if you need them," Hal said, glancing toward the dish on the counter.

Con crossed the room to inspect the petri dish. A tiny, oddly shaped bottle containing a dark, oily liquid lay next to it.

"What's this?" he asked, peering through it as he held it to the light above.

"Opium," Hal answered. "Found it in his pocket."

"So, you're saying I just compromised evidence with my fingerprints," Con stated, blushing at his ignorance.

"Yes, but so did we before we realized what it was," Hal answered, shrugging. "It happens."

"Do you think he had used some of the opium before he died?"

"Judging by his injuries, I would have. Look here," Hal went on, lifting the sheet to expose Campbell's left arm. "Wrist is broken pretty severely. Bruises and abrasions on the palm and fingers like they slid on a rough surface." He moved down the table and raised the sheet above the knees. "Bruising and abrasions on the right knee are similar to the hand. He took a pretty hard fall." He laid the sheet back down and moved to the victim's head, revealing Campbell's face. "See that shiner there?" Hal asked, pointing to Campbell's left eye and cheek. "There are no abrasions. I don't think it happened at the same time as the others and it didn't happen where we found him."

Blood had been washed from the face Con had seen in the garden. "Which happened first?"

"It's hard to tell," Hal answered. "Joe?"

"I'm less experienced than Hal, but comparing the bruises and swelling, I think the shiner came a little before the fall."

"Exactly!" Hal exclaimed. "Maybe even an hour or two."

Con returned to examine Campbell's left hand. A white circle showed on the ring finger where a wedding band had shaded it from the sun. "What about the knuckles?" he asked the two men.

"Most likely from the fall," Dr. Anderson answered.

"Or maybe he slugged somebody beforehand," Hal added. "Might explain the shiner."

"Thanks for your help, Dr. Anderson. Hal will give you the forms for your report. You each have to fill them out separately," Con told him then turned to Hal. "Drop them by my office when you're finished, and be sure to seal the envelopes."

Con drove across town to Robert Westcott's office. It did not surprise him to see the red Buick roadster parked out front. The fact it had already been washed since Mrs. Westcott had returned to town, however, caught his attention. A pretty blonde receptionist occupied the desk in the foyer. A ceiling fan dropped a slight breeze from above. It amazed Con, in general, how cool it was in the building. Large tropical-looking plants occupied the corners of the lobby. It smelled fresh and clean.

"Mr. Westcott asked to see me," Con told the receiver. "I apologize for not calling ahead."

"That is not a problem, Sheriff. Please be seated. I will tell him you are here," she told him and walked down the hallway, her high heels clicking their way down the hardwood floor. When the footsteps stopped, he heard a quiet knock on an office door, then an imperceptible conversation followed by returning footsteps. A few seconds later, heavier footsteps followed.

Con remained standing in the waiting area, toying with the hat in his hands.

"Mr. Westcott will see you in a moment," she said when she entered the reception area.

"Thank you," Con replied, barely getting the words out before Westcott appeared from the hallway.

"Thank you for stopping by, Sheriff." Westcott offered his hand with a smile. "Please," he gestured Con to precede him down the hall. "The open door on the left, Sheriff. Please bring some iced tea, June."

Con proceeded at a casual pace down the hallway. The door opened into a spacious office. Across the room, Amelia Westcott sat cross-legged on an over-stuffed leather sofa, thumbing through a magazine. Robert Westcott's ornate desk dwarfed the one in Brice Campbell's study, and Con presumed that the matching sideboard concealed a set of decanters similar to those belonging to his deceased father-in-law. A wooden box with decorative carving occupied the center of the piece of furniture, accompanied by a small silver vase. Red and white-tipped matches protruded slightly from its rim. *Cigars*, Con thought, but no hint of the lingering pungent odor accompanied them.

"What can I do for you?" Con asked, turning to Westcott as he entered the room behind him.

"Please, sit down." Robert Westcott indicated one of two leather chairs that, along with a coffee table, formed a sitting area near the couch.

Con remained standing, as June entered the room and placed a silver tray with a crystal pitcher of iced tea on the sideboard. When she opened the cupboard to retrieve matching glasses, Con spied the decanters he suspected would be there. He watched as she filled four glasses, offering the first to Amelia Westcott and the second to him. Had their hands touched for a moment longer than necessary when she handed him the glass of tea? When he raised his eyes to her face, they met a warm smile wearing red lipstick. A sprinkling of freckles adorned her nose and cheeks beneath the pair of sapphire blue eyes looking directly into his. Was she flirting with him?

"Thank you," he said, regaining his composure.

"Please, sit down," Robert Westcott repeated, taking a seat himself in the chair nearest his wife.

June returned with a glass of tea for Westcott and poured one for herself as she sat down with a steno pad and pencil in an office chair near the desk. So, this was an interrogation Con surmised as he deposited himself as gracefully as possible in the armchair. Complete with a paid witness taking notes. So much for flirting. The seat resembled the one in the Campbell's sitting room. Too low and too soft for Con's taste. He would have preferred trading places with June had he been given the option.

"So, what can I do for you?" Con mimicked Westcott's repetition with the slightest bit of sarcasm.

"I just want to help you, Sheriff. I want to resolve this tragedy as quickly and painlessly as possible, so our family can properly mourn the loss of our loved one." Con could not decide if Robert Westcott sounded more like a funeral director or a snake oil salesman with his implied sincerity. "I have already spoken to key personnel at the company and business will continue as usual until," Westcott paused, searching for the precise word he wanted on record in June's notes. "Until whoever should take control of the company can be decided by the family." Now Conor understood it, or so he thought. The family attorney was already maneuvering the pieces of the puzzle in a direction in which he and his wife could leave the party with all of the prizes. *No wonder so many lawyers become politicians*, he thought. Deceit pulses through their bodies like the very blood in their veins.

Con swallowed a large gulp of tea, trying to overpower the sour taste in his mouth. "That is exactly my goal, also," he choked out.

"When can Mr. Rogers have father's body?" Amelia Westcott interjected.

The question interrupted Con's train of thought. "Palm Funeral Home?" Con asked.

She nodded, her face flushed. Clearly, she was on the verge of tears. The Amelia Westcott he saw now was not the same woman he met this morning at her parents' home. Nor the one who sat nonchalantly on the very same sofa just moments ago. She dropped her guard. She lowered the domineering shield of pompousness that protected her from commoners like himself. She sat upright in her seat with both feet on the floor, anxiously waiting an answer. For this instant, he felt comfortable in the room with her. And sorry for her.

"Dr. Martin and Dr. Anderson have completed their autopsy. I should have their reports by tomorrow, I think. If everything is in order, Mr. Rogers should be able to proceed in a couple of days."

"Dr. Anderson?" Robert Westcott blurted out. "Why is he conducting the autopsy?"

"Dr. Martin conducted the autopsy," Con answered calmly. "Under the circumstances, I asked that Dr. Anderson assist."

"Circumstances!" Westcott roared. "What circumstances?"

"Brice Campbell, one of the most prominent and well-respected men in this county, known across the state, appears, for no apparent reason, to have taken his own life this morning in the garden beside his house. That's the circum-stances." Con's voice gradually increased in volume, reaching a climax. "Excuse me," he said more calmly, looking at Amelia Westcott. "I didn't mean to raise my voice."

"I understand," she replied evenly. "We are all anxious under the," she paused, not wanting to repeat the word *circumstances*. "The situation," she finished, for lack of a better word.

"My apologies, Sheriff," Robert Westcott added, coolly regaining his equanimity. "I did not consider the depth of your responsibility."

Con looked over at June. Her face was flushed. She did not raise her eyes when she lifted her pencil from the pad.

Westcott sat staring at the glass of tea in his hand. Con could see a solemnity he had not previously noticed. He had allowed his emotions to escape beyond his stoic courtroom persona. He had spoken freely without regard to any penalty enforced by a judge if such an outburst had occurred before his bench.

Westcott took a sip of his tea. Looking at Con, he cleared his throat. "Shall we proceed?"

"Yes," Con answered directly.

"How can we help you, Sheriff?" Westcott began.

"Did Mr. Campbell use opium?" Con asked them.

"Sheriff," Amelia Westcott began. "My father had a very bad back. Much of the time, he could not physically lie in bed for more than a half hour without severe pain. A normal night's rest for him might be a couple of hours. Four hours would be extreme. He used to take laudanum on occasion when he felt too much pain to sleep."

"Has this been going on for some time?" Con asked, glancing back and forth between them.

"A few years ago," Robert Westcott began, "Brice experienced somewhat of a psychological breakdown. He had a very profitable business, but he felt he had missed out on much of a *young man's life* by working many long hours building that business." He paused, gathering his thoughts. "Where should I begin? Brice and Gary Wagner were business associates. They had met contracting in the oil fields near Circle Cliffs in Utah. They both did well there. After the business peaked about ten years ago, Brice looked for new challenges and did not wish to return to Wyoming where he had lived most of his life. Gary, who lived here, suggested he might find ample work for his construction business here in Nevada. The mines west of here were growing, Brice made some good connections, and soon after, he moved his family here."

"That all sounds pretty positive. What's the catch?" Con asked.

"Gary was ten years younger than Brice and an avid mountaineer when not chasing after his trucking company," Westcott continued. "The sport intrigued Brice. He began climbing several peaks with Gary and soon fell in love with the adrenaline-inducing diversion. Coaxed on by four fellow climbers, the six men decided to take on the north face of the Eiger in Switzerland. No one had ever climbed it. Still haven't. I have no idea how far they made it, but somewhere along the line, someone fell and took the rest of them with him. Gary Wagner and another climber were killed, and Brice broke his back. Brice came home and decided he wasn't as young as he thought he was, and that ended it. That was seven years ago."

"I remember it," Con stated. "Didn't he spend quite a while in the hospital?"

"Yes," Amelia interjected. "Two months in Europe and

another month with the Mayo brothers in Rochester, Minnesota."

"Who was his doctor?" Con asked.

"Here?" Amelia asked.

"Of course."

Amelia and Robert Westcott shared several questioning glances at each other.

"Dr. Joseph Anderson," Amelia finally answered.

Con was speechless. The Westcotts' hesitation, Robert Westcott's blow up about the autopsy, they obviously had a problem with Dr. Anderson, and he doubted he would uncover the answer here. Conversation gradually subsided without serious consequences. When Con rose, he asked Robert Westcott for a copy of June's notes.

"Certainly," he answered. "You can make the sheriff a copy now, June," he told her. "Do you read shorthand, Sheriff?" he asked, turning to Con.

"No. I'm afraid I don't."

"I do some," Westcott commented with a smile. "Not very well, I must say. In long-hand, please, June."

June smiled at Con knowingly as she left Westcott's office and Con listened as her high heels clicked away down the hallway. *She is very pretty*, he thought to himself. Westcott's voice broke Con's contemplation.

"Sheriff Armenta," he said as he offered Con his hand. As he held Con in an extended handshake, he continued, "I cannot say it has been a pleasure, but rest assured, sir, I am at your service if there is anything further I may be able to help you with."

"I thank you, Mr. Westcott. I will keep in touch with you. Mrs. Westcott," he nodded in farewell. At that, Con turned and escaped down the hallway. He heard the door to the office close behind him. He would rest more assured, he thought, had Westcott not slipped back into the same implied sincerity he had started out with.

At the end of the hall, June diligently copied her notes onto another pad of paper. "I'm nearly finished," she told Con politely.

"No hurry," he told her as he feigned examining the leaves of the exotic plant nearby.

"I'm sorry if Mr. Westcott bothered you in there," she commented as she wrote. "He seldom loses his self-control like that."

"Oh, it's not a problem. He must not care for Dr. Anderson."

"No, he certainly does not," June replied, then quickly bit her lip before saying too much. As she finished the notes, June carefully folded them and placed them in an envelope. She then took a business card from her desk and handed it and the envelope to Con. "Here is Mr. Westcott's card also, should you need to call him."

"Why, thank you, Miss," Con said as he accepted the envelope.

"Sommers," she said, offering her hand. "June Sommers."

"Thank you, Miss June Sommers," Con added, blushing as he accepted her handshake. Her hand felt cool and soft, her grip gentle as he held it slightly longer than he should have.

"I need to be going," he stammered, tipping his Stetson slightly as he placed it on his head and walked out the door.

6

The clouds dissipated into white fluffs of feather in the stratosphere, drifting lazily on a sea of brilliant blue sky. Juan slept deeply. Last night's treatment weighed heavily on his weakened physique. Con had risen early and stirred the coals of the fire long before sunrise. He added fuel, bringing it back to life, and refilling the coffeepot, positioned it over the flame. As dawn broke, he carefully lifted the cloth from Juan's back and examined his condition. To his surprise, the inflammation had improved. Much of the swelling had gone down, and the surrounding redness moderated. He placed a canteen full of water alongside the flask of whiskey within his father's reach.

After slicing the dried crust from the end of the bacon for the dogs, Con left to check the sheep. Birds darted about among the brush, chirping and singing their morning songs.

Scant flowers showed themselves before the scorching desert heat drove them closed to preserve their precious moisture, and bees bustled from one to another, thieving a drop of nectar and pollen in their morning rituals. Skip and Ranger had established themselves in a favorite clearing across the small valley, holding the sheep in view between them and the camp. Their tails wagged fervently when Con came into view. He smiled to himself that they had become too accustomed to these treats he brought to them regularly. He did not mind. They joyfully performed their duties without complaint.

Con was not as adept as his father at evaluating the herd, but he was becoming better at it. Juan could tell at a glance if a lamb was missing from the flock. He could spot an ewe limping from three hundred yards away. Someday, Con wished to be as knowledgeable and observant as he was. As he walked around them, he made careful inspection of every member as he passed them. He tried to memorize specific traits of the animals he encountered. His father might say, "The young ram with the scar on the bottom of his left ear is acting strangely. We need to watch him and make sure he is not sick." *How can he do that?* Con wondered to himself. All of the rams looked the same except for a couple of real old ones with great big horns.

Vowing to learn more about them, he continued around the flock to Ranger and Skip. They anxiously awaited his arrival. He pulled the bacon from his pocket and eventually hacked it in two with his dull jackknife. He thought he should have cut it with the big butcher knife at the wagon. Then, recalling his father's comment last night, he vowed to sharpen his own knife later today. Con petted and played with the rambunctious duo for a few minutes, then sat with them, watching the sheep for nearly an hour when they settled down. Regaining his feet, he gave each dog a playful farewell pat before continuing around the herd to camp.

Juan continued to sleep as Con chastised himself on his return to the camp for leaving the coffeepot on the fire. It had nearly boiled dry. Adding more water, he replaced it over the freshly stoked flames. With their dwindling supply of water, he needed to return to the spring today. In the meantime, he sliced bacon and soaked beans in the dutch oven. When water in the coffeepot returned to a boil, Con added grounds and sat it back to simmer, refilling the position over the main heat of the fire with the skillet to fry bacon.

The smell of brewing coffee and cooking bacon roused Juan from his sleep. *"Buenos días,"* he said, grinning, embarrassed by his late rising.

"Good morning," Con said, returning the smile. "Your back looks better. How does it feel?"

"Much better," Juan replied as he lay on his side under the shade of the tarp. "You did a fine job."

Con did not answer. The recollection of last night's experience nauseated him still. Finally, as he poured a cup for his father, he commented, "I added cold water to settle the coffee grounds. The bacon is nearly ready and I have beans soaking for later. We're out of bread and peaches, though."

"I can make some frybread later, if you will get the ingredients from the wagon," Juan told him.

"We should have everything. I can find it, but I'll need to go for water this afternoon. Both canteens are nearly empty, and the barrel is getting sour."

"How far is it?" Juan asked. "It's been a long time since I've been there. I'm surprised you remembered it. You've only been there once, I think, and you were only seven or eight then."

"About a mile and a half, I think. I found a way to get the wagon there, but I will just fill the canteens again for now."

Juan thought for a moment. "That will be good."

With the bacon cooked, father and son made quick work of consuming it and the last of their cheese.

Con and his father stored most of their equipment and supplies in an assortment of wooden crates. Some had hinged lids that could be latched to keep creatures from helping themselves to precious food supplies. One such box was built to hold two fifty-pound sacks of flour and lined with tin to deter even the most persistent scavengers. Cheese, bacon, and jerky were wrapped in cloth then placed inside canvas bags, and then inside a latched wooden box. If kept from the scorching sun, the cheese would last several days, and cured bacon would not spoil for a few weeks, and mutton jerky for months. It worked well for a life without refrigeration.

With the unusual sensation for the last few days of a full belly, Juan returned to his blankets to lay face down in the shade. The wounds on his back were greatly improved. Con carefully washed them with whiskey and dampened the cloth from the flour sack to loosely cover them. Juan's face looked much better. The swelling around his eye now had little effect on his sight as scrapes and bruises began to mend themselves. When kept immobile, his fractured leg offered only minor discomfort. Movement brought back the nagging throb and sharp pain shot through him when even slightly jolted.

Rummaging through the wagon, Con secured the crate of flour, utensils, and a few other ingredients Juan required for frybread. He lightly stoked the fire and placed the pot of beans over it. The fire would burn down to coals before the beans would boil dry. Covering the skillet of bacon grease, he sat it aside and placed the half full coffeepot nearby in the sun. Con then drained the last of the water from the keg into a bucket and sat it under the wagon in the shade, then emptied the canteens into the keg.

As suspected, his weakened father had fallen back to sleep. Con slipped four pieces of jerky into his pocket. With the two canteens slung over his shoulder, he circled the grazing sheep, looking them over as he passed, and shared his jerky with Ranger and Skip. Ranger smelled the remaining jerky in Con's pocket, nuzzling his hand for more, but obeyed his command to stay when Con departed. The sun had risen to midmorning, and the wrens quieted from their sunrise chorus as temperatures began to climb. With everything in order, he trooped toward the spring.

Aligning the red rock wall over his shoulder, he covered the expanse in half an hour. More vegetation surrounded the spring, allowing the area to remain a few degrees cooler during the day. Con filled the canteens with refreshing water and then soaked his face and head in stimulating splendor. After taking a short reprieve in the tranquility, he drank his fill from the spring and headed back.

The sun lay high in the sky when Con topped the hill near the watching dogs. He petted them briefly before circling the flock and returning to camp. Juan sat in the shade of the lean-to, mixing dough for frybread.

Con handed him a canteen of water. "That's a little fresher than what we had," he said, taking the skillet from the wagon. "I saved the grease from the bacon."

"Good. Set it on the fire."

Con checked the beans simmering in the oven and placed the skillet over the hot coals.

"The sheep look pretty good, but I should probably move

them tomorrow," Con reported. "They've about drank up what water the rain left."

"Yes, and I should be recovered enough to ride to town then also." He half crawled and half scooted the few feet to a rock nearby the fire from where he could reach to fry the bread.

"It might be difficult," the thirteen-year-old commented, trying to visualize his disabled father negotiating the wagon through the brush.

"I've been thinking about it. I'll need to ride Trueno without a saddle, and I can't hold on with my legs," Juan responded, gently patting his splinted member. "We will have to rig something to her harness."

While Juan fried slabs of bread at the fire, Con made a patch from the remaining portion of the flour sack and proceeded to mend his father's tattered shirt with the small sewing kit they carried in their supplies. The wounds on Juan's back were greatly improved and no longer weeping. When Con finished the repairs, his father gingerly donned the ragged garment, thankful for the protection it provided from the blazing sun. Con gave Trueno the bucket of water he had saved from the keg. After again emptying the canteens into the small barrel, he returned twice more to refill them at the spring. When at last he came back to the wagon, he found Juan seated not far away in a position to overlook the herd of sheep. As the sun lowered in the afternoon sky, the intensity lessened, and they resumed cropping scattered clumps of foliage. Con sat down beside him and handed him a canteen of water.

"They're in good shape, Conor," his father began. "You've done well. Not by choice, but out of circumstance, you were given a man-sized load to carry on your shoulders, and you've borne it well. I am very proud of you, son," he finished, putting his arm around his son's shoulder and embracing him. "Thank you."

Con blushed under the praise, at the same time beaming with pride from his father's approval. The two sat there together discussing sheepherding, dogs, growing up, coyotes, wolves, and mountain lions. The first adult conversation he could recall having with his father...or with anyone, for that matter. Over just a few days, he had left his childhood behind and become a man. Surely there would be a wealth of experience gained throughout his adolescence to come, but he had matured. He recognized it. And so, too, did his father.

* * *

As the sun began to set, the sheep bedded down in the hollow with Ranger and Skip among them. Con helped his father up and back to the wagon. They ate beans and frybread and drank muddy, tepid coffee that had sat in the sun all day. The conversation had waned to an occasional word, but an unspoken communication between them remained. An understanding perceptible only to them. Before he rested, Juan had his son again wash his back with whiskey.

As he pulled his shirt on, he said, "Thank you for the shirt. You're smart. You think of things. You'll do well." Then he laid down on his blankets and slept.

Con was weary, but too filled with emotion to sleep. He added some larger sticks to the fire and laid on his blankets, staring at the stars. The moon had yet to rise, and even with the firelight, they shone brightly against a sea of blackness. *So close you could almost reach up and touch them*, he thought to himself. The faintest cry of a coyote in the distance joined in the music of the crackling fire, lulling him into slumber.

* * *

SUNDAY, JULY 7, 1907

As the sun rose in the east, Con had already been busy for an hour. A late full moon allowed him ample light to fuel the fire and start heating fresh water for coffee. He fed Trueno a handful of grain, then watered and harnessed her before dawn. He cut in half one of the long reins needed to pull the wagon, making two shorter ones. He fashioned a stirrup from a branch of sagebrush pulled back to itself into an eye and lashed together, then lashed it to a strap of leather made from the leftover rein and tied to the harness. He then folded his blankets into a rectangle several layers thick and tied it to the harness with rawhide strings to form the resemblance of a seat. Finally, he fashioned a loop of leather across the horse's withers tied fast to the harness. In case his father slipped from his seat, he had an emergency grab handle. He knew in his father's condition he could not withstand a fall.

When the first morning rays shone on the camp, Con poured fresh grounds into the boiling coffee pot and sat it off the direct heat to brew and simmer. As he sliced bacon from the slab, Juan awoke to the smell of the fresh coffee.

"You've been busy," he said, eyeing the apparatus tied to Trueno. "You in a hurry to get rid of me?"

Con smiled. "No, but it must be fifteen miles to town, and you'll be moving slow. I figured you would need to take advantage of the coolest part of the day. It may take a while to get there."

"Well, let me have some coffee and think about it." He paused. "What's all the stuff hanging from the mare's harness?"

Con explained his modifications as he fried bacon over the fire. "I set it all up to fit me, and she didn't mind when I tested it," he said. "I don't think you will be able to get down once you start, and if you did, you probably couldn't get back up."

They ate a hearty breakfast of bacon, beans, and frybread and drank fresh hot coffee. Juan had made a flour sack full of frybread. Enough to last Con several days when he left. He had plenty of beans and mutton jerky and enough bacon for a few more days.

When they finished eating, Con helped his father up onto the wagon and brought Trueno alongside. Tying her there, he helped Juan mount up—a difficult task with only one operable leg. Settling in and trying the single stirrup, Juan adjusted to the awkward seat. He tested the grab handle and appreciated his boy's ingenuity. Con took a short piece of rope and fashioned a sling for his father's broken rifle. He handed it to him. Then a full canteen of water. He gave Trueno another handful of oats, then took a swig of water and gave her all that remained in the keg and in his canteen.

Con removed his hat and gave it to his father. "You'll need this more than me today. Good luck," he said, choking back a tear as he handed his father the reins.

"I'll be sending her back to you with fresh supplies and a working rifle in a few days," Juan answered. With a cluck of his tongue Trueno moved off at a slow walk as if she fully understood the frailty of her precious cargo. She disliked the feel of the wooden splints gouging into her left side, but tolerated it.

Juan left his thirteen-year-old son without instructions. After Con's actions in his absence and their conversation yesterday, Juan knew he did not need any.

The young Conor Armenta picked up his empty canteen,

put several chunks of jerky in his pocket, and headed around the band of grazing sheep toward the trustworthy dogs. He frisked and played with them for nearly a half hour, doling out jerky until he had only two pieces left. Then he headed for the spring to fill his canteen.

* * *

SATURDAY, JULY 13, 1907

Con had moved the sheep twice and his camp and most all of the supplies to the spring since his father's departure. The wagon remained at his previous campsite, along with a few non-essentials stored beneath the tarp in its bed. Today, he watched the sheep grazing beneath him from a low rise. In the late morning, Ranger began to bark at something beyond Con's view over the next small hill. Skip soon joined in as the two barked at something in the distance, but held their position within view of both Con and the sheep. When he went to look, he saw a horseman, perhaps a half mile off, leading a packhorse in his direction. As the rider came nearer, Con recognized his father's good friend, Luis Garza. He rode his own horse and led Trueno under a heavily loaded packsaddle.

"*Buenos días, Señor,*" Luis greeted him with a grin. "An old crippled man in Las Vegas told me there was a herd of fine sheep that could be easily stolen from a young herder in this area. Have you seen them?" He laughed.

"That old man must have lost his senses wandering around in the hot sun. These are the only sheep around here, and they are guarded by two vicious dogs and the meanest hombre in all of Nevada," he added, barely controlling his laughter.

Luis could not let the young man have the last word in the

charade. "Where can I find this bad man? I would like to meet him."

"Perhaps you should reconsider, *Señor*. He might not treat you kindly since I see you've already stolen his horse." Con continued grinning.

"Oh, but stealing the horse was so easy," Luis kept on. "How difficult could it be to steal a few lazy sheep from this man? Perhaps he's gone daft in his loneliness with no one but his dogs and the sheep to talk to."

"You have convinced me, *Señor*. This can be a very lonely place," Con conceded. "Could you possibly join me for some beans and frybread? My camp is not far."

"Oh, *Señor*," Luis answered. "Beans are very good for a man who has been out here for a long time, but I have fresh cantaloupes and peaches that will go to waste if they are not eaten fairly soon. Possibly we could share?"

"Follow me." Con laughed and led off toward the spring.

Arriving at camp, the game concluded. Among the provisions, Luis brought Con a new hat, a pair of long reins for Trueno's harness, and a new canteen in addition to the one Juan had taken with him. After unloading the necessities, they loosened the cinch on Luis' saddle and picketed the two horses near the rivulet that ran a short distance below the spring before disappearing beneath the desert floor. They ate beans and drank coffee that had been left in the sun to keep warm. They finished their meal by splitting the largest of three cantaloupes. Luis had thought his young friend should save the melons for himself, but Conor insisted on sharing one.

He enjoyed the older man's company, and Luis updated him on Juan's condition. He told Con how Dr. Martin had commended him on the treatment of his father's injuries. The infection was gone and wounds nearly healed. Hal had replaced his father's splint with a plaster cast, but could not reset the broken bone. It had already knit itself together in the disfigured position. The result would leave Juan with a misshapen left leg about an inch shorter than the right. In addition to the fractured thigh bone, Juan's left hip had been dislocated and his right cheekbone broken.

When they had finished their meal, Luis stood and lit a small cheroot with a stick from the fire and handed Con six peppermint sticks. "Your mother sent these," he said with a straight face. "I considered keeping them for myself, but I have these," he said, indicating his cigar. "Besides, some bad hombre might take them from me for stealing his horse." Luis could control himself no longer. Laughing, he reached out and flipped the young man's new hat from his head in play. "I've got to go, but you're doing well." He collected his horse and tightened the cinch. "I have to check on my own herders, but I'll be back to check on you in two weeks.

"Your father has been my friend for a very long time," Luis told him as he slipped a nearly new Winchester Model '94 from the scabbard on his horse. "He asked me to get his rifle fixed and bring it to you. The gunsmith could not do it right away." He paused for a moment. "You know how to shoot?" he asked seriously.

"Yessir."

"Take this," he said, handing Con the rifle. Con stood there speechless as Luis reached in his saddlebag and pulled out two new boxes of .30-30 smokeless cartridges. "You'll need these, too."

"But I can't pay for these," Con finally managed to respond. "These rifles cost a hundred dollars. I'll never have that kind of money!"

"It is not new," Luis replied as he mounted his horse. "And it's a gift."

"But—"

"For saving my friend's life," Luis interrupted him.

The young man stood in shock, staring behind him as Luis rode away.

7

The heat of the day slapped him in the face as Con stepped from Robert Westcott's office. Though it was past six o'clock, the sun remained and temperatures had yet to abate for the evening. He drove to the sheriff's department to check in. Dottie had arrived to assume her duties for the nightshift, and she chatted with Hazel at the clerk's desk.

"Anything new?" Con asked as he entered the room.

"Nothing of note," Hazel replied. "That young reporter from the *Evening-Review* is a bit peeved not to have gotten a report on the Campbell situation for today's edition. She glanced and nodded toward the door to Con's office.

"He's in there?" the sheriff asked.

"Since three o'clock. When the paper went to print, I suppose."

"Okay," Con sighed. "Why don't you go home to your husband? Have a glass of lemonade on the porch swing?"

"He's working out at Boulder City, building a commissary or something. He won't be home until after dark," she replied, seemingly disappointed as she stood. Gathering her purse from a desk drawer she moved toward the door. "But lemonade on the porch does sound inviting."

As Dottie went to her desk, Con strode through the door to his office. "Good morning, Stanley," Con spoke loudly, startling the dozing reporter awake.

"Good morning?" he asked, quickly glancing out the window to determine the hour. "It's hardly morning, Sheriff!" he retorted. "I've been here repeatedly today and now it's evening and I still haven't gotten any information."

"I'm sorry, Stanley," he responded in a consoling tone. "I've been so busy with this Brice Campbell thing. The day has totally slipped away from me." Con rounded his desk and took a seat in his oak swivel chair. "How can I help you?" he asked as he slipped the envelope containing June Sommers' notes into his center desk drawer.

Dottie could hardly stifle the urge to laugh aloud as she sat at her desk in the outer office, listening to the conversation through the open door.

"But I," Stanley stuttered. "But that is precisely what I need to know about! Brice Campbell committing suicide!" he blurted.

"Who said anything about suicide?" Con asked calmly.

"For crying out loud, Sheriff!" Stanley exclaimed. "It's all over town!"

"Really?" Con asked innocently. "What do you know about it?"

"I don't know anything!" the exasperated reporter answered. "That's why I'm here!"

At that point, Dottie could no longer contain herself and burst into laughter sprinkled with several stifled snorts. Stanley looked out the door at her and knew he had been taken for a rube. He turned back to Con who leaned back in his chair, grinning.

"Really, Sheriff? Am I that gullible?"

Con remained quiet, but the reporter knew the answer.

"What I can tell you, Stan," Con finally spoke seriously, "is Brice Campbell is one of the most prominent businessmen in our county. He died outside his home at around 4:30 this morning."

The reporter sat with pad and paper, waiting for Con to continue. He didn't.

"That's it?" he finally asked in disbelief. "He shot himself, right?"

"The case is under investigation. I may have more information after I have reviewed the reports from the autopsy," Con finally responded.

"Was he drunk? Did somebody see him? Did he leave a suicide note? What?" Stanley shook his head.

"Who? Brice Campbell. What? He died. When? Around 4:30 this morning. Where? Outside his home. Why and how? The case is under investigation," Con answered. "That's your story."

"That's it?" Stanley asked again, waiting for an answer in silence. Then answered himself as he stood and turned to the door. "That's it."

"You're welcome, Stan"

"Thank you, Sheriff," he mumbled as he passed through the outer office.

"Sorry, I couldn't help myself," Dottie said as she came to Con's door, still grinning. "I feel sorry for him, really," she added. "He worked so hard to get *the big scoop*."

"He'll get his story. Just not before we have the answers."

They chatted briefly before Dottie returned to file the reports and paperwork of the previous day, a regular part of her evening ritual.

Con could hardly believe that only twenty-four hours ago he and Luis Garza were dissecting the week-old remains of sheep in search of the bullets that had killed them. It was a dirty job, but he and Garza managed to recover three of the culprits. They were all copper-jacketed bullets and seemed to be about .30 caliber. After cleaning up, Con spent the evening scouring the area surrounding the crime scene in search of evidence. He discovered nine .30-40 Krag cartridge casings on a hill about two-hundred yards away. A seldom-traveled dirt road passed another hundred yards further along. Alongside the road, he found another spent Krag casing and an empty whiskey bottle with a Tennessee maker's "For Medicinal Use" label. Yet another loophole in the controversial prohibition law, he had thought to himself. Any remaining sign of tracks had long become unidentifiable.

The casings and the whiskey bottle were in a small wooden crate where he carried a few tools in the back of his pickup. When he went to the truck to retrieve them, he realized the bullets were still in the pocket of the jeans he'd worn yesterday. He climbed in and drove home to recoup them and change from his uniform shirt into a plain chambray one.

When he returned to the office, he noticed Dottie's Model T runabout parked outside.

"That's your runabout?" he asked her as he came in the door.

"Yes," she answered quizzically.

"Could I borrow it for a few hours this evening?" he asked. "For a little undercover work," he added, noting her questioning look.

"You're not going to bring it back all shot full of holes or something, are you?" she asked, eyeing the forty-five still strapped to his hip.

"Oh, no!" Con answered, noticing her gaze. "Nothing like that at all. In fact, I'll leave my gun here in the safe and return your car unscathed with a full tank of gas," he added with an encouraging smile.

"Well, okay," she answered, knowing the gas tank was nearly empty. "You might need to fill it up before you go very far."

"And my pickup will be here to use, should any emergency arise," Con noted as he entered his office.

Taking a seat at his desk, he re-examined his evidence from Luis Garza's ranch. Leaving the pieces sitting on the corner of the desk, he pulled two new file folders and a large envelope from office supplies. On the envelope, he listed the evidence he had secured in the Garza case and sealed the casings and mangled bullets inside. Then he unlocked the safe and added the envelope, the whiskey bottle, and his holstered Colt automatic to its contents and closed the door.

When he sat back down, Con scrawled pertinent details of the sheep shooting on a notepad. He wrote "Luis Garza" at the top of one of the folders, added his notes, and placed the folder in the file drawer in the lower right of his desk.

On the other folder, he wrote "Brice Campbell," then proceeded to review the notes in his tally book. On the notepad, he made subsidiary notations and attached all of the sheets together with a large paperclip and slipped them into the folder. From his center desk drawer, Con extracted the legal-sized envelope he had placed there earlier. Holding it in both hands he scrutinized it momentarily: "Robert J. Westcott —Attorney-at-Law," imprinted on the upper left corner, and "Sheriff Conor Armenta" penciled in elegant penmanship across the center. He opened the envelope and laid aside West-cott's business card as he began reading. The documentation was precise and accurate to the best of Con's recollection, all recorded in the same lovely handwriting. A note followed at the foot of the last page.

I hope you can read my writing,
June Sommers, ph. 142.

Con glanced at Westcott's business card. Phone 366.

He trimmed the note and number from the bottom of the page, and folding the strip of paper, placed it in his wallet. Inserting the pages back into the envelope, he placed it with his own notes in the folder and filed it in his desk.

Just past seven o'clock, Con left the office and drove Dottie's runabout to the county garage where he filled it with gasoline and signed the ticket. From there he drove the eight miles to his younger brother's small sheep ranch. This had been their parents' homestead. One hundred and sixty acres of desert surrounding a small spring at the base of the hill behind the house. Con was born here. No house existed back then. Only a sheep camp with an eight-by-ten shed. The house came two years later. When he pulled into the yard, Patrick watched the unfamiliar vehicle from the porch.

"How are you, Paddy?" Con yelled from the car as he pulled to a stop in a cloud of dust.

"I must be doing better than you," he answered, curiously staring at Con's vehicle. "You get sacked from the sheriff's department?"

"No, nothing like that. I borrowed it."

"What brings you all the way out here?"

"I need a horse."

"How long?"

"Just tonight."

"It will be dark before I can get a horse loaded to take somewhere."

"I will ride from here."

"Where are you going?"

"I'd rather not say."

"No gun? No badge?"

"I shouldn't need them."

"How far?"

"Six, seven miles."

"That white horse with the black mane in the corral should do you. She's solid," Patrick suggested.

"Got something darker? Should be more than a half-moon tonight."

"This whole thing is a bit peculiar," Patrick replied.

"That's what Lorenzo said. *Curioso.*"

"You talked to Lorenzo?" Patrick asked. "What's going on?"

"It looks like Brice Campbell killed himself this morning."

A long descending whistle was Patrick's only response.

"Yep," Con confirmed.

"I've got an eight-year-old bay in a little pasture behind the house," Patrick said, shaking his head. "I don't know. He's a real fireball. Only been gelded about a year. Old Trueno's great-grandson and he hasn't outgrown his adolescent streak yet."

Patrick grabbed a carrot as the two men walked past the house. The horse trotted up to them at his whistle. He handed Con the carrot who rewarded the horse with it. The horse was calm at Con's touch and received scratching and rubbing in return. Noticing the horse was not shod, Con picked up a front foot and examined the hoof.

"Barefoot," Con remarked.

"Yeah. He's got good feet. Not many rocks around here. I don't shoe him very often." He waited, watching Con check each of his feet. "He must like you, letting you mess with his feet like that. He doesn't usually tolerate much contact. Thank your rodeo-star brother-in-law for that."

"What?" Con asked.

"Stu and Olivia had him for a couple of years. Stu broke him and roped off him some. Didn't want to geld him. I guess he thought it made him look more macho to the ladies if he rode a stud horse. I don't know which one was the bigger knot-head. Him or the horse."

"I won't answer that," Con chuckled. He loved his little sister dearly, and contrary to his teasing, she was a true beauty. The combination of her Hispanic and Irish genes melded into a rare amalgamation that complemented each another. Her clear olive skin had earned her her name at birth, and Olivia had coal-black eyes whose sparkle had melted the hearts of many suitors when she reached adolescence. Among her several callers, she fell in love with Stuart McLeod, a rodeo cowboy from Oklahoma, five years her senior. Stuart was handsome in a rugged sort of way, athletic and charming. His sandy blond hair and sterling gray eyes were as mesmerizing to women as Olivia's dark orbs were to men. The problem arose that neither his skills nor his work ethic lived up to his ego. When Olivia became pregnant with their first child, their rent and his entry fees far outweighed Stu's winnings. Olivia went to work waiting tables full time at the Mesquite Café to support the family. The day their son David was born, she put her foot down and Stu started driving a truck in between rodeos to help support their family. Stu may not have been Con's first choice for a brother-in-law, but he was her choice and the whole Armenta family respected it.

"What's his name?" Con queried.

"Roberto," Patrick responded.

"Roberto?" What kind of a name is that for a horse?"

"Some character in a book she was reading. Olivia named him," his brother replied, shaking his head. "I call him Bob. He knows it."

"Well, Bob," Con said, taking hold of his halter, "let's go for a little ride."

Con led the horse around the house to the small barn and the brothers quickly had him saddled. At dusk, Con shoved the flashlight he brought along into a saddlebag. As he prepared to mount up, Patrick came from the house and handed his brother a canteen of water. He then drew a Smith and Wesson .38 from behind his belt and slid it in with the flashlight.

"Six shots. They're all loaded," he said. "If my horse comes back and I hear about some prowler getting himself shot over around the Campbell's place, I'll know who it was."

"I'll try not to disappoint you."

As he rode off into the darkness, the desert began to cool off, and the moon peeked over the horizon.

"Paddy was right!" Con told his mount as the big horse

stepped out through the desert night. "You're all horse and plenty of it."

As the three-quarter moon rose to light up the wasteland before them, Bob broke into a gaited lope. It ate up the ground in front of him and rode as smooth as sitting in a porch swing.

"If old Stu taught you that, I need to give him a little more credit."

Con wasn't worried about leaving a trail to follow through the desert. There were enough wandering mustangs in the region to draw little attention to the tracks of an unshod horse crossing the inhospitable surroundings. A good tracker, however, would recognize immediately that the tracks from this smooth-gaited stride weren't left by some broom-tailed cayuse on the move.

In less than an hour, Con neared the Wagner rancho and slowed Bob to a walk. He reached down and patted the horse's neck as they continued on, and as he suspected, Bob had barely broken a sweat. As he crossed the road, he kept the horse walking at a steady pace to avoid drawing attention to his tracks, but stopped not far beyond to get his bearings in the dim light. Not long after they resumed, Con spotted the secluded house in the distance. In its setting, the residence offered no view of itself from the road or any other inhabitance. It appeared daunting, unlighted in the darkness.

The property was fenced, and as Con recalled from his investigation of Katherine Wagner's disappearance a few months earlier, his nearest access would be from the rear of the house. That also would be the direction Brice Campbell had come from on foot the night before.

He and Bob made a wide swing around the property, gradually closing in until Con could see the barbwire fence then continued on, staying a few yards out until he had reached the area he wanted. He then rode further away from the boundary looking for an appropriate place to leave Bob while he investigated on foot. Finding a likely spot, he dismounted and tied Bob to a large clump of brush. He took a long drink of water from the canteen and poured several handfuls that he let Bob suck from his palm. Not a lot, but enough water to pacify him for a while.

Con hung the canteen back over the saddle horn and found his flashlight in the saddlebag. His fingers touched the steel of the revolver as he reached it. At first, he shirked the idea, before reaching back in and taking it. He hefted the gun in his hand, then slipped it into his waistband behind his belt buckle. As he moved toward the fence, Patrick's farewell came into his thoughts. He returned to Bob and retied him in such a way the horse would stay there in his absence, but could break loose fairly effortlessly if he did not return. Giving Bob another friendly pat and rub on his neck, Con turned back toward the house. As he neared the fence, he began walking along it, periodically using his light to look for Campbell's tracks.

Within a few yards, he came upon a wire gate. It was partially open, and from the look of Campbell's boot tracks, he may have made several attempts to get the top hooked closed before he abandoned it. A difficult task for a man with a broken wrist. Inside the gate, the trail led directly toward the garage before disappearing in the gravel near a side door. Taking the bandanna from his pocket, Con tried the knob and found it unlocked. He pushed open the door. The garage smelled of dust, oil, and gasoline. Once inside, he closed the door and turned on his light. Directly before him sat a tan Auburn Speedster with dark green fenders. Undoubtedly the car that passed him on the road the previous night.

A Graham Brothers panel truck sat backed into the stall

beside it. A large variety of boxes and crates were stacked behind the truck. As Con approached the boxes for a closer look, the sound of crunching gravel beneath his feet was drowned out by that of a vehicle pulling up outside. Quickly scanning the building, he spotted a place to hide. Squeaking brakes signaled the vehicle's stop, followed by the slamming of a door, then another a split-second later. A large steamer trunk sat between the two stalls and slightly in front of a workbench at the back of the garage. Con scrambled beneath the bench behind it. He pulled the .38 from his waist and struggled to control his breathing as hands rattled the latches of one of the doors. The one in front of the truck, he thought.

As the doors swung open, headlights from the idling vehicle outside flooded the room before him.

"What are we taking?" a man's voice asked.

A second, deeper and more commanding voice answered, "All of it."

Con could not distinguish the face of either man. They only appeared as black silhouettes before the glaring headlights. The man obviously in charge had a deep voice and a large build, six feet or perhaps a little taller with broad shoulders. He wore a straw skimmer. He did not avoid doing his share of the work as he lifted the heavy boxes with ease and carried them outside. The other man called him Drago. He had a medium build and wore an eight-panel flat cap like those the newsboys wore. The two men spoke casually as they went about their work, but gave no hint of their destination nor their employer. Drago called the smaller man Wesley.

The tiny clinking together of glass bottles as the men toted their freight outside helped solidify Con's suspicion they contained illegal liquor. The vehicle they arrived in had to be a truck of some kind. More cargo had been carried out than any type of automobile could carry. The minutes seemed like hours as Con lay silent and motionless in his hideout. The pile of cartons and crates diminished. With each box they lifted, the men came closer and closer to Con's refuge. On the final row, their faces were no more than five feet away, yet he still could not make them out in the shadows.

Unable to control the elevated pulse of blood rushing through his veins, Con could barely regulate his breathing as he waited in anticipation of being discovered with each box the men picked up. When the wide doors of the garage closed to leave him in total darkness, he finally took in a deep breath and exhaled it very slowly. He listened to the slamming of two doors on the truck and the whine of gears as it backed away from the door. The driver ground the gears as he re-engaged them to head down the driveway. Listening ever so carefully, Con could hear the truck stop to close the gate at the county road.

As the truck accelerated and the driver shifted through the gears, the sound gradually faded into the night. Con, at long last, allowed himself to begin to relax. He had been confined behind the trunk for scarcely more than a half hour, but the stiffness in his body reminded him he was no longer a teenager. He laid his flashlight on the workbench as he stood fully erect, and after stretching his back and legs, tucked the .38 behind his belt buckle again. Little brother had shown wisdom, and his parting comment had implanted a seed of doubt in Con's own self-assurance. Had anything gone wrong in the past hour, Paddy's pistol may have been the difference between seeing the sunrise tomorrow and Bob returning home alone. Fumbling in the darkness, he recovered the light and turned it on.

No remnant of evidence suggested the contents of the

crates and boxes, or that they had even been there. Con held little reservation he stood in the midst of a bootlegging operation. He turned to get a closer look at the Auburn. A layer of dust and dirt remained from traveling unpaved roads. The grime failed to disguise the sleek look of the car, beginning at the long hood required to cover the Speedster's massive engine. He could hardly imagine driving any car at a speed of 100 miles per hour, but this car was reportedly capable of it and perhaps a little more. It may have been approaching that speed when it swept past him last night. The forty miles per hour he drove at the time made it difficult to estimate. He imagined the long rear decklid covered ample space to conceal several cases of illegal liquor it probably carried.

The interruption by the bootleggers had upset the surprise of finding the Auburn here, but now his thought pattern began to put itself back into order. Brice Campbell had been driving the Speedster when it passed him on the road southeast of Las Vegas. The car must belong to Katherine Wagner, or had belonged to her. Maybe not. Recovering the scrap of paper with June Sommers' phone number from his wallet, he jotted down the license plate numbers from both vehicles. Knowing who actually owned them may help fill in some of the blanks regarding Brice Campbell's death.

Looking around, he saw the back of the panel truck was empty, as was the Auburn. What about the trunk by the bench? Con examined the latches, which were locked. Most of these locks were pretty simple in design. A bent nail from the workbench proved sufficient to pick the mechanism, and it fell open easily. He did not know what to expect when he raised the lid. Con hoped it wasn't Katherine Wagner's body. It wasn't. It was her clothes—or some woman's clothes—all clean, neatly pressed, folded, and packed tightly into the trunk. He did not rifle through the contents. He would have enough to explain if anyone found out he had been here without incriminating himself further.

Con relocked the trunk, checked carefully around the garage for any evidence of his trespass, and left through the door he had entered. When he passed through the wire gate at the rear of the property, he closed it with the loop the crippled Brice Campbell had been unable to secure the previous night.

Bob patiently awaited his return and nickered when Con approached. Con patted his neck before returning the pistol and flashlight to the saddlebag. After taking a drink from the canteen and giving Bob a sip from his hand, he saddled up and headed back toward his brother's ranch. Anticipating their destination, the long-legged gelding soon found his comfortable ground-eating lope and stepped out for home. Bob had nearly rocked the weary sheriff to sleep before rousing him from his drowsiness with a bone-jarring trot for the last few yards before stopping in front of Patrick Armenta's barn.

Con felt beyond his years as he swung to the ground. His tired and sore legs and backside reminded him that it had been quite some time since he had ridden more than a dozen miles through a sleepless night. He pulled Bob's saddle and bridle off and hung them on the rack where Paddy had gotten them. He put the flashlight in his hip pocket, left the revolver in the saddlebag, and hung the canteen from a nail near the saddle.

Tired as he was, he scrounged up a brush and gave Bob a good rubdown. The night was not terribly cool, but Bob's back was barely damp beneath the saddle blanket. "You got to like this horse, Paddy," he said out loud to himself. "He's a good one."

"Yes, he is," Patrick's voice broke the quiet night air as he walked up behind his brother from the darkness.

"You should be more careful," Con exclaimed, half startled by his brother's sudden appearance. "I might have shot you."

"Not without the pistol I loaned you." He grinned. "Did someone take it away from you, or did you lose it out in the desert somewhere?"

"Neither." Con chuckled as he tossed the brush back into the box where he had found it. He then reached into the saddlebag and retrieved the .38, handing to Patrick butt first. "Thank you," he said seriously. "I nearly needed it."

Patrick almost unconsciously rolled the cylinder, checking the six bullets in their chambers. "Go home and get yourself some sleep, big brother."

"What time is it?" Con asked, looking at the moon sitting low in the morning sky.

"You'll know when the sun comes up," he answered, pointing toward the dim light appearing on the eastern horizon.

Con dropped his flashlight onto the seat beside him as he climbed behind the wheel of Dottie's car. "Good night, little brother," he called as the runabout came to life.

"Yeah," Paddy answered as Con sped out of the yard.

The sun warmed the morning air by the time Con pulled up in front of the sheriff's department. The cool breeze blowing in his face as he drove the runabout refreshed him on his way to town. When he stopped at the county shop to top off the gas tank, he had also given the car a quick rinse with the wash bucket and garden hose near the pump. Dottie looked relieved to see him when he walked in the door.

He pitched the keys to her. "Full tank of gas, like I

promised," he said, walking into his office. His voice was cheerful, but he looked terrible.

"Are you okay?" she finally asked as he returned, strapping his pistol around his waist.

"I'm fine," he said. "Just tired. I'm going to get some breakfast at the Mesquite then home to take a nap." Con retrieved the scrap of paper from his wallet and handed it to Dottie. "Ask Hazel to check those two vehicles and see what she can find out about them."

Dottie looked at the two numbers scrawled on the paper. "Sure," she said as Con walked out the door. Holding the paper in her hand, Dottie noticed something written on the other side. She turned it over.

I hope you can read my writing,
June Sommers, ph. 142.

8

C on woke at eleven o'clock. He had slept for about four hours. He estimated he'd had a total of around seven hours sleep in the last three days, but felt refreshed considering the circumstances. He started a pot of coffee on the kitchen stove, then shaved. Dressed in a clean uniform shirt and jeans, he collected three days of the *Evening-Review* from his front porch and sat down with a cup of coffee. As he opened yesterday's edition, the bold "BRICE CAMP-BELL IS DEAD" headline dominated the front page.

The subsequent half-column article did not support the grandeur of the headline. Coroner, Dr. Harold Martin, M.D. brought the body of the deceased to the morgue and identified it as that of Brice Campbell. When asked where and how Campbell had died, Hal had answered only that he was not at liberty to say. Stanley Olsen had done his best. Sheriff Conor Armenta was not available for comment and all personnel with the sheriff's department had given the same statement. Leanora Campbell had not answered her telephone. Robert and Amelia Westcott had stated they had no announcement. Mr. Rogers at the Palm Funeral Home stated the family had contacted him, but no arrangements had been made. Both the receptionist and field superintendent at Campbell's Fremont Construction Company stated all current contracts were proceeding as planned. Stanley filled the rest of the space with a common knowledge history of Brice Campbell and his contributions to the community. Numerous other tidbits from around the country occupied most of the front page. It appeared obvious the editors had rushed to fill the columns they had planned for the Campbell story with anything they could fit into the vacant space.

"Good job, Stan," Con said aloud as he sipped his coffee.

Glancing through the rest of the paper, an advertisement by the Desert Chevrolet garage drew his attention on page three. It boasted their manufacturer's new six-cylinder engine. "It's wise to choose a SIX!" headlined the two columns with a $495 price tag for a roadster at the bottom. Looking through his back door, he eyed the disabled Plymouth Phaeton parked in front of his sheriff's department pickup. *I really need to get a dependable car*, he thought to himself as he downed the last of his coffee. Strapping his holstered Colt around his waist, he donned his Stetson and exited out the kitchen door.

Con arrived at the office with a sandwich from his parents' café in a brown paper bag.

Hazel greeted him cheerfully, "Coroner's reports are on your desk. Would you like coffee?"

"Sure, that would be great."

As Con opened the first envelope from Hal Martin, Hazel sat a fresh cup of coffee on his desk and casually handed him a page from a notepad with Con's scrap of paper clipped to it. "Thank you, Hazel."

"No problem at all, Sheriff," she replied and turned before he could catch her eye.

He sat Hal's envelope aside without looking at its contents. There were three sections on the note she had handed him. The first read, "1927 Graham Brothers delivery truck. Dutch's Oasis, 251 North 1st Street, Las Vegas." The establishment had some notoriety in Las Vegas. Dutch Wagner, son of Gary and Katherine, owned a saloon, billiard hall, and brothel in Block 16. Though thriving on the questionable morals of his patrons, all were legitimate forms of business in Nevada. His saloon occasionally attracted the scrutiny of federal agents searching his and others' for more potent beverages than sarsaparilla and ginger ale, but it seemed outwardly that he ran a pretty clean operation. Located within the city limits, the enterprise fell under the Police Chief's jurisdiction and consequently had not attracted Con's analysis.

The second section read, "1929 Auburn Speedster. Katherine Wagner, Pine Canyon Road, Las Vegas." Neither notation surprised Con. The fact he could not recall ever seeing the Speedster before it passed him on the road from Searchlight two nights ago did surprise him. This was no ordinary automobile. He certainly would remember if he had seen it. Perhaps she had purchased it just prior to her disappearance?

The third notation caught the sheriff completely off guard. "June Annette Sommers, employed by Robert Westcott, Atty. at Law, 33, widowed, 469 South 3rd Street, Las Vegas, since 1925. Previous residence, Riverside, California."

As he approached the door into the main office, Hazel already had a slightly guilty look on her face. "You didn't intend for me to run a check on her. I know. But Dottie and I were just too curious." She tried to assess Con's reaction. "Especially after you borrowed Dottie's car and were gone all night and brought it back all washed up." He still had not replied. "I thought you would want to know, too."

"You're reading way too much into this," Con finally answered. "I spent last night out in the desert checking evidence in the Brice Campbell case. The dusty roads left Dottie's black car a mess, so I rinsed it off when I filled it up with gas. It had nothing to do with June Sommers."

The look on Hazel's face told Con she did not believe a single word he had just spoken, and he had already divulged more information about last night's escapade than he planned on sharing. Unable to think of anything to convince Hazel— and probably Dottie—otherwise, he finally said, "Thank you," and returned to his desk.

Wondering how he could keep this latest little rumor from spreading, it suddenly dawned on him he had proof of his statement. "Where did you think I got the license plate numbers?" he yelled out to Hazel.

Con returned to his coroners' reports. He ate his sandwich and drank his coffee while he read. Everything coincided with his discussion with the two doctors. Hal had included a complete set of the victim's fingerprints. An evidence envelope contained the opium bottle, a set of keys, and bullet fragments wrapped in tissue paper. Con telephoned the state crime lab in Carson City and asked about ballistics tests. The cost to be billed to the county did not seem excessive to him, so he made arrangements to have them done and also to have the revolver checked for fingerprints. He packaged the pistol, bullet fragments, and fingerprint samples in a box and addressed them to Carson City.

As he prepared to leave the office with his parcel under his arm, he told Hazel, "I will be out on West Charleston Boulevard for a while. I should be back before you leave." He turned back at the door. "Don't let your imagination get ahead of you," he winked and departed before she could respond.

After dropping the package at the Post Office, he drove down the main street toward Charleston Boulevard. He could not help noticing a new chocolate brown coupe at the Desert Chevrolet garage as he passed by. He turned right onto Charleston and motored on out to the Fremont Construction Company where he pulled up in front of the office. With his tally book in his hip pocket and hat in hand, he entered the front door. A friendly secretary occupied the first desk.

"May I help you, Sheriff?" she asked with a smile.

"I was told to talk to Mr. Goldstein."

"I am afraid Mr. Goldstein is out of town. Is there anyone else who could help you?"

"Mrs. Campbell suggested I talk to him regarding financial matters."

"Well, that would certainly be correct, but unfortunately, he is out of the country right now."

"Oh. Evidently, Mrs. Campbell did not know of that. When is he expected back?"

"According to the wire, he cut his trip short and should be leaving Zürich tomorrow."

"Switzerland?"

"Yes?" she replied quizzically.

"Mountaineering?" Con asked.

She giggled. "Elmer? No, I am sorry." She giggled again. "I just cannot picture him in the outfit. No, he is there on business."

"I am the one who is sorry. Knowing Mr. Campbell had

been a mountaineer, I thought perhaps they may have shared that passion."

"Certainly not. The passion Mr. Campbell and Mr. Goldstein shared was money." She thought perhaps she had overspoken her opinion and added, "Not that there is anything wrong with that."

"No, nothing at all. Why would they be in business if they did not expect to prosper?"

"Right," she replied.

"So, when might he be back here?"

"I think it's a day by train from Zürich to Amsterdam, maybe two. Then Amsterdam to Boston is six or seven days by steamer, depending if they stop in Great Britain. Then four more days by train from Boston to here if they are on schedule." She totaled the score in her head. "It's Friday so, about a week from next Wednesday if the trip goes well."

"I see. The newspaper said the superintendent expected all contracts to be continued on schedule. Is that correct?"

"He is out by Boulder today, but that is the word we all have here."

"Thank you, miss. Could you have Mr. Goldstein call me when he returns?"

"It would be my pleasure," she replied as she wrote a note on a green pad of paper and tore the sheet from it. "Is there anything else I can help you with?"

"No, thank you. You have been very helpful." He gave a slight tip of his hat and stepped out the door.

He sat for a moment in his pickup and jotted a few notes. The secretary knew from memory how long it took to travel from point to point on the journey from Zürich to Las Vegas. She was even familiar with the options in sailing from Amsterdam. Mr. Goldstein or Mr. Campbell must have made the trip

frequently. Somewhat disappointed with missing Mr. Goldstein, Con turned his truck back toward town. He had not
planned it, but as he approached the Wagner Trucking Company's facility, he decided to stop. When he entered the office, he
noticed a striking similarity to the layout of the Fremont
Construction Company office. A pleasant, matronly woman
seated in the same position asked nearly the same question.

"How can I help you today, Sheriff?"

"I know your company has worked closely with Fremont
Construction in the past, and I wondered if Brice Campbell's
death is going to affect any of your contracts?"

"I don't believe so, but Mr. Wagner is in today. Perhaps he
can answer your question. Excuse me," she added as she rose
and crossed the room to a door at the rear. She knocked on the
door, then opened it. After speaking to someone from the
doorway, she motioned to Con. "Come right this way," she
said. Con followed her across the room. Before reaching the
doorway, Dutch Wagner filled it, and the secretary stepped
aside. Wagner extended his hand. "Dutch Wagner. I believe we
met a few months ago."

"Yes, Mr. Wagner," Con answered without bringing up his
mother's disappearance. "We have met." Wagner's handshake
was firm, but his palm was clammy.

"What brings you out here today, Sheriff?"

"I was just over at Fremont Construction. They seem to be
moving ahead. I know you have worked together extensively
in the past. Is Brice Campbell's death going to affect your
business?"

"I certainly hope not," Wagner answered, as he motioned
Con to a seat near the desk. Both Bob Westcott's office and
Brice Campbell's study were more elaborate than Wagner's
nicely appointed office. It was not dirty, but not quite clean.

The air smelled stale and heavy. Recalling the cleanliness of Katherine Wagner's home when he had been there, there must have been a freshness to the atmosphere here when she occupied the space. "I have a couple of large contracts coming up with Fremont that would break this company if they fell through."

"What do you mean?"

"We have fifty brand-new dump trucks coming. The first twenty-five begin arriving in six weeks. Five a week for five weeks, then another twenty-five the same way later this year." Wagner fidgeted in his seat, possibly fearing Con would inform him Fremont was busted.

"Well, sir," Con offered, "that is a big responsibility. It must nearly double the size of your fleet."

"More than double. We currently have thirty-two. Most of them haul freight. The few dump trucks we run are aging. They won't stand up to the beating they will get when things really get rolling next year." Unable to figure out why the sheriff had called on him contributed to Wagner's obvious nervousness.

"Well, if it's any consolation, I didn't talk with him directly, but Fremont's field superintendent is assuring everyone all current contracts will be filled on schedule."

Wagner let out an audible sigh of relief. "Well, that's the best news I've heard all week."

"I was out at the Campbells' yesterday," Con mentioned, changing the subject. "I noticed fresh tire tracks into your mother's place when I drove by. Might be somebody messing around out there." Con watched the man closely. His statement brought back a slight bit of Wagner's discomfort, but nothing like a few moments ago.

"Those would be mine," Wagner lied. "I go out there once a week or so to check on the place. Everything is okay."

"Ever hear anything from your mother? A letter? Ransom note?" Con asked cautiously.

"No, not a word," Wagner replied dispassionately. "I'm sure she's off on an adventure somewhere. Might be on the Mediterranean with some lover basking in the sun for all I know. Probably afraid to upset me and my sister with romantic details."

Wagner's indifference left Con dumbstruck. More importantly, Wagner never looked up when he answered. A dead giveaway to his deceit in Con's book. The treachery he suspected six months ago seemed to be coming closer and closer to fruition.

"What does your sister think?" Con asked, though he really wanted to end the conversation.

"The same, I suppose. Mom's been pretty flighty since Dad passed." He appeared a little more confident in his answer, but still would not look Con in the eye when he spoke.

"Well, good luck to you," Con stated flatly as he rose to his feet.

"Thank you," Wagner replied, walking the sheriff to the door. "I appreciate your concern." He offered Con his hand, and he accepted. Still clammy. The sensation left Con longing to wash the slimy feeling from his hand. When he crossed the outer office, the secretary's agreeable smile helped compensate for the unpleasantness of her employer.

"I was just at Fremont Construction's office earlier and couldn't help noticing that both this office and theirs are nearly identical," Con offered casually.

"This used to be Fremont's office," she responded cheerfully.

"When Freemont Construction outgrew this facility, Mr. Campbell built their current one. A short time later, he sold this property to Mrs. Wagner. We had also outgrown our previous yard."

"Have you worked here long, ma'am?"

"Nine years."

"Then you knew Mr. Wagner as well as Mrs. Wagner?"

"Yes," she answered. "Katherine and I became pretty close after Gary died."

"I forgot to ask Dutch. What kind of car did she drive?"

"An Oldsmobile coupe. Why do you ask?"

Her answer puzzled Con. "Do you know where it is?"

"Certainly. It's in the shed behind the shop out back. Dutch brought it to town a few months ago. He said he was afraid someone would steal it if he left it out in Katherine's garage."

"Never drove an Auburn?"

The secretary turned white. "How did you know about that?"

"She had an Auburn?"

"Yes, a fancy roadster. I only saw it once."

"Why didn't she drive it?"

"It was a gift…and she was afraid."

"Afraid of what?"

"Dutch," she answered, staring at his office door.

"Who gave it to her?"

She sat at her desk in fear, staring at Dutch's door. She did not answer.

"This is just between you and me," Con whispered. "You will never have to repeat it. Who gave her the car?"

"Brice Campbell," she answered, barely audible. "Excuse me," she said only slightly louder and rushed to the restroom as tears flowed down her cheeks.

The statement had set Con on his heels. He glanced at

Dutch Wagner's office door, making sure it had not opened.
Then he left the building. As he drove down Charleston Boulevard, heatwaves danced on the graveled surface ahead. The
phenomenon of the mirage only compounded the daze the
information had left him in. His mind raced through random
thoughts as he tried to grasp what he had just learned. What
had gone on out on Pine Canyon Road that left Katherine
Wagner missing and Brice Campbell dead?

Con motored down Main Street and again eyed the new
Chevrolets as he passed. Turning on Fremont, he pulled in
across from the First State Bank, then casually crossed the
street and entered the lobby. Thomas T. Cooke, the bank presi-
dent, had known Con since his teens. He leaned over the desk
of a younger man engaged in conversation.

"What brings you in today, Con?" Cooke asked when he
looked up.

"Just a couple of questions, Mr. Cooke," Con answered.

"Come on back," he said, motioning the sheriff behind the
polished banister that divided the lobby from the desks of
several clerks. Tom Cooke then ushered Con through the
etched-glass door into his private office. With his hand on
Con's shoulder, he guided him into a chair across from the
desk where he took his seat. "Well then. What can I help you
with?"

"I'm thinking about buying a new car."

"That is wonderful," the banker responded. "You probably
have enough in savings to pay cash, if you care to. What do
you have in mind?"

"I haven't begun to shop actually, but maybe a new
Chevrolet. I'd like to finance a portion of it."

"It certainly won't be a problem," Mr. Cooke replied. "You
have banked here your whole life and I certainly don't

consider you a credit risk. It is getting rather late today. If you would like, I can call Mr. Collins and arrange to handle the financing on Monday for whatever car you might choose?"

"That would work great for me. I will probably go there tomorrow."

"Mr. Collins usually requires a ten percent cash deposit or a trade in of equal value to confirm the sale."

"That will be fine," Con agreed, nodding his head. He then waited while Mr. Cooke called Desert Chevrolet and made the arrangements. With that, the two men shook hands and Con stopped at the teller to withdraw the cash he might need from his savings.

The afternoon waned as Con returned to his office. Hazel had nothing new to report. He called Palm Funeral Home and talked to Steven Rogers. The Campbell family had spoken to him, but no arrangements had been made regarding services for Brice Campbell. Con decided to pay Leanora Campbell a visit. He did not look forward to another meeting with the Westcotts right now, and needed a representative of the family to authorize a recipient in order to release Brice Campbell's body from the county's custody. The drive out to Pine Canyon Road gave him an opportunity to contemplate the circumstances of Brice Campbell's death. It also provided another chance to compare the layout of the neighboring estates of the Campbell and Wagner families and perhaps provide a glimpse into the Campbell's affiliation with Katherine Wagner.

As Con pulled up in front of the Campbell home, he could not help admiring the serenity of the hacienda. The abrupt trauma had supplanted its peacefulness.

A tall thin woman in an apron responded to his knock at the door. She asked that he wait there and left the door ajar as she retreated behind it. A moment later, Leanora Campbell appeared in her place.

"To what do I owe this visit, Sheriff?" she asked pleasantly.

"I am sorry to intrude, ma'am. I hope I am not interrupting your supper."

"Not at all, Sheriff. I dine late in the evening this time of year, and quite frankly, I have not had much appetite lately anyway."

"I understand perfectly. I came to tell you the coroner and his assistant are finished with their autopsy. I can release Mr. Campbell's body now. Your daughter suggested the Palm Funeral Home might be handling the services, but Mr. Rogers advised me no arrangements had yet been made. Consequently, I need your direction as to who you would like me to discharge to."

"Oh, that would be Mr. Rogers. We just did not want to proceed until Newt gets here."

"Newt?"

"Yes, our son. Newton Campbell. He will arrive from Cheyenne tomorrow. He runs our company there."

Con hoped he didn't have a stupid look on his face as he tried to gather this whole new factor into perspective. "I apologize, ma'am. I had no idea you had a son or a company in Cheyenne. Wyoming? Correct?"

"Yes, that is where we started out. A very small company then. Brice borrowed money from his father to get it started. Before we paid him back, Brice felt obligated to follow his father's rules. Afterward they butted heads on management philosophies almost continually. When the opportunity arose to contract the work in Utah, we needed additional financing to pursue the venture. Brice's father refused the loan, so Brice went to his father's former partner, a competitor, for the money. The Utah project was a huge success, but Brice's father never forgave him and never spoke to him again. After Utah, Newt returned to Wyoming with a portion of our equipment and resurrected our operation there. We moved here. Newt's business is small in comparison to here and nearly dried up completely with Wall Street the way it is."

"Wow, that certainly is interesting," Con replied, still trying to regain his composure. "If you could sign this authorization, I will release Mr. Campbell's remains to the Palm Funeral Home," he added, indicating the paper in his hand. "You might wish to ask Mr. Rogers to begin his procedure before you decide on final arrangements."

"Yes, I will call him. Please come in, Sheriff, no need to stand out here," she said, leading the way to Brice's study. At first glance, he thought the room looked exactly as he had seen it before. When Leanora Campbell took her place behind the desk, he noticed several differences. The inkwell had been moved to a position near the top right corner of the desk pad and the telephone to the left side of the desk. There were three ledgers now stacked on the right-hand side of the desk. Not large like those used in most businesses. More the size of a notebook or business letter. Con suspected the drawers' contents were also significantly different now than the empty spaces he observed on his previous visit. He also supposed the notations in the ledgers would explain why they were hidden the morning of Brice Campbell's death.

Leanora scanned the release form with the eye for detail of a legal secretary, not the naïve eye of a housewife who had no idea what financial condition the family's construction company might be in as she had suggested herself to be. Taking a pen from the stand and dipping it in the inkwell, she quickly filled in the section naming the Palm Funeral Home as the recipient, the person responsible as herself, wife of the deceased, and signed it. When she opened the top desk drawer to retrieve the blotter, he noted the previously sparse contents were now struggling to contain themselves in limited space. She blotted her inscriptions with experienced care not to blur them, blew on them to ensure their dryness, and handed the document back to the sheriff.

A quick glimpse showed Con everything in order. "Very good," he commented. "Thank you for your assistance, and again, I apologize for the intrusion." As he prepared to leave, Leanora Campbell rose from her seat. In doing so, she bumped the ledgers and the top one fell to the floor at Con's feet. He picked it up and handed it to her. She quickly placed it carefully on the stack, but not before the notation on the front of the second ledger caught Con's eye. *Dutch.*

9

Con woke to birds singing outside his bedroom window. It reminded him of the days he herded his father's sheep near Red Rock Canyon. No criminals or outlaws had stalked the canyons those two decades earlier beyond what he had imagined or joked with Luis Garza about in the little game they played with each other anytime he visited Con's camp. Times were simpler back then. Now, gangsters, bootleggers, and con men lurked in the backstreets and alleys, ready to take the hard-earned wages of railroad workers, miners, and dam builders by swindle or outright robbery when they came to town to celebrate in the saloons and brothels of Block 16. Somehow, Brice Campbell and Dutch Wagner were tied up in it, maybe separately, but probably together.

Con called Hal Martin. He thanked him for the autopsy report and told him to release the body to Palm Funeral Home.

Hal told him he would contact Steve Rogers and make the arrangements. Recalling the rearranging of Brice Campbell's desk, Con brought up a new question to Hal. "Do you suppose Brice Campbell was left or right-handed?" he asked Hal casually.

"Well, he was shot in the right temple."

"True. Could you shoot yourself in the temple with your left hand?"

"Yes, I believe I could."

"Same here."

"Let me think about this some. I'll call you if I come to any conclusions."

"I don't want to raise any suspicions or I'd just ask the family or someone at Fremont Construction. Keep this to yourself, okay?"

"You know me pretty well, Con. I won't show my hand."

Con made coffee and took a cup to his front porch. He picked up Friday's *Evening-Review* and sat down to enjoy his coffee and the fresh morning air. Scanning the paper, he found little of interest. No mention made of Brice Campbell. He took a bath and shaved before dressing in clean civilian clothes and strolling to Mesquite Café.

"Well, if it isn't our lazy sheriff," his sister taunted when he walked in. "Nine o'clock in the morning and he's finally out of bed. It must be a nice job, getting paid to drive around doing nothing all day."

"For your information, I'm off duty today…and walking. And even at that, I may go out to Luis Garza's later to see if he is still losing any sheep," Con responded, taking a seat at the counter as Olivia filled a cup with coffee in front of him.

"Huevos with chorizo on special," she said as if she hadn't heard him.

"Sure," Con answered just as his mother leaned over him from behind and kissed him on the cheek.

"Good morning, Conor," she said happily as she continued toward a table of patrons with coffee pot in hand.

"Are you sure she is your mother? You didn't inherit her kindheartedness," he told his sister.

"Neither did you," she replied as she called his order back to their father.

"Oh, I'm nice enough...just not to you," he retorted as she moved to the far end of the counter. While he finished his coffee, Olivia returned with his breakfast and refilled the cup. The banter continued between them intermittently as Con leisurely consumed his food. He could not recall having time to actually enjoy a meal recently. When finished, he stood and doled out his payment on the counter.

"Why are you walking?" Olivia asked as she collected the money.

"Just got tired of driving around, doing nothing," he winked. Grabbing his hat, he walked out the door. He crossed to the shady side of Fremont Street and wandered toward Main, occasionally stopping to peer into a store window.

At Main Street he paused before leaving the shade of the Hotel Nevada. Leanora Campbell, Amelia and Bob Westcott, and a tall man about his own age were leaving the Union Pacific Depot. Con guessed the stranger to be Newt Campbell. He held the driver's door of her car for his mother. Amelia scrambled behind the wheel of her Whiskey Six unassisted as Bob took the passenger's seat. Newt threw two bags in the rear of the touring car and climbed in beside his mother. With little chance they would notice him in civilian attire, Con still turned to face the hotel when the two cars pulled out toward

Pine Canyon Road. *Perhaps the prodigal son has returned*, he thought to himself as he proceeded to the Chevrolet garage.

He had difficulty identifying the reason, but Con had recently acquired an overwhelming desire to purchase a new car. He hadn't even looked at it, but the chocolate brown coupe with black fenders he had seen became the center of his attention. When he began to look it over, Abner Collins appeared from inside.

"Good morning, Sheriff," he greeted, offering his hand for a shake. "Tom Cooke told me you might stop by. How can I help you?"

"Well, I would like to buy a car, Mr. Collins."

"Call me Ab. Everybody does. This one right here is a beauty," he offered, referring to the car he looked at. "It has the new six-cylinder engine," he said as he lifted the butterfly hood. "This is the Deluxe Model, with a rumble seat in the back." He walked to the rear of the car, tilted back the lid, and pointed toward the rear fender. "With the step here, it's quite comfortable for even an adult to climb in. We could install a rear rack if you need to carry a trunk," he added, noticing Con examining the rear spare tire mount. Ab then stood back for a moment, allowing Con to study the vehicle. As Con returned to the side of the car, Collins opened the driver's door. "Climb in and see how she fits."

Con felt obliged to accept the suggestion and took his place behind the wheel. The more spacious interior than his sheriff's pickup surprised him. With the soft, comfortable mohair-covered seat he imagined a more pleasant ride, also.

"Would you like to take her for a turn around the block?" the proprietor asked.

"Sure."

"Go ahead and fire it up while I batten down the hatches," Ab grinned.

A moment later, Collins climbed in beside him. "Don't let it surprise you. These sixes have considerably more pep than a four-popper," he commented as they pulled onto the street.

Con turned down Fremont. The smooth sound of the six-cylinder engine surprised him and he sped up slightly for a few blocks, then slowed to make a right turn down 3rd Street. As they rambled down the way, a blonde woman and little girl laughing on a porch swing caught Con's attention. June Sommers. Had he subconsciously taken this street in hope of seeing her, he wondered. He did not know. He did know it pleased him.

"So, what do you think of her, Mr. Armenta?" Ab Collins asked.

Had Collins noticed him staring at June Sommers? "Well, sir, she's very nice," he answered with dual meaning for himself as reality quickly rejoined his thinking.

"You'll notice the smooth ride," Collins continued. "The new, longer leaf springs really iron the wrinkles out of a rough, choppy road."

When they reached Charleston, he made a right-hand turn and picked up his speed as he sprinted down the lightly traveled thoroughfare back to Main Street.

"I told you she had some horsepower." Collins laughed as they returned to the garage. "I know you like her. Are you ready to take the girl home?"

Con's mind kept drifting back to June Sommers. He kept comparing Collins's comments about the car with June—she was a beauty, nice, and he certainly did like her. "Well, let's see what we can do," he said, wrestling his thoughts back to Ab Collins and the coupe.

"Come on in and we'll put a pencil to it," Collins offered. "Do you have anything to trade in?"

"I have a Plymouth Phaeton at my house. It quit running a few months ago. I think it needs a fuel pump, but I haven't had time to work on it. I have some cash to make a down payment."

"I'll tell you what, Sheriff," Ab began. "Let me send Max, my mechanic, over to take a look at your Plymouth. You can take the coupe out for a ride and get a better feel for it. Meet me back here at say," he looked at the clock reading a quarter to twelve, "let's say two o'clock. Then we can put some numbers together."

"That sounds fair to me," Con agreed. The two men rose, shook hands, and Con departed.

He jumped back in the coupe and turned south. At Charleston he headed back to 3rd Street and pulled up in front of June Sommers' house. She still sat on the porch swing with the cute little blonde girl. Con quickly saw a resemblance.

He removed his hat as he walked to the porch. "Good day, Miss June Sommers! How are you this fine day?" he asked.

"Very well, Sheriff Armenta," she answered with a smile. "And you?"

"I could not be better," he replied. "But as you can see," he said, motioning to his attire, "I am not the sheriff today. Please call me Con."

"Very well, Conor Armenta. What brings you here today?"

"Well, June Sommers," he replied. "I passed by this house a little while ago and saw you and this charming young lady sitting on this swing. I said to myself, perhaps you should pay these beautiful women a visit and gain an introduction to this lovely upcoming debutante. So here I am."

"I saw the car drive by earlier, Mr. Armenta. I had no idea

it was you," June fibbed. She had noticed Con's stare when he drove past earlier. "Please forgive my ill manners. Mr. Conor Armenta, may I present my daughter, Princess April Sommers. And Princess April, I present to you, Mr. Conor Armenta, the Sheriff of Nottingham, oh excuse me," she giggled, "the Sheriff of Clark County, Nevada."

Con swept his hat before him and bowed deeply to rest on one knee before the shyly smiling young girl and gently took her hand, "My lady," he said without rising, "I am at your service." Then he gently kissed the back of April's hand as he grinned ear to ear before releasing it. The pair on the porch swing giggled profusely and Con broke into a pleasant laugh as he regained his feet.

"Well Mr. Armenta, would you care for a glass of tea?"

"I would like that very much, but please, my father is Mr. Armenta. I'm Con."

"Very well." She blushed slightly, turning to her daughter. "Princess April, could you bring Con and me a glass of tea?"

"Yes, Mama," April answered and disappeared into the house.

"She is lovely," Con commented as April scampered away.

"Yes, she is. I would die without her." June patted the swing beside her. "Please sit down."

"Thank you," he answered, setting his hat on the floor beside him as he took a seat beside her. He could not quite find a place to put his hands until the one nearest June finally settled on his knee and the other on the arm of the swing.

"It's a beautiful car," June commented. "It looks like a brand-new one."

"It is. I am trying it out. They are looking at my old car right now. I need to be back to the garage at two o'clock with it."

"Shouldn't you be driving it then?"

"When we've finished our tea, perhaps you and April could join me for a jaunt?"

"Perhaps."

April returned to the porch with three glasses of tea on a serving tray which she proudly presented to Con and her mother before taking her own and a seat on the top step of the porch. Con and June engaged in casual conversation, occasionally including April as they sipped their tea.

At twelve-thirty June asked April, "Would you like to go for a ride in Mr. Armenta's new car?"

"You're supposed to call him Con," she answered.

"Would you like to go for a ride in Conor's new car?" she repeated.

"Do you have a rumble seat?" she asked Con.

"Why yes, I do."

"Can I ride in it?"

"That would be up to your mother."

"Yes, you can ride in the rumble seat," June replied.

"Yes!" April cheered.

"Will you please excuse us for a moment?" June asked, and Con stood as the two took the glasses and tray into the house. He then went to the coupe and opened the rumble seat just as the ladies stepped from the porch. April had donned a sunbonnet. When she reached the car, Con helped her up the steps and into the rear seat as she beamed with joy. Con then held the door for June and she gracefully took her place in the front. Con climbed in and the three drove up Fremont Street to Main where they headed north on Arrowhead Road toward Salt Lake City. Con did not look to see if any of his family saw them passing the Mesquite Café.

With the windows down and April grinning broadly from

the rumble seat, they motored up the highway at a pleasant clip. The quiet engine made for comfortable conversation at a normal volume.

"Did it surprise you to find out I have a daughter?" June asked.

"Yes, it did," Con answered, "but it didn't scare me."

"You're a nice man, Mr....Conor." She blushed.

The conversation remained casual until June explained about her husband being killed in the war in France three months before April was born.

"I am very sorry to hear that," Con commented. "It must be terribly difficult for you and April."

"Yes, it has been," she replied. "It has been easier for April. She has never known anything different than the two of us. It was harder for me in California. There were sad memories there and I had a hard time financially. I have a much better job now and can better support us here. It has helped me."

"What brought you here?"

"The right circumstances at the right time. Mr. Westcott placed an ad for a secretary in a Los Angeles newspaper. I called him, he purchased a train ticket for me to come for the interview, and everything just fell together. I sold our house in Riverside and my sister kept April for two months while I lived in a boarding house here. I bought our house and brought April here five years ago. That's pretty much it."

"And they lived happily ever after," Con grinned.

"Yes." June smiled in return. "Pretty happy, I think."

"Good for you!" Con added cheerfully.

"Thank you."

Time had passed more quickly than either had expected. When Con turned around to return to Las Vegas, he stopped to make sure April was doing all right in the rumble seat. Her smile answered the question before he could ask it. He jumped back in, and they motored down the road at a renewed tempo. At five minutes before two, they pulled up in front of June's home. He opened her door and helped April down from the rumble seat.

"I'm sorry to rush off," he said as he walked them to the front step, "but I have to get going."

"I enjoyed your company and I'm sure April is ecstatic over her ride in the rumble seat," June replied as April bounded up the steps into the house.

"I had a good time, too," Con added, stammering slightly in unfamiliar territory.

"Go, buy your car," June told him, giving him a peck on his cheek and dashing up the steps so quickly it took a moment for him to realize what had happened.

Con turned, jumped in the coupe, and dashed off to Desert Chevrolet. The clock on Ab Collins's wall read 2:05 when he walked in the door.

"Thought I might have to call out the sheriff," Collins laughed when Con walked in.

"I was having so much fun, I lost track of time. Had to see what the six could really do to make up for it on the way back to town."

"Well, Max tells me he thinks you guessed right on the fuel pump," Collins told him. "By how he describes the car other-wise, I can give you a hundred dollars for it toward the new coupe."

"I've got another hundred cash to go with it," Con added.

"That's great. It leaves about three seventy difference, if that's agreeable to you?"

"With what you're offering on the Plymouth, it's a little better than I figured. I'm fine with it."

"I'll put it all down on paper and have you sign it. I'll give you a receipt for your cash and you'll be driving out of here in about ten minutes." Mr. Collins filled out two or three forms and asked Con back into his office, where he gave Collins the cash and signed the paperwork.

"I'll send Max over in about an hour with the tow truck to get your Plymouth and Tom will have the paperwork at the bank first thing Monday. Everything else is between you and him." He reached out to Con and offered a firm handshake. "It has been a pleasure doing business with you, Sheriff. You should have a lot of good miles ahead of you."

"Thank you, Mr. Collins. I plan on enjoying it for a long time."

Con drove home and parked the coupe on the street beside his house. He moved his sheriff's pickup to the street behind the coupe and prepared his dinner while waiting for Max to arrive. Before long, the tow truck pulled up outside and backed up to the Plymouth in the yard. Con helped Max hook the Phaeton to the tow truck, and he soon made his way down the street. Con moved the sheriff's pickup and the coupe into the yard, side by side at his back door, then went inside to eat his supper.

He turned on the radio in his living room and stepped through the screen door to sit down and listen in the shade of the front porch. The music playing came from a station in California. Con found himself restless and had difficulty relaxing. He had been so busy lately, and he had had very little time to even slow down, let alone enjoy leisure time. He went back in and retrieved a bottle of Coca-Cola from the icebox and a Zane Grey novel he had started reading a few months ago. He sat down in the worn-out, over-stuffed chair that inhabited the

porch. He soon became engrossed in the novel and experienced a tranquility he had been missing for months.

Before he knew it, the shadows were stretching across the
street and temperatures were fading into a cool evening. He
sat quietly, watching his neighbor's cat pouncing and playing
with a grasshopper in the yard. From somewhere in the
distance, a dog barked, momentarily catching the cat's attention. The fleeting lapse in concentration provided the perfect
diversion for the grasshopper, which sprang into a jumble of
weeds and escaped.

The cattle rustlers in the novel reminded Con of Luis Garza
and his sheep. He should drive out tomorrow and reexamine
the situation. As one thought drifted into another, anticipating
the drive to the Garza place brought June Sommers into his
meditation. The time with her today had been a pleasant
departure from recent days. As dusk approached, he reentered
the house and started toward the kitchen. A glance at the telephone in the living room interrupted his chain of thought. He
picked it up and called 142, the number she had given him.

On the third ring, she answered. "Hello?"

"June?"

"Yes."

"This is Con."

"Well, good evening Mr....Conor, how are you?"

"I'm fine. Can I call you June?" he clarified after already
greeting her that way.

"Certainly."

"Are you and April busy tomorrow afternoon?"

"April is attending a friend's birthday party tomorrow.
What do you have in mind?"

"I'm driving to a ranch out toward Searchlight in the afternoon and wondered if you could accompany me? It might be several hours."

"April's party begins at three o'clock. My next-door neighbor can probably watch her before and after, so I don't foresee any complications," June answered, a hint of anticipation in her voice.

"It's a date then," Con confirmed enthusiastically, before fear struck him that his choice of words and tone may have been over-eager.

"Definitely. Should I prepare a picnic?"

"Only if I can contribute."

"What will you bring?"

"I have some wonderful cheese and Coca-Cola. And I know where we can pick up some cantaloupes or fruit along the way."

"Perfect. I'll bring the rest. What time?"

"Is noon okay?"

"Definitely."

"So, I'll see you then," he concluded, still a bit afraid of a misstep.

"Yes, good night, Conor."

"Good night."

Con hung up the telephone. Sitting in his favorite chair, he stared into infinity, contemplating his day. He felt at peace. June made him nervous, he mused. A pleasant kind of nervousness. Not anxious. As he grabbed another Coca-Cola from the icebox, he glanced out his back door. He sure liked his new car. He then returned to the porch to enjoy the quietness. Even the boisterous Saturday-night-din from the clubs of Block 16 failed to reach his ears tonight.

10

SUNDAY, APRIL 6, 1930

Con rose early, greeted by another pleasant morning. He shaved and tried the lotion his niece, Donna, had given him last Christmas. Finding a clean white shirt, he dressed and left for morning Mass. He had not attended for several months and arrived late, but before Father Francis O'Malley began the service. He had difficulty understanding the priest's Irish brogue, but his mother loved him and gloried in seeing Con there. Con surprised his father when he squeezed by him in the pew and bent over to hug his mother. He leaned down between Donna and Olivia, and whispered in Donna's ear that he was wearing her shaving lotion. As she drew a deep sniff at his collar, he turned and gave Olivia a quick peck on the cheek that drew a startled gasp and an uncertain glare. As he moved along, Stu nodded, sitting bolt-upright and looking very uncomfortable in a jacket and bolo tie. David sat looking down at the small toy horse he played with in his lap as Con took a seat beside him. When he looked back, his mother faced straight ahead with a broad smile, and Olivia stared at him with a look of disbelief.

Con nestled in and did his best to pay attention to Father O'Malley's sermon, but his mind continually wandered from Brice Campbell to Dutch Wagner to Luis Garza to June Sommers. Following the benediction, the family flowed single-file from the sanctuary, each taking a moment with Father O'Malley at the top of the steps.

"Sheriff Armenta, 'tis a pleasure to see ya' with us today, sir," the clergyman greeted with an outreached hand.

"Thank you, Father. My new duties haven't seemed to know which day of the week it is lately," Con replied a bit sheepishly.

"The Lord understands, my son, and assists his flock in their toils. Keep a strong heart, and he will help resolve your prayers," O'Malley continued, still holding Con's hand in a firm grip.

"Thank you, Father...for your guidance," Con finally managed to blurt out.

"My confessional is always open, my son. You need not wait for Sunday evening." The priest finally released Con's hand. "Should you require it."

"Thank you, sir," Con said as he hurried down the steps toward the mixed huddle of family, awaiting his explanation for the surprise appearance.

Juan confronted his son first. "I seen the O.K. wrecker dragging your car down Fremont Street yesterday afternoon."

"Yes, I traded it." Juan eyed him skeptically. "I needed a dependable car. I haven't had time to work on the Plymouth."

"You smell pretty, Uncle Con." Donna's interruption rescued him temporarily.

"Thank you, sweetheart. I wanted you to know I haven't forgotten your thoughtful gift."

"So, what kind of car did you get?" Stu queried.

"That brown coupe, there." Con pointed it out.

Stu whistled. "Nice." "Sheriffs must get paid better than I thought."

"Payments," Con answered, grinning.

"So, who you all spiffed up for?" Olivia chimed in.

"Actually, I'm going out to Luis Garza's this afternoon," Con responded not quite as pleasantly. "But I plan on changing first."

"Don't get testy," Olivia countered. "We don't often see you all shined up, new car, shave-lotion."

"Well, I'm delighted to see you in church this morning," Maggie Armenta said, still smiling. "It's not often I get to see my son…not here this way. I, for one, am proud of you…and you look handsome."

"What's going on with Luis?" Juan asked. "More trouble with his sheep?"

"Nothing that I know of. Him without a telephone, it's hard to tell. I'm just going out to follow up with him."

"Well, tell him hello. If there is anything he needs, let me know. I should really go see him myself."

Before Con allowed his father to congeal his thoughts and ask to join him on the trip to Luis',s he kissed his mother's cheek. "Well, I need to be going."

He drove home. Though keeping his white shirt, he changed into jeans. Almost certain he had a picnic basket, regardless of his searching, it eluded him. Settling on the small wooden crate from his sheriff's pickup, he placed four Coca-Colas and a thick wedge of his mother's Irish cheddar cheese in the box wrapped in a couple of towels to help keep them cool. While looking for the basket, he found his canteen in the closet and decided to carry it along, just in case. He placed them in the foot-space of the rumble seat. Remembering the situation a few nights ago in Katherine Wagner's garage, he stowed his holstered 1911 Colt automatic under the front seat, then as an afterthought, returned to add the Winchester '94 Garza had given him as a young teenager. He covered the guns with a blanket to avoid alarming June. He didn't intend to need either of them, but circumstances had been known to change quickly in recent days.

He then drove to the sheriff's department. Deputy Jesse Slater, the only one on duty, sat behind Hazel's desk.

"How are things today?" Con asked.

"Early this morning, we had a couple of railroad workers throwing punches over some unknown difference of opinion out south of town. By the time I got there, they had settled it, and their foreman had them back working side by side. That's been it," Slater told him.

"Good. I'll be going out to Luis Garza's this afternoon, to follow up on the sheep killing. Dottie isn't working tonight, so when you leave, have the telephone operator call me if she needs to, or you if she can't reach me, until Hazel comes in in the morning."

"Got it, Sheriff."

Con topped off the coupe's gas tank at Sam Arguello's filling station on 3rd and Fremont, then drove down the street to June's house at a quarter to twelve. June and April shared the porch swing awaiting his arrival when Con pulled in.

"Well, how are the two most beautiful girls in the county today?" he asked, strolling up to the steps.

April giggled, and June blushed. "If you are talking to us,

we're fine. However, you may have mistaken us for someone else," June replied coyly.

"Not likely, I think," Con responded. "I hear Miss April is going to a big party this afternoon. Is that right?" he asked the youngster.

"Sure is, Con. We're having ice cream and playing games until we fall asleep."

"That sure sounds like a swell time. Maybe I should join you?"

"Nope! Just us girls. No boys allowed!" April exclaimed.

"Well, that's too bad. I bet you'll have a whole lot of fun," Con responded with a note of disappointment in his voice.

"Maybe I'll have a party someday for girls AND boys, then you can come," April offered.

"That would be splendid!"

"Okay, April. You run on over to Mrs. Wright's so Con and I can go."

April sprang to her feet with a birthday gift in one hand and a pillow case in the other that Con guessed held a night-gown and toothbrush. She pranced down the steps and skipped to the porch next door. A woman a little older than Con answered the door to let April in.

"Thank you, Joyce," June yelled. "I will pick her up before work in the morning."

"Goodbye, Mama. Goodbye, Con," April yelled.

"Goodbye, April," Con and June replied almost in unison.

"I'll be just a minute," June told Con and stepped in the door. Seconds later, she returned with a picnic basket that undoubtedly weighed a bit. Con scrambled up the steps and relieved her of it as she closed the door behind her.

"My word," he said when he lifted the heavy basket. "How many folks did you invite to share this?"

"Just us," she said with a snicker. "Hope you're planning to be hungry."

"I will be." Con opened the rumble seat and placed the basket on the floor beside his wooden crate, then opened the door for June, and the duo soon motored down 3rd Street to Charleston Boulevard, where they turned east to intersect Fremont for a short dash on pavement before turning to the graveled highway to Boulder City and Searchlight. Within a short distance, Con turned onto a side road that led to Hernando and Juanita Chavez's farm. Con pulled up to a small barn near the house. Juanita shaded her eyes from the sun when she greeted them from the large, wide doorway.

"Conor, what brings you here?"

"We would like some cantaloupes and peaches, if you have them?" he answered as he opened June's door. "Juanita, this is June Sommers. June, Juanita Chavez."

"My pleasure, Mrs. Chavez," June said and offered her hand.

"My hands are dirty," Juanita remarked, wiping them on her apron. "I've been picking all morning."

"That is quite alright," June returned as she continued to hold out her hand. Juanita accepted.

"I have plenty of cantaloupes," she said to Con. "Peaches are just beginning to ripen, but I have a few."

As they chose their fruit, Juanita glanced at June and spoke to Con in Spanish. "Ella es muy amable...y bonita."

Con blushed. "Yes."

He paid Juanita, and as they returned to the car, June asked, "What did she say to you?"

"She said you were very kind."

"Oh."

Con stored their produce behind the seat. June climbed

into the car and as Con closed the doors, she added, "So, why the red face?"

"And pretty."

"Oh," she blushed.

As they pulled out onto the road, she asked, "So, where are we going?"

"To Luis Garza's sheep ranch. He's an old friend of my family." Con told June of the shooting of Luis' sheep. He then related a condensed version of the story of the puma and his father's injuries. He shared how Luis had given him the rifle and brought food while Con herded the family flock for the rest of the summer of '07.

"In the fall, Luis bought most of our family's sheep. They made enough money to buy the café and have been there ever since."

"What café?"

"The Mesquite Café."

"I have eaten there," June exclaimed. "It allowed a pleasant variety from meals at the boarding house. Very good food."

"Yes, I agree."

June contemplated the realization for a moment. "So, Juan and Maggie are your parents?"

"And Olivia is my sister."

"April goes to school with Olivia's daughter," June added cheerfully, suddenly aware she knew Con's family.

"Donna is a sweetheart," Con offered, "though I have to confess partiality. She and April have similar qualities."

The lighthearted conversation continued as Con shared experiences he had been part of in Donna's childhood and June compared those of April's.

When they turned onto a seldom-traveled track, Con explained it to be the road the shooter had used to assault

Luis' sheep. When they reached the spot, he and June walked out to the point from where the person had fired his rifle. As they turned to walk back to the coupe, a delivery truck approached on the deserted road. They began walking. As it came nearer, Con identified it as one made by the Graham Brothers and his pulse raced slightly. He took ahold of June's hand. She smiled in surprise, but when she looked toward Con, he stared at the truck with a grim expression on his face. He stopped, and his grip tightened slightly when the truck halted beside the coupe in a cloud of dust. They were still a dozen yards from the car. The driver peered over its roof from his seat in the truck. His gaze shifted from inside the car up to them. He looked large and surly to June and wore a flat-brimmed straw hat.

"You're on private property," he said in a loud, sour tone.

Con recognized the skimmer and the voice confirmed the identity. Drago. "I know," he answered clearly, contemplating the pistol under the coupe's seat. "Luis Garza's ranch."

An imperceptible voice spoke from inside the truck, and the driver sped around the car. Con did not move until it disappeared over the next hill, then realized how tightly he held June's hand and released it.

"You know that man?" June asked seriously, watching Con's face as his stare finally turned to meet hers.

"Yes, sort of," he responded, forcing a smile.

"You don't care for him?"

"That's a nice way to put it. I don't trust him."

As they continued toward the car, he struggled to recover the pleasantness of a few minutes ago. He desperately wanted to reassure her.

June recognized immediately the change in Con's nature when they encountered the men in the truck. She suspected by the grip Con had on her hand, that their situation may have been much more dangerous than it appeared. It frightened her, yet she felt completely protected in his presence. Safe.

"Thank you," she responded as cheerfully as she could muster when he held her door. She hoped to encourage Con with her trust in him. She suddenly felt oddly overwhelmed with the revelation. It almost took her breath away. She had not fully trusted a man, or woman for that matter, since she lost her husband.

As they began to continue up the remote track, he finally began to return to the gentler demeanor that had attracted June to him at Robert Westcott's office.

"I'm quite certain the men in the truck are bootleggers," he began as they ambled up the road in the opposite direction the truck had traveled. "They must have a relay station or a still hidden out here somewhere. It concerns me that they are working so close to Luis' ranch. We'll go on out here and circle in the back way to Luis' house."

Con kept a steady eye on the tracks from the delivery truck. Two miles further, the backroad to Luis' angled off to the right.

"The truck probably came from the bluffs up there." Con pointed ahead into the distance.

"How do you know?"

"The tracks come from straight ahead." They turned right.

"How do you know they are from the truck?"

"I've watched them. Never lost sight of them the whole way."

"I thought you were ignoring me. I hoped maybe you were just afraid of wandering off the road and damaging your new car." She looked at him in near misbelief as he turned and looked her in the eye with a smile. "You're teasing me."

"No, I swear."

They continued down the old wagon road at a crawl. Like many other roads in the area, some sheepherder had driven a wagon out through the desert decades ago. Someone else followed that track hoping it would not lead them to a dead end, then another and another. If it pointed in a popular direction, it became a road. No one built it or planned it. It just gradually grew. Someone might remove an obtrusive boulder or other obstruction occasionally, but no one actually improved or maintained it. Consequently, Con took his time enjoying June's company and being careful of his new car.

Gradually, the road became more well-traveled, and they topped a hill to see a small house, barn, and corral under the shade of a dozen cottonwood trees.

"How do these trees grow out here in the middle of the desert?" June asked.

"There's a spring, and a good one."

The road passed between the barn and corral. When the coupe emerged into the ranch yard, Luis stood in front of them with an old, tired-looking dog by his knee and a double-barreled shotgun pointed in their general direction. A couple of hens scratched the dirt nearby.

Con came to an abrupt stop and stuck his head out the window. "Don't shoot, Luis, it's just me."

"What are you doing coming from that way?" he asked.

"Showing this lovely lady the attributes of your beautiful ranch."

"You got the wrong place," he answered, moving the shotgun to rest in the crook of his left arm. "Who's with you?" He tried to peer through the dusty windshield.

Con opened his door, but before he could get out, June hopped from the passenger seat, smiling. "I am June Sommers,

Mr. Garza." She beamed as she sauntered ahead with an outstretched hand.

Con scrambled to catch up. "June Sommers, Luis Garza, Patrón of this fine Rancho. How are you, Luis?" Con asked.

"I'm okay."

"No more sheep lost?"

"One." He pointed back up the road they had come down. "Back up there...the day after you were here."

"How far?"

"Couple of miles."

"How close to the upper road?"

"Three hundred yards, maybe."

"I've got a hunch," Con began, "but let's eat first."

Luis looked at him skeptically.

"We brought lunch with us," June chimed in, which brought a smile to Luis' partially bearded face.

Con pulled the cantaloupes and peaches from behind the front seat and handed them to June as he opened the rumble seat and retrieved her picnic basket. Luis brought two chairs from his kitchen to join the one already at the small table on his porch. Con sat the basket on the porch and returned for his little crate. Luis brought out plates and utensils along with a large knife to cut open a cantaloupe. Con retrieved three Coca-Colas and sat them on the table. Then he brought out a bundle wrapped in brown paper. Removing the wrapping exposed a creamy-colored triangular object covered by cheesecloth.

"Mama's homemade cheddar cheese."

"Hope you're hungry," June said, producing a large potato salad, baked beans, and plenty of fried chicken from her basket.

"My gosh," Con gasped. "No wonder it was so heavy."

It was nearly three o'clock. The trio did not hesitate to dig into the sumptuous feast. In the shade of the porch and trees, the warmest hour of the day remained comfortable.

Con remarked to June between mouthfuls, "I can't believe you cooked all of this food since we spoke last night."

She blushed. "I was inspired." The tension of the encounter on the road seemed long ago to her as they all relished the wonderful meal. The old dog lay at Luis' feet, feigning sleep, but one eye remained open and nostrils on alert in anticipation of a displaced morsel leaving the table above him. They talked and joked. Luis shared tales of Con's young manhood that embarrassed him and delighted June. After the Armenta family moved into town, Con worked many summers for Luis, herding sheep and other seasonal labors. The conversation rolled around to Luis' recent loss of sheep. Con wanted to investigate this last episode. When their meal had somewhat settled, the old dog received the reward he hoped for with a few scraps and chicken bones tossed from the porch while leftovers were stowed in Luis' springhouse. Luis chose riding in the rumble seat of Con's car and let the youngsters ride up front as they took the rough road back toward the ridge. Luis' dog trotted behind the car as Con carefully maneuvered the coupe over the uneven terrain. About two-thirds of the way to the fork in the road, Luis tapped on the roof of the coupe and they came to a stop.

"Just over there. He's been there four days. The coyotes have been at him."

"This will probably smell pretty rank," Con told June. "You may not want to get much closer."

"I have changed dirty diapers and been in an outdoor privy on a hot summer day...it can't be all that bad, can it?" June responded.

Con shrugged, and they followed Luis three or four

hundred yards toward the foot of the ridge. Sure enough, a large ram lay partially eaten and rotting in the late afternoon sun. The stench reached them before they could see the animal and Con had to admit, he had been in several privies that had smelled worse. Con did not plan on looking for a slug, but viewed the ridge above for the most likely locations for a shooter. He took the lead, holding June's hand as the trio scrambled up the hillside. From the top, he tried to visualize being the shooter. There had been no rain for several days and they were only a short distance from the road that the men in the delivery truck had driven down earlier in the day.

Seeing no tracks where they had crested the ridge, Con chose to search along the road for a place the perpetrator had left his vehicle. All three walked straight to the road.

"Luis, you go left. Look for any sign of a vehicle pulling off the road or any footprints. We'll go this way," Con instructed. He didn't know Luis' tracking skills, but he had lived out here for longer than Con had been alive. He would be a better tracker by accident than most who considered themselves adept in the art. "Holler if you find anything," Con added as he watched the faithful old dog follow his master down the road.

"Stay behind me. So you don't accidentally spoil anything." June followed diligently about three yards behind. Fifty yards down the road Con discovered tire tracks that left the road for a dozen yards before reentering. Midway there was a bobble in the tracks where the front tires had been turned slightly while stopped.

"Come over here a minute," he beckoned June. "I'm going to teach you a little tracker's secret. See this little dig here and how this first track came to the left, making it look a little bit wider when the second track rolled over it?"

"Yes, I see it," she answered with pride.

"The driver grabbed ahold of the steering wheel when he climbed back into the vehicle. It made the tires turn, just a little bit. That caused them to dig in ever so slightly, making this dimple right here." He pointed into the slight indentation in the middle of the track. "You can see it straight across over there on the other side, too." He pointed to the parallel track a few feet away. "The only way that can occur is if the vehicle is at a complete stop. If he didn't get out, he at least turned the wheel slightly before he went back out and on down the road." Con paused for a moment, considering the possibilities. "I'll bet he got out. Now stay put for a minute while I look for footprints."

He soon spotted a footprint pointed toward the ridge on the desert surface. "Come stand right here," he told June and she obliged. He carefully continued to scan the immediate area for a return pair of footprints. He didn't locate any.

"Okay, stay behind me while I work this trail out some." He carefully progressed ahead, still scanning from side to side for any print pointed toward the road. Nearly to the crest, he spotted the return tracks slightly off to the side.

"Stay right here." He then followed the return tracks for several yards, where he stopped again. Then gazed off for a moment toward the road. He returned to June.

"What did you find?" she asked, fascinated by this new adventure.

"Our suspect is definitely a male, and he turned back to the road."

"How can you tell? Couldn't it be a woman whose stature resembled a man?"

"That might be possible." He stared into the distance for a moment as if contemplating her suggestion. "But he relieved himself right over there, and I'm not quite sure how a woman could accomplish the task in quite the same way."

June's face turned bright red as she slapped him playfully on the shoulder. "I would suppose not."

"You are welcome to take a look for yourself, if you would like," he teased her.

"I don't think that will be necessary," she responded as her face began to return to its normal hue.

Con continued carefully on the trail in the direction of the crest of the ridge as June followed a few paces behind him. As he neared the edge he could see where the shooter had knelt to steady his aim. The decomposing ram lay in plain sight below. Con found a spent casing a few feet away to the right. .30-40 Krag, same as the others he had found last week. He hollered to Luis in the distance, who looked up at the sound of Con's voice and turned to join Con and June.

"Same culprit," Con told Luis, holding up the casing as he approached.

Luis nodded in agreement.

"I think a gang of bootleggers are using this road," he told Luis. "I suspect they are the shooters. I'm not sure why, unless they want to keep you and your sheep out of the area."

"That would explain the traffic on the road lately," Luis added.

"I don't remember ever being much past the fork up here. Where does this road go from there?"

"Up into the bluffs."

"Nowhere else?"

"No, just to the bluffs. I have grazed sheep up there in summer. There is good water in the canyons."

"They need good water to make moonshine," Con

remarked as he stared at the distant cliffs. "How far to the canyons, where the water is?"

"About four miles from the fork."

"Seven from your house?"

"About that."

"Do you still have a horse?"

"Oh, no. It's too hard for me to get up on one anymore."

"Paddy might bring one out to you in the next couple of days," Con suggested. "If a big bay gelding shows up in your corral, that's where he came from."

"I've got hay and water. Tell him to bring some grain, if he wants to. I don't keep any around anymore." He looked at June. "It'll kill a sheep." "What are you planning, Conor?"

"June?" Con turned to her.

"Yes?"

"Can you keep a secret?"

"Yes," she replied curiously.

"It's important," Con added somewhat sternly.

"Yes, I can keep a secret."

"Luis, I want to ride out there after dark and get a good look at their operation. It's nearly a full moon right now. I need to do it in the next few days to keep from using a lantern."

Luis confirmed his understanding, nodding his head thoughtfully.

"Where is the best source of water near the road?" Con asked, looking toward the bluffs.

"See the dark gap above that Joshua tree?" Luis pointed. "The road goes into that notch. The narrower one just to the right has a really good spring. Water flows for a hundred yards or more from it, before it sinks in the desert."

"That's probably where they are," Con surmised, wishing

he had his field glasses. He mapped the layout of the land in his mind. He particularly tried to identify landmarks that might be visible on a moonlit night.

"Let's go have some nice cool cantaloupe," Con proposed cheerfully after a few more minutes of study. Without hesitation, the trio headed down the hill to the coupe.

Dusk entered the valley surrounding Luis' house while they enjoyed more of June's picnic dinner and pleasant conversation.

"We should head back to town before long," Con suggested. "It'll be dark before you know it."

With everyone in agreement, June dished out a healthy portion of the leftovers to leave for Luis. Con added two cantaloupes, a dozen peaches, and half of his mother's cheese that they carried to the springhouse.

"I should be seeing you in the next couple of days," Con told Luis as he loaded June's basket in the car. He grinned as he shook Luis' hand. "Keep your head low, *amigo*."

"It was very nice to meet you, Mr. Garza," June added, also taking his hand.

"You don't need to wait for this fellow to bring you," Luis responded, smiling. "You can come visit anytime."

Con held June's door as she climbed in and closed it behind her. It was nearly dark when he started the coupe down the road to the Searchlight highway.

"He is very nice," June soon offered cheerfully.

"He has been a good friend to my family and to me for a long time." Con thought for just a moment. "He is family to me."

"Doesn't he have anyone of his own?"

"None I've ever heard mentioned."

They turned onto the graveled highway and motored

toward the city at a pleasant clip. Soon, Las Vegas came into view.

"What a splendid sight!" June remarked at the scene. "It looks so much bigger at night!"

Con agreed, and the coupe ate up the miles in comfort as their pleasant conversation flowed without cease. It seemed only minutes had passed when they pulled to a stop in front of June's house. The shadowy street produced a foreboding presence as most of the residents of the block had shut off their lights for the night. Con retrieved June's picnic basket from the floor of the rumble seat and walked her to her darkened door. She reached inside to flip the switch in the living room that emitted a subdued glow through the windows to the porch.

"Would you like to sit down?" she asked, indicating the porch swing.

"Sure, but just a little while. It's already late."

She took her seat and waited for Con to join her. He sat the basket by the door, removed his hat and laid it on the floor beside him as he sat down next to her.

"I had a great time today," he said cautiously. "I hadn't intended to drag you through the desert the way it turned out."

"That was fine. I might have worn different shoes had I known, but these did fine. I have a whole new perspective on your position as sheriff. I am sure most citizens have no comprehension of the knowledge and character needed to perform your duties."

"That's very flattering, but most folks around here still consider the sheriff just another gun-toting cowboy."

"That's what I mean!" she exclaimed. "When you pointed out how to read the tracks by the road, even where the man... you know. You have to really know what you're doing to see all of that. To me, I would have never looked past the tracks by the road. It just looked like someone drove off the road and back on without even stopping. I'm sure most other people would have seen it that way, too. You look at all the pieces and fit them together...you think the guys in the truck did the shooting, and I bet they are hoping that you don't make that connection." She stopped talking, afraid she had rambled. She had been looking at Con through the entire oratory and he had not moved. He faced straight ahead, but she could not make out his expression in the darkness.

"I haven't dated very much," he finally said. "And that was quite a while ago. Take a girl to a dance or something. You know." He felt extremely awkward. "Not much social life in Las Vegas. Until this last couple of years, anyway. Never drank much, even when it was legal."

"I had a really good time. You have been very kind and gentle. I admire that."

"I bet you didn't think I was being very gentle when I nearly squeezed your hand in two when those fellas in the truck showed up."

"When you grabbed my hand, at first I thought you were flirting. When I saw your face, I knew otherwise. I recognized then that they were dangerous men. I realized you were protecting me. I felt safe...with you there." She still could not make out the expression on his face. She chose not to share how it had frightened her, but comforted her at the same time.

"I like you, June," Con finally said. "I shouldn't have gotten you into that kind of a situation." He stood up abruptly. "I apologize."

She rose with him. "Apologize for what, not being able to see into the future? Not knowing some thug would come along out in the middle of nowhere? How could anyone know?" She faced him, gripping the front of his shirt in both hands. They were so close, she could feel his breath on her face, yet she still could not detect his expression. She nearly cried. Then he wrapped her in his arms and gently held her. Neither uttered a word for several minutes.

"I was afraid you might get hurt," Con finally admitted. "I didn't realize how tightly I held your hand until they left."

"You defended me. I felt...I *feel* safe with you."

He kissed her forehead and slowly lowered his arms from around her.

"Thank you, Conor."

"Good night, June." He reached down and picked up his hat. "It's late."

"Yes, it is. You are a remarkable man, Conor Armenta."

11

MONDAY, APRIL 7, 1930

When Con dressed in the morning, he realized he had unintentionally left his Colt and Winchester in the coupe. "Must have been more tired than I thought," he told himself. In actuality, apprehension over the situation at Luis' place and his association with June Sommers left him distracted when he got home. Even at the late hour, he had lain awake, staring at the ceiling, trying to sort out his thoughts after going to bed. He had a much better grasp on the state of affairs with the bootleggers than with June. The sensation left him unsettled.

Retrieving the Colt from his car, he strapped it on and left the Winchester hidden beneath the seat. He drove the sheriff's pickup to the office.

Hazel brought him a cup of coffee and a handful of notes as he sat down behind his desk. She waited a moment. "Am I forgiven?" she finally asked sheepishly.

"For what?"

"For jumping to conclusions and running a check on June Sommers."

"Forgiven. Running a record check on someone could draw unwarranted suspicion toward them by other departments. It's not something you should do unnecessarily."

"Yes, sir," Hazel responded and left the room without lifting her gaze from the floor.

Con read through the various notes she had given him. Steve Rogers had recovered Brice Campbell's remains. Jesse arrested the same two railroad workers from Sunday morning's incident at 8:00 o'clock last night. Their fisticuffs had resumed at the railroad camp near Arden. Both men were intoxicated and refused to divulge the source of their liquor. He locked them both up in the county jail. The other notes were insignificant.

"Is Jesse on the board today?" Con called out to Hazel.

"Yes, he's not in yet," she called back.

"I have a couple of errands. Have Jesse wait for me when he comes in." A few minutes later, Con walked to the bank to sign for the loan on his new car. When he returned, Jesse waited in his office.

"What's the story on your two boxers?" Con asked.

"They're going before the judge at ten o'clock. I just called the clerk."

"Okay. We'll both go to the hearing."

At nine thirty the sheriff and his deputy walked two blocks to the county jail. Retrieving the inmates, they escorted them handcuffed together back to Justice William Tucker's courtroom. There, Con and Jesse rearranged the restraints, and each prisoner's wrists were cuffed together in front of them. They seated the men in front of the bar on chairs facing the judge's bench.

The two prisoners sat quietly in front of the nearly empty gallery as the bailiff entered. "All rise," he summonsed in a commanding voice. Judge Tucker entered the courtroom. He eyed Con, seated in the first row and nodded in recognition before taking his seat. The bailiff continued in his imposing tone, "The Court of Clark County, the Honorable Judge William Tucker presiding, is now in session. God bless this honorable court and the State of Nevada. Be seated."

Tucker's gavel struck the block with an ominous ring as he announced, "I hereby call this court to order. Sheriff Armenta, do you wish to participate in some portion of these proceedings?"

"Yes, Your Honor. I wish to testify in the case of these two railroad workers," he responded, indicating the two men seated on the bench.

The bailiff handed Deputy Slater's report to Justice Tucker. He looked it over. "Nicholas Logan," the judge began. Logan looked up, but remained slouched in his chair. "You are charged with possession of illegal liquor, assaulting your partner there, and disturbing the peace. How do you plead?"

"I—" Logan began.

"You will stand while addressing my court, Mr. Logan!" the judge roared, "or I may add contempt to the list."

Logan slowly rose to his feet. "I was minding my own business when Harv here attacked me," he stated.

"You are out of order, Mr. Logan. That was not my question. Guilty or not guilty?" Tucker admonished.

"Not guilty."

"What?"

"Not guilty."

"Not guilty, what? Mr. Logan, you can call me Judge or Judge Tucker, or Your Honor, or just plain sir, but you will respect this court and me while I preside over it. Do you understand?"

"Yes, sir," he answered, standing a little straighter.

"How do you plead?"

"Not guilty, Your Honor."

"Be seated, Mr. Logan. Harvey Rae, you also are charged with possession of illegal liquor, assaulting Mr. Logan, and disturbing the peace. How do you plead, Mr. Rae?"

"Guilty, Your Honor," Harv Rae stated clearly, looking straight at the judge as he stood before him. "Could I make a statement, though?"

"We're about to that point in the proceedings. What would you like to say, Mr. Rae?"

"I'd like to give my side of the story, sir."

"Bailiff," Judge Tucker beckoned, "swear Mr. Rae in as a witness."

The bailiff gathered the Bible from the corner of the judge's bench and approached the prisoner. "Sheriff Armenta, could you remove Mr. Rae's handcuffs?"

Con came forward and did as he was asked and turned to retake his seat.

"Stay right here please, Sheriff," the bailiff requested. Facing Rae, he began, "Raise your right hand and place your left hand on the Bible." He did as was told. "Do you, Harvey Rae, swear to tell the truth, the whole truth, and nothing but the truth, so help you God?"

"I do, sir."

"Sheriff, you may replace Mr. Rae's handcuffs." After Con completed the task, the bailiff added, "Thank you, Sheriff. You may return to your seat. Mr. Rae, please take your seat on the witness stand." When Harv sat down, the bailiff returned the Bible to its assigned resting place and stepped aside.

"Harvey Rae, the purpose of this court today is to perform a preliminary hearing of your case," the judge began. "Since you have pled guilty to the charges brought against you by the Sheriff's Department of Clark County, Nevada, your case will not be bound over for trial. At the end of this procedure, since all of the charges are misdemeanors, you will be levied a fine which will include court costs. If you are unable to make arrangements to pay those fees, you will be sentenced to a comparable time in jail. Both the fine and jail time are completely up to my discretion within the limits of the laws of Clark County and the State of Nevada. Do you understand, sir?"

"Yes, Your Honor."

"You have asked to tell your side of the story. Do you wish to change your plea?"

"No, sir."

"You are under oath, Mr. Rae. Should anything you say while on the witness stand here today become evidence in Mr. Logan's trial, you may be asked to testify in that case. If anything you testify to today is false, you will be charged with perjury, a far more serious offense than anything you have pled guilty to thus far. Do you understand?"

"Yes, sir."

"Please tell us your story."

"It sort of begins Saturday evening. Nick and some others of the crew went into town after we got off work. They ended up at Block 16, which is supposed to be off-limits for us, but nobody pays much attention to that rule anymore. Anyway, they rode into town with one of the conductors that lives here and hitched a ride back to Arden on the southbound early yesterday morning. They had been up all night and that would have been okay, except that a switch had broken at one of the spurs to the mines and we had to fix it yesterday morning. Mr. Browne was pretty mad when he woke us up and found out half the crew had been up all night."

"Excuse me, Mr. Rae. Who is Mr. Browne?"

"Amos Browne. He's our boss. Foreman of the track crew." Tucker nodded. "All those boys were grumbling that we were supposed to have Sunday off, but everybody knows that if something broken is urgent, we work 'til it's fixed. Anyway, it takes five fellas to do the job we had, and only three of us had been to bed. Counting Mr. Browne, we had four. Nick volunteered to round out the team and we took two jiggers and headed down the track a couple of miles. Pump trolleys," he added, when he noticed everyone but Nick had puzzled looks on their faces. "Nick offered to run one of the cars. Said it would wake him up.

"We'd been working a couple of hours. It was getting hot, and Nick was getting surly. I figured he had a hangover kicking in. So, we're all getting a little tired of his foul mouth and then he called my sister a disrespectful name. It was more than I could take, and I hit him. I hit him as hard as I could and he went tumbling down the grade. Just as he got up, I tackled him, and it was a free-for-all for a while there. Mr. Browne and the other two fellas pulled us apart. After a short break and a drink of water, we went back to work. It wasn't long before the deputy showed up. I guess someone had seen the fight and thought the whole crew was trying to kill each other. They called the sheriff. Mr. Browne told the deputy that it was all a mistake, no hard feelings and stuff. So, the deputy turned his car around and drove back toward town."

"What you're saying is that it wasn't all over like Mr. Browne had told the deputy?" Judge Tucker asked.

"No, it really kinda was. We finished up our work and went back to the camp. We washed up and ate. Nick went to bed. I laid on my bunk reading. At around six, Nick woke up growly. He rummaged through his stuff and pulled out a bottle of hooch and took a long swig of it. 'Hair of the dog!' he said and took another big swallow, then passed it to me. Having booze in camp will get you fired immediately. Nick was hungover and hurting. He'd really stepped up to the plate to go to work that morning when no one else would. I figured he needed a break and I wanted to show him I could forgive his earlier remark so I took a swig. We passed the bottle back and forth. I don't drink much and my little swigs were adding up fast. Nick's big swigs were, too. Before long, he was getting pretty loud. I tried to quiet him down, but he'd have none of it. He knew how riled I got that morning when he called my sister that name and he did it again with the same result. We had half the camp tore up when the deputy got there."

"What did he call your sister?" Judge Tucker asked.

Harv looked down at his cuffed hands and shook his head.

"Answer my question, Mr. Rae. What did he call her?"

So quietly it was barely audible, he said, "A whore, sir." He answered with a mix of sadness and shame. He did not look up.

"Is your sister employed?" Judge Tucker asked softly.

"She entertains gentlemen at Dutch's Oasis," Harv answered without raising his face.

"I see," the judge continued in the same consoling tone. "Is there anything else you would like to say?"

"No, sir."

"You may step down." Judge Tucker cleared his throat and

calmly took a sip of water from a glass that had been hidden from view of the gallery. "Sheriff Armenta," he said somewhat regaining his normal voice, "would you like to come forward?"

"Yes, Your Honor." Con rose and crossed through the bar in front of the gallery.

"Please proceed, Sheriff."

"I had thought to bring to the attention of the court that Clark County only has one deputy on duty to serve the entire county on Sundays. Because of these two men's tomfoolery, Deputy Slater spent most of the morning, the evening, and much of the night making two trips out to Arden. Had some incident arisen during that time endangering the lives of other citizens, it could have been disastrous. I wanted to say that these men are both adults. They should have outgrown their schoolyard behavior long ago. Now, it appears, however, that perhaps the circumstances are much more complicated than they seemed. I apologize for interrupting the court with my shallow observations, Your Honor."

"You are not out of order, Sheriff Armenta. Your points are all well taken and your apology, though not necessary, is accepted. I will take your comments into consideration when making my ruling. If you have nothing further to add, you may be seated." He looked past Con to Jesse seated behind him. "Deputy Slater, please come forward." Jesse and Con passed each other as they crossed through the gate in the bar that separated the gallery from the front of the courtroom. Jesse looked nervous and Con winked at him in reassurance as they met.

"Deputy Slater, I have read your report. After hearing Harvey Rae's testimony, is there anything you would like to say regarding this case?"

"Yes, Your Honor. It was very late last night when I wrote my report. In my haste to complete the paperwork, I may have arbitrarily omitted details from eyewitness accounts taken at the scene that Mr. Rae included in his testimony."

"So, you are saying that Mr. Rae's testimony is more thorough than your report?"

"Yes, Your Honor. There was nothing in Mr. Rae's testimony that conflicted with information I received from eyewitnesses at the scene."

"Anything else you'd like to add?"

"No, Your Honor."

"Please take your seat." Tucker looked over at Nick Logan. He sat upright in his chair now and looked much less confident in himself than he had earlier. "Mr. Logan, please come forward."

Logan stood and took a couple of steps toward the bench. "Yes, Your Honor."

"You were out of order earlier, Mr. Logan, when you interrupted this proceeding with a statement regarding your innocence. You have heard the testimony of Mr. Rae and statements from Sheriff Armenta and Deputy Slater. Your earlier statement is not on the record. Do you wish to make a statement at this time?"

"Yes, sir. I didn't do anything wrong. Harv attacked me for no reason."

"You don't consider calling a member of someone's family a derogatory name offensive?"

"It's the truth!"

"What?"

"It's true!"

"It's true, what?"

"It's true, Your Honor."

"Being disrespectful is not against the law. Being disrespectful in my courtroom is, Mr. Logan. I consider the term you used to be an obscenity. If someone called a female member of your family an obscene name, would you be offended?"

"No one in my family—"

Tucker lowered his gavel with a slam that rattled the windows and startled everyone in the room, including the bailiff. "You are out of order, sir!" he boomed. "Answer my question!"

"Yes, sir."

"Did you think Mr. Rae was offended after he had struck you down in the morning for using that term?"

"Yes, sir."

"But you don't think it was offensive to use that same term again a few hours later?"

"But I was drunk then—"

Judge Tucker's gavel again struck the block with ominous force, but those present were slightly more prepared. "So, you are changing your plea?"

"No, sir."

"But you just admitted your guilt on the first count brought against you."

"But the liquor was gone!" Logan argued under Tucker's portentous glare. "Your Honor," Logan added just before the judge reprimanded him again.

"It was in your stomach. Did you strike Mr. Rae?"

"But he hit me first…Your Honor."

"Answer my question, Mr. Logan."

"Yes, sir."

"Was everyone in the railroad camp content with what was going on there?"

"Well," Logan mulled the question over for a moment, trying to find a justification for his actions, "no, Your Honor."

"Mr. Logan, you have just admitted your guilt on all three charges. Do you wish to change your plea?"

"Yes, sir," Logan answered, staring at his feet, much like the schoolboys the sheriff had described earlier.

"Nicholas Logan, you are charged with possession of illegal liquor, assaulting Mr. Harvey Rae, and disturbing the peace. How do you plead?"

"Guilty, Your Honor."

"Very well," the savvy judge concluded. "At this time, I will recess to evaluate the case. Court will reconvene tomorrow morning at ten a.m. at which time I will pronounce sentencing. This court is adjourned." With that proclamation, Judge Tucker struck his final blow of the gavel for the day.

"All rise," the bailiff called out as the judge stood, leaving the courtroom.

"That went well, don't you think?" Con asked Jesse.

"Well, for you, maybe. I thought he was going to hang me out to dry for my weak reporting after the way he went after that Logan fella."

"You'll write a better one next time, won't you?"

"Yep."

"He made his point without a public reprimand then, didn't he?" Jesse nodded. "He's been around for a long time. I saw your report. I knew you were tired when you finished up last night. I wanted to make sure that he knew that, too."

They walked the two prisoners back to jail in silence. After turning them over to the jailer, Con looked up at the clock. A quarter to twelve. "I'll bet you jumped out of bed late this morning and haven't eaten a thing, have you?"

"A cup of Hazel's coffee."

"Come on. I'll buy you lunch."

They walked the one block to the Mesquite Café. When they entered, Con looked around for a table instead of his usual seat at the counter. The place was filling up pretty fast with the lunch crowd, but they managed to get a two-top near the corner. Olivia appeared out of nowhere with two Coca-Colas which she sat in front of them and a menu she handed to Jesse.

"Who's buying?"

"I am," Con answered.

She looked at Jesse. "The chicken fried steak is the most expensive thing on the menu. He doesn't feel generous very often, you better take advantage of it. Oh," she added as she started to walk away, "it's really very good, too."

"She's a little pushy. Doesn't she know you're the sheriff?" Jesse noted.

Con nodded. "Downright rude somedays," he concluded, "but just to me." Jesse stared with mouth open, completely confused. "She's my sister."

His mouth reshaped into a broad grin as he bobbed his head in understanding. "Got it."

"Olivia is right. The chicken fried steak is very good, and I'm really hungry." Both men ordered the same accordingly. The two enjoyed their lunch with intermingled cop-talk between mouthfuls of mashed potatoes.

When they were nearly finished eating, Olivia swung by their table. "Papa wants to talk to you before you go."

"What about?"

She shrugged. "Just said he wanted to see you."

Con walked back to the kitchen to see what his father wanted.

Juan paused in his duties and greeted Con. "Hernando

Chavez brought some produce by this morning," Juan began. "He said Juanita saw you yesterday. She told him you have a new girlfriend. Very pretty. Is that why you were all dressed up for Mass Sunday morning?"

"Partially," Con answered. "But what I have is a new friend who happens to be a pretty girl. There is a difference, you know?"

"I know," Juan replied. "Just, why such a big secret?"

"I just met her for crying out loud, my sister is the biggest nosey gossip in all of Las Vegas, and I'd like to get to know her a little bit before Olivia runs her off or has her picture on the front page of the newspaper." Con realized he had begun to raise his voice. "I'm sorry, Papa. I'm an elected official now and I have to be aware of rumors. I certainly don't want my family to be the center of them, or the source. Can you keep this under your hat for a little while? I just don't want anything blown out of proportion."

Juan reached up to hug his son. "I understand. Our secret, okay?"

"Yes, Papa. You're the one who said I should have a girl-friend. Well, I might. I just don't know yet."

"Okay," he said. "I've got food to cook. Go back to work."

Con headed back toward the front of the café, but was accosted by his mother in the hallway before he made it there.

"What was that all about?".

"Oh, nothing."

"You and Papa hugging in the kitchen and it's nothing?"

"It's nothing. Can't my father hug me occasionally?"

"Is he sick? He's not dying, is he?" At that, she burst into tears and fell into Con's arms.

"It's nothing! No one is dying! He just wanted to tell me

something Hernando Chavez told him about this morning. It's okay."

She lifted her apron to dry her tears as she recomposed herself. "What did he tell you?"

"Something suspicious Hernando had heard."

"Why did he hug you?"

"Why did you hug me?"

"Because I thought he was dying!"

"He's not dying. Everything is okay. Okay?"

"Okay. What did Hernando say?"

"It's sheriff's business. I can't say. Jesse and I have to get back to work."

Con returned to the front, paid Olivia for their lunch, and he and Jesse walked out the door.

"What was that all about?" Jesse repeated his mother's question curiously.

"If you ever have to go before Judge Tucker, I'll send you over to talk to my mother first…for practice. She could put Tucker to shame in the art of interrogation."

"I'll remember that."

As they walked to the sheriff's department, Con felt guilty for lying to his mother. As he considered the situation, he reassured himself. He hadn't actually lied to his mother. "I am the sheriff and it is my business," he announced aloud with a smile.

"What?" Jesse asked, bewildered.

"Oh, nothing. Just thinking out loud," Con replied. *By now, Jesse probably thinks that I and my whole family are nuts*, he thought to himself. They walked toward the office, sharing bits of casual conversation as they went.

"Anything new, Hazel?" Con asked as they walked in.

"Jim Thomas called in from the airfield."

"And?"

"Are you sure you want to hear this?"

"Crazy Jim?"

"Yes."

"Okay, hit me with it."

"He said someone stole the propeller off his airplane."

"Are you sure?"

"That's what he said."

"Did he sound like he had been drinking?"

"Maybe."

"Jesse..."

"I'm already headed that way."

"Be careful. He owns a revolver and if he's been drinking... well, make sure he knows who you are and maybe...well, just be ready to duck."

"Got it."

"Hal called. Wants you to call him," Hazel added as the door closed behind Jesse.

"Okay. Anything else?"

Hazel looked around the room as if someone may have been lurking behind a door. "A pretty blonde girl dropped this by right after you left and before Jesse arrived this morning," Hazel said as she pulled a small folded paper from her top desk drawer. It had a red wax seal over the fold with a rose imprinted in the middle of it. "She said it was personal and asked that I give it to you privately."

Con's face was as red as the seal on the paper when he took it from Hazel's hand.

"Are you okay?"

"Uh, yeah...sure." Con stared at the seal on the note as Hazel stared at him, trying to read his facial expression without any success.

"It won't open itself."

"Yeah." Con moved toward the door to his office.

"Coffee?"

"Sure," he answered as Hazel started toward the pot.

"No, actually not. No thanks." He entered his office and closed the door.

Bewildered. That's the word she was thinking of. Con looked bewildered. Hazel had seen Conor Armenta around town since he was a teenager, but had never really met him until he became a deputy three years ago. He had always been a real solid kind of kid, she thought. She had never seen him act so peculiarly.

Con leaned back in his oak chair and stared at the note he had laid on his desk unopened. He was certain it was from June. She was the only pretty blonde girl he knew. Well, the only one he cared to know. Was it a dear John letter? Was she afraid to tell him face to face that she wasn't interested in knowing a simple-minded cowboy sheriff any better? The thought scared him. *It shouldn't*, he thought to himself. *I barely know her.* That idea side-tracked him in a different direction. *I'm afraid of a piece of paper. How can paper hurt me? I can throw it away or burn it up if I don't like what it says. It's just paper*, he said again to himself as he hurriedly leaned forward, grabbed it, and tore it open before he lost his courage.

It was from June. He recognized her beautiful handwriting the instant he saw it.

Con –

I had a wonderful time with you this weekend.

June.

PS I think that April did, too.

What? No, "sorry it didn't work out?" He turned it over to see if he had missed anything. No. She had a good time. That was all.

A different man opened the office door than the one who had closed it just minutes before. He placed the note in his pocket as he said to Hazel cheerfully, "I'm going to see Hal at his office, then I'll be out west of town for a while. Hold down the fort."

"Okay," was all she managed to reply as she sat in total disbelief. She didn't know what happened to the other guy, but Conor was back.

Con drove to the coroner's office to see Hal. The old doctor sat at his desk reading a forensics investigation magazine that Con was unfamiliar with. "What's up my friend?"

"As you suspected, Brice Campbell was left-handed. I'm certain of it now."

"What convinced you?"

"I thought about it ever since the moment we talked Saturday morning. It suddenly came to me last night."

"What's that?"

"Campbell was a pencil pusher, right?"

"Yeah."

"Did you ever notice that someone who writes a lot gets a little callus on the side of their middle finger right by the first knuckle?"

"Well, no, but I guess it makes sense."

"Well, they do. It's where the pencil rides while they're holding it. Just like a ditch digger gets calluses on their palms, a pencil pusher gets them on their fingers. Campbell had a callus on the inside of his left middle finger…right at the first knuckle."

"How'd you check that with the body already at Palm Funeral Home?"

"I ran over there this morning. Roberts had the body all fixed up and in the casket, ready for the family to come over later this morning. Did a real fine job making over the gunshot wound. A real artist, he is. I told him there was something that I forgot to look at. I checked it with him standing right next to me. Did it so fast he didn't even know what I looked at. Made it look like I was checking the scratches on the back of his hand. I'm pretty stealthy when I need to be, Con."

"Now the question is, how did he get shot in the right temple."

"You said yourself that you could probably shoot yourself in the temple with your off hand if you put your mind to it. If you were really set on killing yourself and the wrist on your shooting hand was broke, I guess you'd figure out a way."

"Or someone else could help you, whether you wanted them to or not," Con added.

"Well then, there's always that possibility."

12

MONDAY, APRIL 7, 1930

Con drove home from the coroner's office and switched vehicles, then drove the coupe to his brother's ranch. Patrick was working in the barn when he pulled into the ranch yard.

"Well, that's a little suspicious, Mr. Sheriff. You come here at night in an old jalopy that barely runs looking for crooks a few days ago. Next time you come back in the daylight in a shiny new car. You taking a little kickback from some of these moonshiners around here?"

"I need to borrow a horse."

"That's what you said the last time. Still doesn't explain the new car."

"Well, my little brother gave me such a hard time about the runabout I borrowed, I figured I better step up my style a little," he countered. "Actually, I needed my own car that runs.

I traded off my old Plymouth. Besides, Dottie's little car ran pretty well. I just don't like borrowing things."

"Except my horse, that is."

"That's different."

"Oh, I see."

"Can you get him over to Luis Garza's?"

"That's a long way away, Con" he answered, staring at his brother incredulously. "He's clear across the other side of town and halfway to Searchlight. Borrow a horse from Luis!"

"He doesn't have any anymore. Says he's too old to get on one."

"I suppose you want Bob?"

"Of course."

"Another midnight ride? Never mind. I don't want to know. I can jump him into the back of the truck if it will start and get him over there. When do you need him?"

"Tomorrow night if I can."

"This is going to cost you, you know."

Con looked in his wallet and extracted a five-dollar bill. "This will get you out there and back to town. I'll get some money to Sam to fill you up with gas on your way back home."

Patrick eyed Con skeptically. "Okay."

"When this is all done, you can bill the county for renting Bob twice, driving to Luis's, everything. Right now, nobody can know what I'm doing. Too many eyes and ears around. You know?"

"Yeah, I get it. He'll be there tomorrow."

"Take a little grain for him, too? Luis has hay."

"Anything else, Your Highness?"

"I could use a rifle scabbard. Maybe a lariat, just in case."

"You're changing your tactics."

"These guys are pretty serious."

"How far are you riding?"

"Fifteen, maybe twenty miles."

Patrick's face was solemn as he shook his head. "Don't get yourself killed, big brother. Mama would never forgive me."

"Stop in and see her. She'd like that." Con gave Patrick a hug. "Thanks Paddy, I owe you one."

"You already owe me one from last time," he said, laughing as they broke their embrace. He tried to make light of the seriousness of his brother's mission, knowing little of what that mission might entail.

Con drove back home. He went into his house and took some cash from his hideaway. Then he switched to his sheriff's pickup and drove to Sam Arguello's filling station. He left ten dollars to fill Paddy's truck with gas and gave Sam two dollars to keep for himself. He felt the note in his pocket and looked down 3rd Street as he climbed back into his truck. *I had a wonderful time, too*, he thought to himself.

He stopped in at the sheriff's department and spoke to Dottie. Jesse and Hazel were gone for the day, and Dottie seemed particularly cheerful this evening. Con suspected she and Hazel had shared a fair amount of speculation about the pretty blonde lady with the note and Con's response, both before and after reading it. It didn't bother him as much now as it had a few days ago, particularly since he had gotten June's note. He read Jesse's report on the stolen propeller. It was very thorough. Judge Tucker had made his point and would be pleased to see how well Jesse had accepted his covert criticism and improved his documentation.

* * *

Crazy Jim Thomas was about half inebriated when Jesse arrived. He asked Jim where he'd gotten the liquor. He promptly produced a pint bottle of American Medical Spirits bourbon. When asked where he got the bourbon, Jim immediately provided a prescription from Dr. Joseph Anderson. The report read that Jesse had not yet contacted Dr. Anderson to confirm its authenticity.

When he continued questioning Jim, Jesse asked if perhaps Jim had removed the propeller and just misplaced it. The question may have been considered condescending by some, but knowing Jim Thomas's occasional lapses from reality, it was not unreasonable. After some discussion, Jim convinced Jesse that when he went into town Saturday evening to fill his prescription, the propeller was on his airplane. He had not looked at his airplane when he got back last night, but when he got up this morning the propeller was gone. When Jesse asked if he had asked around looking for witnesses, Jim claimed that no one else was at the airport during the day. Jesse could clearly see Martin Fisk, another local aviator, in his hanger across the taxiway. When Jesse asked about Mr. Fisk, Jim replied that he and Fisk had not been friendly in recent weeks.

Jesse then crossed the taxiway and spoke to Mr. Fisk who, it turned out, had loaned Crazy Jim fifty dollars several weeks earlier and Jim had failed to pay it back. Payment being well past due, Jim had been ducking the creditor persistently. When asked if he knew where Jim's propeller might be, Fisk claimed that he did not, but that if Jim paid him back the fifty dollars, he would help look for it. When asked if Fisk had a lien on the propeller for the fifty dollars, he said no, but reassured Jesse that if he had his fifty dollars, he would help find Jim's propeller.

Jesse went back and asked Jim if he owed Mr. Fisk fifty dollars and he said yes. When told that Fisk would help find his propeller when he got his fifty dollars, Jim went looking for his revolver. Jesse got Jim back under control and took his revolver away from him. It soon became apparent that Jim did not have the money, however, he had a customer coming in an hour that was paying him one hundred dollars for a flight from which he could then pay Fisk back. Jesse also found out that it would take about a half hour to reinstall the propeller if he had it. Jesse asked if the customer would pay in advance for the flight and Jim thought he would.

Jesse went back to Fisk and negotiated that if he found the propeller and helped put it back on Jim's Alexander Eagle-rock, Jesse would stay and not let Jim out of his sight until Fisk had his money. Jesse went back and asked Jim if he was sober enough to fly his client when he arrived, to which Jim told Jesse that he was sober enough to fly his client upside down and backward, in a hurricane, to his destination. By that time, Fisk was carrying Jim's propeller across the taxiway. When Jesse asked where he found it, Fisk said that it was out under some bushes in the desert. Jesse stood guard while the two men worked together as if they were the best of friends, and he learned how to install an airplane propeller while watching them and occasionally handing them tools.

When the customer arrived, the Eaglerock was finished and ready to go. He was skeptical of Jim's idiosyncrasies, however, and refused to pay more than half in advance. Jim said that he also needed enough to fuel his plane before they left, which he estimated at twenty dollars. Jesse asked if Jim would take ten dollars for his pistol, which Jesse paid him, and then convinced the client to up his advance to sixty dollars. Jim got his propeller back, Martin Fisk got his fifty dollars,

Jesse got an old worn-out Smith and Wesson revolver, and the client got his airplane trip to wherever it was that he was going. After Jim and his client left, Jesse asked Fisk if he thought they would make it alright. He told Jesse that Jim was the best pilot he had ever seen. Flew all over western Europe in the war. Awarded an Ace and other commendations for valor. If he was sober enough to climb in the cockpit, he could fly anything with wings on it.

The report was indeed thorough. There was no other urgent business and Con drove back home. He didn't feel like cooking dinner or eating alone. He thought about it for a few minutes, then picked up the telephone and dialed 142.

The sweet voice of a young girl answered on the second ring. "Hello?"

"Is this Princess April?" Con asked.

There was a giggle then, "Mama, it's Con!"

"Good evening, Sheriff. Is this a business call, or social?" she asked comically.

"Oh, purely business, ma'am."

"And what sort of business might that be?"

"The business of dinner. It appears that the hour is very near, and with no other arrangements made on my behalf, I was wondering if you and Miss April would care to join me at one of Las Vegas' finer dining establishments?"

"Well, that is a very appealing business offer, but I was just putting together some leftovers from our picnic of chicken, potato salad, and baked beans for April and me. There is more than enough to share, if you would care to join us."

"Well, ma'am, that is a very tempting counter-offer, and I'm afraid that I may just be forced to accept it. Would you allow me to furnish a few Coca-Colas to supplement the fanfare?"

"Absolutely. But hurry, dinner will be on the table in about ten minutes."

"If you don't mind me being in uniform, I'll be there in five."

"We don't mind at all."

Five minutes later, Con's footsteps crossed the Sommers' porch. April was waiting at the screen door for him. He hung his hat on an empty coat-tree by the door as they passed it, while April led him into the kitchen, grinning ear to ear and chattering all the way. June was placing a steaming platter of chicken she had just reheated onto the kitchen table, wearing a flowery apron and a smile, looking as if she had just stepped off the cover of *Good Housekeeping* magazine.

"Can I help?" he asked as he sat the drinks on the counter.

"I think I have things covered. You can wash up if you like while I finish setting the table. The bathroom is the first door on the left from the living room."

Being his first time inside June's home, Con could not help noticing its pleasantness. The living room was clean and nicely furnished. Not luxurious, but comfortable looking and in good condition. A photograph of a soldier adorned one wall, and Con was sure he must be April's father. A smaller photo that seemed to be a wedding picture sat on an end table across the room. Con hastened to wash his face and hands. He almost regretted using the towel in the spotless bathroom. He did his best to leave it precisely the way it had hung where he found it.

As he reentered the kitchen, April had taken her seat and June was placing Coca-Colas at each place setting. Con held June's chair as she sat down. He seated himself after removing his gun belt and hanging it on the back of his chair.

"Would you like to say grace, April?" June asked.

The three bowed their heads. "Thank you, God, for the food we have and thank you for having Con eat dinner with us. Amen."

"Amen," June and Con responded.

"How was your day?" June asked as she passed him the plate of chicken.

"Nothing exceptional. I was in court most of the morning, then out west of town seeing about a horse this afternoon."

"I love horses," April chimed in cheerfully.

"You do? Do you ride horses, April?"

"I did once. It was really fun."

"Well, that's very interesting. I'll have to remember that," he said, giving June a wink. "And your day?" he asked June as she handed him a bowl full of potato salad.

"I was not very busy. The office is open from nine to five-thirty. Mr. Westcott left shortly after I arrived and spent most of the day with his wife's family. Funeral arrangements, business and family issues, I suspect."

"Yes, I am sure he had important matters to attend to." He considered mentioning Newt Campbell arriving Saturday, but decided not to jeopardize anyone's confidentiality.

"The telephone only rang once all day, and that was the newspaper reporter. I told him Mr. Westcott was out for the day. I spent most of my day reorganizing old files. Mr. West-cott returned after five, gathered some paperwork, and followed me out at five-thirty with his briefcase in hand. He locked up behind us and said he'd see me in the morning. That about sums up my entire day."

Con was grinning slightly.

"What?"

"Sorry, I was just thinking about Stanley."

"Stanley?"

"The reporter, Stanley Olsen. A very diligent young man. But very honest, too. As badly as he wants a big scoop, he doesn't make anything up. Won't compromise the story."

"Yes," she agreed, smiling, "but he is indeed very persistent."

They chatted on through dinner, April joining in occasionally. She pointed out to Con her discovery that Donna McLeod, her best friend, was also his niece. They remained at the table talking for most of an hour afterward. June apologized for not having a dessert prepared, and Con assured her that he could not eat another bite. She promised to bake a pie for a future visit. April insisted that it would be a peach pie, her favorite. June sent April to retrieve her homework while she cleared the table. Then she washed dishes and Con dried. While April continued her schoolwork at the table, Con and her mother retired to the sofa in the living room and continued visiting.

"You have a very pleasant home," Con said as he scanned the room more thoroughly. "April's father?" he asked, indicating the photograph.

June smiled with the memory. "Yes. I loved him dearly. I still do, but in a different way than then."

"You should," Con replied, but he could not quite find the right words to tell her how he respected her deceased husband and their marriage. Con envied the man he would never meet. Maybe admired him and at the same time felt sorrow. The man had a beautiful daughter he had never met. A family he could not enjoy and share in. This evening, Con began to feel, ever so slightly, what it might be like to have his own family.

April finished her homework and prepared for bed. She came back to her bedroom door to announce that she was ready.

"I'll be in to tuck you in in a minute, sweetheart," June replied.

"Could you come tuck me in, too, Con?"

"Maybe not tonight, Princess. Can you come give me a hug instead?"

She raced across the room to comply. Con hugged her and gave her a peck on her forehead. "Good night, princess."

She kissed him back on his cheek. "Good night, Con."

June held April's hand as they returned to her bedroom. A moment later, she reappeared and closed the door behind her, returned to the sofa, and sat down beside Con. She paused, contemplating the situation. "Thank you," she said finally.

"What for?"

"For handling an awkward situation gracefully. She has no concept of the implications of a man being in her bedroom, even if I was there, too. It stunned me when she invited you. My mind was racing for a response when you answered so fittingly. It completely defused the situation...she is very fond of you, you know. Perhaps it's missing a father figure."

"I am fond of her, too. She is a wonderful little girl. You should be very proud of her."

"Oh, I am. I depend on her in an indirect way. She has kept me stable through some very emotional times."

"I had siblings, so I can only guess, but being an only child, she's been growing up in an adult world. Even if it was only one adult much of the time. She's not had brothers or sisters to learn from, so even though she is very mature for her age, in some ways, maybe she's more naïve in others?"

June looked at him, almost in disbelief. "You see all of that and don't have any children of your own. I do have a child, that very same little girl in there, and I have missed it completely."

"Maybe it's because I'm on the outside looking in and you're right in the middle of it. Or maybe I'm just a simple-minded cowboy sheriff who doesn't have a clue what he's talking about."

"Not a chance," she said as she wrapped her arms around him, then kissed him deeply on the lips. "I'm pretty fond of you, too, you know," she added as she gradually released her embrace.

"I think we're pretty fond of each other," he whispered.

They sat there in silence for several minutes. June leaned against Con's chest on the sofa. He contemplated his feelings. The sensation of her presence next to him. His arm still around her shoulder. The tender kiss that had come unexpectedly.

"I will be working tomorrow night," Con said, breaking the silence.

"The man with the horse?"

"Yeah, my little brother."

"And Luis?"

"Paddy is taking the horse there tomorrow."

"Is it dangerous?"

"Maybe. I might be dealing with the men in the truck. You can't tell anyone that you know where I'm going."

"I won't. Be careful...and smart."

"That last one is the hard part."

She slapped him playfully on the chest. "I think it might be the other way around. Too brave for how smart you are."

"I should be going."

"Yes, I know. Call me Wednesday."

"I will."

"Brice Campbell's funeral is Thursday morning."

"Okay, I should be there. Probably half the town will be there."

June leaned back from him, allowing Con to stand up. He went into the kitchen and strapped the Colt back around his waist. She watched with mixed emotions. June did not like that he had to wear a gun to work, but at the same time understood the necessity and the message of authority that it carried with him, even if he did not use it. She was certain he was skilled with it, even if he might not admit it. He seemed to do everything well.

She followed as he crossed to the door, taking his hat from the tree when he passed it. He turned and faced her, silently pausing for a moment. Then took her into his arms and kissed her passionately.

"Good night," he said, stepping out onto the porch.

"Good night."

"I will call you."

"I will be waiting."

"Yes, he does seem to do everything well," she whispered to herself as he disappeared in darkness to his car.

13

S heriff Conor Armenta seldom lingered around his house in the morning. This particular morning, he picked up doughnuts at the bakery on his way to the office. Hazel had arrived before him. Her conversation with Dottie ended abruptly as he entered the room, suggesting to him that he was the topic of their chat. They stared appraisingly at him as he placed the doughnuts by the coffee pot.

"Is something wrong?" he asked as he turned toward them. He spread his arms and looked himself over. "No, I remembered to put my pants on this morning. What is it?"

"Oh no," Dottie replied, hiding behind her coffee cup and taking a sip. "You look fine. Cheerful, in fact."

"I told you," Hazel said to Dottie under her breath while Con poured himself a cup of coffee and took a doughnut from the sack. He pretended not to hear Hazel's comment.

"Well…" He took a bite of the doughnut. Seeming to be

deep in thought momentarily, he chewed and swallowed. His serious expression returned to a slight smile. "I suppose I am cheerful this morning."

He could hear the ladies' muffled whispers as he sat behind his desk, eating his doughnut and looking over the papers needing his attention.

"Is there anything you need before I leave?" Dottie called from the outer office.

"I'd like to see Jesse's report from yesterday again."

"Why didn't he have you get this?" she whispered to Hazel with a furrowed brow as she sat her purse back down and went to the cabinet to retrieve the file.

"Well, you asked," Hazel whispered back.

"Thank you," Con said as Dottie handed him the file.

"Will that be all?" she asked in a slightly irritated tone.

"No," Con answered, to which she responded with a mixed expression of shock and frustration. "Have a doughnut on your way out." He smiled up at her.

"Yes, sir." She turned and not quite stormed from the room. Grabbing her purse, she headed toward the door. "I'll see you this evening, Hazel," she sputtered in aggravation. Then she turned back and snatched a doughnut before leaving.

"Good morning," Jesse greeted her cheerfully when they met in the doorway.

"Yeah," she answered without looking up or slowing down.

"What's with her?" he asked Hazel as the door slammed behind him.

"She's happy."

"What?"

"She didn't like the subtle way Con told her..." she

answered in a normal tone so Con could also hear her, "and me, too, for that matter, to mind our own business."

Jesse poured himself a cup of coffee and approached Con's open door. "Good morning, Sheriff."

"Good morning. Good job," he added, holding up Jesse's report. "Have a doughnut." He pointed toward the sack near the coffeepot. "Grab two."

Jesse sat his cup on the corner of Con's desk while he procured the pastries. As Jesse handed him the second dough-nut, Con motioned him to have a seat.

"What do you think about the prescription Jim Thomas has for medicinal bourbon?"

"I'm not sure. Almost everyone around here knows that Crazy Jim is a drunk. I can hardly believe Dr. Anderson would write him the prescription, but it sure looked legitimate to me."

"Okay, that's what I wanted to know. I want to talk to Dr. Anderson on another matter, also. If he isn't too busy this morning, I will see what I can find out about this and maybe he can answer my other question, too." Con rose as he polished off the second doughnut and the last of his cup of coffee. "I'll go see the Doc. You hang around close this morning and make sure that our brawlers make it to court on time. I'll stop in here if I'm early, or see you in court if I'm running late."

"Yes, sir, Sheriff. Got it. I'll see you either here or in court later this morning," Jesse confirmed.

"Right. Hazel?"

"Yes?"

"I will be at Dr. Anderson's for a while. If I'm not back before ten, I've gone straight on to court."

"Okay."

* * *

Dr. Joseph Anderson's office occupied the front of his residence. The living room doubled as a waiting room. His wife, who was also his nurse, kept a small desk to one side of the room with a telephone and notebook where she kept track of appointments. Not many patients called or made appointments. Most, like Con did today, just stopped in and hoped the doctor was not too busy to see them.

"Good morning, Sheriff," Mrs. Anderson greeted him as he entered the empty room. "Are you feeling poorly today?"

"Oh, no ma'am," Con answered, removing his hat. "I would like to speak with Dr. Anderson, though, if he's not too busy."

"He has a patient right now. I have no idea how long it might be. Would you like to wait?"

"Yes, ma'am. That would be fine."

Con glanced at a handful of magazines on the coffee table and yesterday's *Evening-Review*. He picked up the newspaper and seated himself in a wing-backed chair near the window. Brice Campbell's funeral announcement graced the front page. Stan had eloquently managed to use a quarter of the page, saying nothing the general populace didn't already know. A half hour later, Con returned the *Review* to the table and exchanged it for a well-worn issue of *Time* magazine. Herbert Hoover, Jr. graced its cover. The related article primarily covered the young Mr. Hoover's involvement in several aviation companies.

A very pregnant young woman soon appeared from Dr. Anderson's examination room. She stopped and spoke quietly with Mrs. Anderson for a moment before departing. She smiled cheerfully at Con upon her exit.

Dr. Anderson emerged from the same room moments later and greeted Con after a short exchange with his wife. "Sheriff Armenta, what can I do for you this morning?"

"I have a couple of questions, if you have a few minutes."

"Come right in," Anderson invited Con into his office. A desk and bookcase overflowing with medical tomes sat in one corner. A cherrywood dining set and hutch seemed to glare back at him. "I'm sorry you have waited so long, Sheriff."

"It's no problem. Gave me time to read yesterday's newspaper. I wouldn't want to interfere with paying patients."

"Well, most of those who can afford it pay when they can," the doctor chuckled. "What can I help you with?"

"Is Jim Thomas one of those patients?"

"Do you mean does he pay? Usually."

"I'm sorry to have misled you. No, I just wondered if he is a patient of yours?"

"Yes, he is."

"Yesterday, Deputy Slater had contact with him. Jim had been drinking and had a bottle of A.M.S. bourbon. When asked how he got it, he produced a prescription with your name on it. I wanted to make sure that it was legitimate."

"It is."

"You are aware that Jim is, in common terminology, a drunk?"

"Yes, I am," Anderson began, unsure of the best way to proceed. "You need to understand a couple of things. Jim was a hero during the war in Europe. Flew hundreds of missions. Received a medal for valor. Shot down countless enemy aircraft. The list goes on." He watched as Con nodded thoughtfully. "Jim suffers from what many men in my profession call shell shock. Battle fatigue...sometimes, it is a result of seeing too many heinous scenes on the battlefield. Or in Jim's case, having too many near-miss experiences where he barely escaped with his life. Jim may never recover from this condition. It's very serious. Do you understand what I'm talking about?"

"I think I have a pretty good idea."

"People call him Crazy Jim, and in many aspects, that is exactly what he is. His recurring memories of those treacherous times literally drive him crazy. So crazy that sometimes he is unable to deal with day-to-day life. Before prohibition, Jim turned to alcohol to deaden his senses and the consequential memories. It may not be the best medication, but in his case, it seems to be fairly effective. I don't just pass out prescriptions of this type. I try to abide by the intention behind the temperance laws."

"I didn't mean to imply that at all, Doc. I just wanted to make sure that we aren't working against each other or that the prescription was forged." Con concluded. He wanted to continue, but was hesitant to broach the next subject. "I have something else I need to talk to you about."

"Go right ahead."

"I understand that you were also Brice Campbell's physician."

"Yes, I was. Hal was aware of that when he called me in to assist with the autopsy. We discussed it and he felt that it wouldn't be detrimental."

"Oh, I agree entirely. The question I have is in regard to some dispute his family had earlier regarding your treatment of him. What was that all about?"

"Well, in some ways there are similarities in the cases of Brice Campbell and Jim Thomas." After seeing the skeptical look on Con's face, Dr. Anderson was careful in continuing with his evaluation. "Brice Campbell had a severe back injury several years ago which you probably know about."

"Yes, I've heard some about it."

"When he came into my care, his pain medications had slowly been graduated down to laudanum. A much lower percentage of opium than his earlier medications of heroin and morphine. Still a powerful narcotic. Brice also suffered from nightmares and depression after witnessing his best friend fall to his death in the same accident that left Campbell seriously injured. It quickly became apparent that Brice had become addicted to the laudanum. The opium in it, to be more precise. He did not deny his dependence on the drug. We discussed the problem and Brice chose to conquer the habit. It was an agonizing process for him, but he succeeded and recovered. As his back healed, he was in much less pain and could tolerate it with much milder painkillers. His family disagreed with the entire process and repeatedly tried to intervene, offering him opium from illegal sources to ease his withdrawal symptoms. The opium also contributed to his depression which became less serious afterward. I am certain that he had not used opium for a half-dozen years. Finding it in his pocket at the morgue stunned me. I had not seen him for a few months. I cannot explain him having it."

"What about the nightmares?"

"Campbell had a lot of trouble sleeping. He, too, resorted to alcohol to help remedy the problem. He never asked for a prescription, so I presumed he had other sources."

"The decanter in his study would substantiate your assumption. Well, thanks, Doc. I sure appreciate the information. I'm not sure that it solved any part of the mystery, but it did answer the question of the Campbell family's animosity.

How severe was his back pain in recent years? Did that contribute to his insomnia?"

"Very little. Once his injuries healed, he became nearly pain-free. His sleeplessness resulted mostly from the nightmares."

"As for Jim, is it safe for him to fly if he's been drinking?"

"Jim is a very gifted pilot. If he's—"

"Sober enough to climb into the cockpit," Con interrupted.

Dr. Anderson grinned as he nodded his head, seeing no need to continue the sentence.

"Yes, and others agree," Con added. "Thanks, Doc."

"No problem, Sheriff."

Con reentered the waiting room. "Good morning to you, Mrs. Anderson," he greeted. "Ma'am," he added, facing another woman seated nearby. He tipped his hat to both of them as he donned it and stepped outside. He checked his pocket watch. "Nearly ten," he mumbled to himself as he jumped into his pickup and headed to the courthouse.

Con entered the rear of the courtroom just as the bailiff proclaimed, "All rise." He worked his way to a vacant seat beside Jesse, just as Judge Tucker told the onlookers to be seated.

"Nicholas Logan, step forward, please."

Nick nearly jumped to his feet and took two or three steps forward to face the judge, standing almost as straight as a soldier at attention. "Yes, Your Honor," he announced, placing his feet nearly together.

"Mr. Logan, you have been charged with possession of illegal liquor, assaulting Mr. Harvey Rae here, and disturbing the peace, all of which you pled guilty to yesterday." Judge Tucker waited a moment, looking at Nick Logan over his glasses.

"Yes, sir," Nick replied, not lowering his gaze from the judge.

"It is of this court's opinion that you are the primary instigator of the disagreement between you and Mr. Rae that resulted in these charges. As noted by Sheriff Armenta, had the need arose for Deputy Slater to respond to another emergency, the ensuing disturbances might have jeopardized the safety of citizens of this county. It is understood by this court that men working beyond hearing range of ladies or small children sometimes use harsh language during the performance of their labors. That does not justify language such as was used in reference to Mr. Rae's sister, regardless of her profession. It is also of this court's opinion that based on your own testimony, had you not been under the influence of illegal liquor, you may not have been so inclined to intentionally provoke your coworker. On the charges of assault and disturbing the peace, you are hereby fined twenty-five dollars each, plus ten dollars in court fees for a total of sixty dollars. On the charge of possession of illegal liquor, I impose six months' probation with the stipulation that should you be involved in any other dealings with illegal liquor you will be fined the minimum of $100 retroactive for this charge, plus whatever punishment results from the later infraction.

"You may pay the clerk following this proceeding. If you are unable to pay your fines, you shall remain in the custody of the Clark County Jail for sixty days after which time the assault and disturbing the peace fines will be considered met. Do you understand the sentence you have received and its implications, Mr. Logan?"

"Yes, Your Honor," he responded.

Judge Tucker's gavel gave a resounding ring as it stuck the

block. "You may be seated, Mr. Logan. Harvey Rae, please come forward."

The next few exchanges nearly mimicked the judge's words with Logan precisely. "Mr. Rae," he went on, "it is in this court's opinion that Mr. Logan was the primary instigator of the altercation between you and he and that you acted in defense of your sister's reputation. Though your intentions may have been honorable, your actions were not. As unkind as it may seem, as long as your sister remains in her current employment, it is not unlikely that similar remarks will be repeated, with similar results. It is also believed that you need to better control your temper in this type of situation. I suggest that if vulgar remarks regarding your sister's profession incite this much anger within you, you should have a long…and calm talk with her concerning a change of vocation on her behalf. I can almost assure you that she hears far worse language at her workplace than you heard Sunday.

"Since you don't seem to normally partake in illegal spirituous beverages, there will be no fine on the first charge. A fine of fifteen dollars on each of the other charges is invoked plus ten dollars in court fees for a total of forty dollars. In addition, I place you under probation on all three charges for six months with a retroactive fine of fifty dollars each for repetition of any of the charges plus whatever fines may be invoked on the later transgressions. If you are unable to pay your fines with the clerk following this procedure, you shall remain in the custody of the Clark County Jail for forty-five days after which time the fines will be considered met. Do you understand your sentence, Mr. Rae?"

"Yes, sir."

"Mr. Logan, will you please join Mr. Rae before this court?"

Nick Logan stood and took his place beside Harv Rae.

"Gentlemen, I have spoken to Mr. Browne. He tells me you are both normally reliable hands. He gave his word that he would hold your jobs until tomorrow morning. As hard as it is to find work right now, I strongly suggest that you both do whatever it takes to pay your fines and get back to work. I also recommend that you keep close to camp and away from trouble. This court is adjourned," he proclaimed as his gavel struck the block a final blow.

Con and Jesse then escorted the two men to the clerk's office. A nice looking, very conservatively dressed young woman awaited them when they walked in. Con had seen her at the rear of the courtroom when he arrived.

"Janet. What are you doing here?" Harv Rae asked.

"You need money."

"Well, I…"

"It's my fault you're in here. I'll pay your fine."

"That's not necessary. I have money in the bank."

"I will pay your fine," she repeated.

Janet Rae approached the clerk's window as Nick stepped away. "I need to pay my brother's fine. Forty dollars," she told the clerk as she peeled off two twenties from a roll of bills in her small drawstring purse.

"I need to talk to you, Harv," Nick whispered.

"What?" Harv whispered back.

"I don't have enough to pay my fine. After Saturday night, I've only got five dollars left 'til this Saturday."

"Ask my little sister," Harv told him.

"I can't ask her," Nick whispered. "Not after what I said."

"Suit yourself. I don't have the money."

Janet Rae looked curiously at them when she turned from the window as Nick and her brother whispered in the corner.

She showed the receipt to the sheriff. As Con uncuffed Harvey Rae, Nick approached Harv's sister.

"Miss Rae, I want to apologize for that name I called you to Harv. I had been up all night drinking. I was at the Oasis and saw you there. I knew who you were."

She did not reply, just looked straight at him. Nick could not look her in the face.

"I'm real sorry," Nick finally said.

"What is it you want from me, Mr. Logan? Do you want me to accept your poor excuse for an apology? I find that possibility highly unlikely."

"I don't have any money," Nick said. He did not look up.

"What?" she asked incredulously. "You expect me to pay your fine?" she nearly screamed.

"But, ma'am...er, miss...I—"

"You must have balls the size of grapefruits," Janet interrupted. "How do you get your pants on in the morning?"

Con and Jesse both nearly burst into laughter. The clerk behind the window was beet red.

"But, Miss Rae," Nick finally managed to get out. "I'm in a really tight spot."

"You put yourself into that spot, Mr. Logan," she responded before Nick could continue.

"Yes, ma'am, miss, I did. This is my fault and I admit it, but I've got to be back to work in the morning, or I'll lose my job." He was becoming even more desperate as the realization began to sink in of how dire his situation really was. "Please, Miss Rae," he pleaded.

"I will loan you sixty dollars, Mr. Logan," she finally agreed. "You get paid every Saturday, correct?"

"Yes, ma'am, Miss Rae."

"You will repay me five dollars every Saturday for twenty

weeks. That's forty dollars in interest. Do you agree to my terms?"

"Yes, Miss Rae."

"If you miss a payment, I'll have one of Dutch's goons find you and beat it out of you. You'll look a lot worse than that bump on your cheek that Harv gave you. Do you understand that?"

"Yes, Miss Rae."

Janet Rae paid Nick's fine. "One more thing," she said before showing Con the receipt. "If I ever hear of you using that name again, for anyone, any reason, you'll receive a visitor for that, too. It will be worth whatever it costs me."

Jesse uncuffed Nick Logan. "You're free to go."

Harv and Janet Rae left the courthouse, with Nick on their heels. Con and Jesse followed them, then turned toward the sheriff's office. Their conversation centered on the quirky ending to the final episode of the Arden boxing match. Both agreed that Nick Logan had felt pretty highly of himself Monday morning prior to Judge Tucker putting him in his place. He arrived in court this morning with a much better attitude. Just when he managed to extricate his tail from between his legs, Janet Rae thoroughly lambasted him. The result would have left Con feeling almost sorry for Logan had it not been so clearly deserved.

The discussion turned to Jim Thomas and his prescription. Con explained what Dr. Anderson had told him. Jesse agreed that it helped make sense of some of his previous observations at the airport. It also reassured him that he had done the right thing by purchasing the old revolver from Jim. In the wrong frame of mind, the veteran may have killed someone without even knowing he had pulled the trigger. After checking in at the office, Jesse left in his car, and Con drove his sheriff's pickup to the Mesquite Café for lunch.

Had he known what he was in for, Con may have chosen another option for lunch.

Olivia began the interrogation. "So, you're dating April's mother." She had learned the tactics well from their mother.

"I don't know what you're talking about," Con answered, trying to deflect the direct assault.

"You *know* what I'm talking about. Evidently, that's all that Donna and April talked about at school yesterday. Her mama has a boyfriend. He's the sheriff. They went on a picnic Sunday," Olivia taunted as Con held up his hands as if attempting to ward off the barrage of accusations assailing him. "New car. All smelled up with foo-foo juice at church that morning. Big story how you're going out to see Luis. Follow up some phony sheriff business. But no, you're actually going out to schmooze Mrs. Sommers. Now we know the real story. I know Mrs. Sommers. She's blonde and she's pretty, but she's no dummy. She's smart. You won't pull the wool over that woman's eyes."

"And you wonder why I never tell you anything. You and Dottie and Hazel. Got it all figured out, don't you? Can't just leave it alone, can you? You know so much, why don't you just call Stanley over at the *Review*? He's aching for a good story. Don't forget to ruin June's reputation while you're spreading around all of this imaginary gossip about me. Papa asked me just awhile back why I never date anyone anymore. Well, this is why!" Con was infuriated. "Mind your own business and keep your nose out of mine."

Maggie Armenta sat a Coca-Cola in front of her son as he took his place at the counter. She did not utter a word. The café full of customers gradually began talking to each other after watching and listening in awe to the battle between Con and Olivia. None had seen Con this angry in a very long time.

There was no longer any point in trying to be subtle about seeing June. By the end of the day, everyone in the café would tell two or three people about the big commotion at noon. By tomorrow, the whole town would know. Con drank his Coca-Cola in silence. Olivia started toward him to take his order when Maggie grabbed her by the arm.

"Don't you dare speak another word to him. Not one step closer, Olivia," she said in a whisper between clenched teeth.

Olivia turned, glared at her mother, and pulled her arm free. "Go wait on your customers," Maggie commanded, reinforcing her previous demand.

Maggie brought Con a steaming bowl of mulligan stew. "It's the special today," she said as she sat it in front of him, then returned with two thick slices of bread with butter. She got a glass of iced tea for herself and sat down beside her son.

"Paddy stopped in this morning. Said he'd been out to see Luis." She waited for Con to reply, but he didn't. "How is Luis?" she asked, trying to prod Con into conversation.

"He's okay. Getting old," Con finally offered. "Someone has been shooting his sheep. I'm working on it."

She didn't tell him what Patrick told her about the horse he took to Luis' ranch, and that it was an absolute secret. Con finished his stew. When he stood and reached in his pocket to pay, she stopped him. "On the house today," she said. When he looked up, she was staring straight into his eyes. "Please be careful, son."

14

Luis Garza sat in the shade on his front porch watching the sun drop toward the western skyline. His faithful companion lay at his feet. The ranch yard would soon be in shadow, followed by darkness in an hour. The brown Chevrolet coupe made its way down the road from the highway, slowly enough that it barely raised any dust. When it pulled into the yard, Con climbed out wearing a khaki shirt and brown leather vest.

"*Buenas noches, amigo mío,*" he greeted Luis.

"*Buenas noches, señor,*" Luis returned as he stood and stepped off the porch. "Patrick brought a fine-looking horse out this morning. He's in the corral."

Luis watched. As Con opened the gate, Bob trotted up to him. The horse nuzzled Con's vest pocket, smelling the chunks of carrot inside. "You think you need some of that?" he asked the horse as he petted him. "He rides as nice as he looks, too," he told Luis while giving Bob a quarter of a carrot.

"Saddle and tack are in the barn."

Bob followed Con untethered out the gate to the door of the barn and waited without complaint while Con slipped the bridle over his head and the bit into his mouth.

"You must know each other well," Luis observed.

"Not very long actually, but we're compadres," Con answered, rubbing Bob's back before throwing the blanket and saddle on him. He tightened the cinch and led the horse to the coupe. Con pulled out a box of .30-30 cartridges that he placed in the saddlebags, then reached under the seat and drew out the Winchester Luis had given him that summer long ago. "Remember this?" he asked, holding the rifle in the air.

"Yes, I do," Luis answered. "Those were hard times for your family for a while."

"You helped us get through it," Con reminisced. "Saved us…thank you."

"Ah," Luis replied, throwing one hand into the air, making light of the seriousness of their circumstances. "We were all friends."

"Good friends."

Con checked to be sure the Winchester was loaded and slipped it into the scabbard. Retrieving his canteen, he walked to the springhouse and filled it. After slipping the canteen over the saddle horn, he added his flashlight, a handful of jerky, and two sets of handcuffs to the saddlebags. He buckled his gun belt around his hips, then checked the clip in the Colt to ensure it was fully loaded, also.

"You're loaded for bear," Luis commented. "Expecting trouble?"

"Don't know. Never hurts to be prepared." He reached

over and shook Luis' hand. "Keep your shotgun handy until you see me again. Just in case."

Darkness had nearly overtaken the ranch yard. A glint of sunshine still glowed on the top of the ridge to the east when Con stepped into the saddle and headed up the back road into the valley. Bob quickly slipped into a lope as they moved through the shadows. By the time they reached the area where the ram had been killed, the sun had fully set and darkness enveloped the bottom of the valley. Con left the lower road. Scavengers had been heavily ravaging the carcass and the stench had significantly dissipated when they passed. Bob trotted up the ridge with ease. When they were just short of the crest, a shot rang out in the distance from further out the upper road. Con brought Bob to an abrupt halt. As they waited in silence listening, Bob's ears focused on the direction of the shot, his breathing only slightly elevated. A second shot split the still air. The horse twitched one ear as Con pinpointed the direction and estimated the distance of the source at perhaps two miles, if it came from a .30-40 Krag as he suspected.

He headed Bob through a scattered group of Joshua trees across the upper road, then paralleled it at a distance of about 100 yards. Bob resumed his comfortable lope and did not flinch as two more shots split the darkening stillness. In ten minutes, horse and rider were back among a sparse group of Joshua trees a mile past the fork in the road when Con spotted the dim outline of a delivery truck. Graham Brothers he would bet. He slowed Bob to a walk as they approached to within thirty yards of the truck. Con quickly dismounted and tied the horse's reins to a tree. He had split the distance on foot just as a large man with a rifle rounded the corner of the truck. He opened the door and slid the rifle under the seat.

"Hold it right there, partner!" Con ordered as he thumbed back the hammer on his Colt. The ominous click of the hammer froze Drago in his place with his left hand on the door, the right on the steering wheel, and one foot up on the running board. "Raise your hands nice and slowly where I can see both of them. It's getting pretty dark out here and I don't want to accidentally shoot you thinking you're trying to pull something, Mr. Drago."

Drago flinched slightly when he heard his name, but very carefully raised his hands. "I need to put my foot down," he said cautiously.

Con had moved to within a few feet of him. "Slowly," he said.

The nearness of Con's voice this time startled Drago. He cautiously placed his foot back on the ground, fearing he might lose his balance at any second.

"Now, move to your right, away from the door where I can see you better," Con ordered, watching closely until Drago reached the side of the panel truck. "That'll do," he said, then placed the barrel of his Colt against the back of Drago's neck at the base of his skull. The cold steel sent a chill up Drago's spine. "Now be real still," Con said and felt around Drago's waist for a pistol tucked in his belt front and back. From there he reached under Drago's left arm and found a new snub-nosed .38 Special in a shoulder holster. "Anything else I need to know about?" Con asked as he tucked the gun in his own belt.

"No, sir," he finally choked out past the frog in his throat.

"Good. Where is Wesley?" Con asked.

"I don't know any Wesley."

Con moved the Colt slightly to remind the thug of its presence.

"He's loading the other truck."

"We're going for a little walk, right over there." He lowered the Colt from Drago's neck and motioned toward Bob with it. "That way." Drago released a noticeable sigh of relief when Con moved the gun. The moon had not yet risen, and Drago shuffled his feet through the desert unsure of his footing in near total darkness, Con guiding him verbally from behind. Bob snorted when they neared, causing Drago to nearly jump out of his skin before seeing the horse. Never taking his gun off of his prisoner, he reached into the saddlebag and handed him a set of handcuffs. "Put those on," he said. "I'm sure you know how they operate."

Con secured the other set of cuffs, putting them in his hip pocket. Then he shined his flashlight momentarily on Drago's hands, making sure the cuffs were secure. In that instant, Drago saw Con and recognized him. He also saw the Winchester in the scabbard.

"Hey, you're the guy with the dame. I never hurt that old man. I was shooting sheep," he exclaimed.

"I know. Walk back over to the truck."

Drago began the return with the same unsure pace on the uneven ground. Con lagged back for just long enough to slip Bob another carrot and a momentary pat on the neck without giving Drago enough time to notice he wasn't behind him. At the truck, he had Drago get in the driver's seat, then hand-cuffed his left hand to the steering wheel with the spare cuffs and removed the other set, leaving his right hand free to shift or steer. He then seated himself behind Drago among many boxes of moonshine.

"Drive."

"Where?"

"To town for now. I'll tell you where to go when we get

there." Two hours later, they pulled up in front of the sheriff's office. He reversed the handcuff procedure, then marched Drago up the steps at gunpoint and into the office, much to Dottie's surprise.

"Point this at him," he told Dottie, handing her his Colt. "It's cocked, so don't shoot me by mistake." He then hand-cuffed Drago to the cast-iron radiator in the front part of the office and got him a chair.

"Call Jesse, get him down here," he said, taking his Colt back from her. He released the hammer, easing it down and holstering the gun.

"Yes, sir, Sheriff."

"You're the sheriff?" Drago asked in surprise, not waiting for an answer. "Shit."

Con then went into his office, closing the door to prevent Drago from eavesdropping. He called the telephone operator. "I need to talk to Ab Collins," he told her.

"But it's nearly midnight, Sheriff."

"I know. I'm running out of time."

A minute later, the telephone began to ring on the other end. It rang several times before a female voice finally answered.

"Mrs. Collins?"

"Yes?"

"This is Sheriff Armenta. I'm sorry to wake you, but I need to talk to Ab. It's a bit of an emergency."

"Just a minute, Sheriff. I'll get him."

After a long silence, a sleepy Ab Collins came to the tele-phone. "What's the problem, Sheriff?"

"I have a panel truck full of moonshine sitting in front of the sheriff's department, and I need it towed and locked up. At least until tomorrow, when I can make other arrangements.

Can you have Max pick it up and lock it in your shop for safe-keeping? The county will pay for everything, but I need to get it out of sight before prying eyes spot it."

"Let me get my pants on, Sheriff, and I'll be there with the tow truck myself in a half hour."

"That's great, Ab. I can't thank you enough."

Con returned to the front office.

"Jesse should be here in about ten minutes," Dottie told him.

"Good."

Con found a clipboard and sat a chair near Drago to begin his report. "Well, Drago. Where should we start? How about your full name?"

"How do you know my name, anyway?"

"I know lots of things. It's my job. So, how about your full name?"

"Alfonso Drago."

"Your friends call you Al?"

"Used to. Now, most everybody just calls me Drago."

"You prefer Al or Drago?"

"Actually, I like Al."

"Okay, Al, how many sheep did you kill last night?"

"I didn't kill any sheep."

"Well now, Al, a couple of hours ago, when you thought I was going to blow your brains out and leave you for the coyotes and buzzards in the desert, you told me you were killing sheep. Something like, 'I didn't hurt the old man. I was just killing sheep.' How many was it, Al? I heard four shots. Were there more? Less?"

"I don't know what you're talking about."

"Oh, Al. I'm disappointed. I'm going to be up most of the night with all of this. You'll go before the judge at ten in the morning. When I go out there at daylight, I'll know how many sheep there were anyway."

"I didn't kill any sheep."

Just then, Jesse walked in. "Good evening, Deputy Slater. This is Alfonso Drago. He is under arrest for not less than twelve counts of destruction of livestock."

"Twelve?" Drago blurted out. "There was only four!"

"Thanks for clarifying that, Al. Deputy Slater, there were four last night, one last week, and seven a couple of weeks ago. That's twelve, right?"

"That's what I count, Sheriff," Jesse replied.

"Would you take him over to the jail, please? Come back here when you're finished."

"Got it, Sheriff."

"Oh, just a minute," Con said as he walked back over to Drago. "Stand up, Al. We never quite finished that search for weapons out there in the desert, did we?" Checking Drago's pockets produced a five-inch switchblade knife. "Now, Al."

"I forgot that was there," Drago whined as he squirmed.

Con continued down his right leg, finding a Derringer in an ankle holster. Moving to his left leg, he found an eight-inch dagger in his sock. "Never mind, Jesse. I'll go with you."

They loaded Drago in the back of Jesse's car and hauled him to the Clark County Jail.

"Watch this man very closely, gentlemen, and do a complete strip search for weapons," Con told the jailers. "Counting the rifle he had when I picked him up, I've already found five deadly weapons on him."

"Yes sir, Sheriff," they replied.

Ab Collins had just pulled up in the tow truck as Con and Jesse arrived back at the sheriff's department. Con sent Jesse to locate a sheet or gloves to protect fingerprints on Drago's rifle.

Con helped Ab hook up to the truck. On the way to town, he counted thirty-two cases of moonshine in the back.

"She's probably pretty heavy Ab, but we don't have far to go. I just want to get it off the street before the recipient realizes it's missing. I want no fingerprints on the steering wheel or gearshift other than those already on them."

"I've got you covered, Sheriff. I have a warehouse in the back of my garage that has room for the truck, and nobody will be accessing it for several days."

"If we can get this thing hidden before anyone sees it, the coroner can get photos and the DA can begin compiling his case. Most important is absolute secrecy."

"You've got my word, Sheriff."

Jesse returned with several large cleaning rags from the supply room. Con carefully extracted the rifle from under the seat and handed it wrapped in the rags to Jesse. "Stand this behind the file cabinet in my office," Con told him. "I'm going to ride with Ab. We're going really slow and staying off Fremont and Main Street. Keep us in sight, but stay back. Take note of anyone you see. No lights."

"Got it."

Ab and Con advanced up Carson Street toward Main. When Jesse returned from Con's office, the tow truck was between Second and First Street. Ab eased across First and continued toward Main before turning in the alley in the direction of Fremont. His garage was a half block ahead on the left. When he arrived, Ab jumped out and unlocked the door. Jesse blocked the alley with his car at Carson Street and walked cautiously toward the tow truck. Con did the same toward Fremont Street. Ab soon had the panel truck backed into the warehouse, unhooked, and the door closed and locked. They had seen no one and hoped that no one saw them. The three men quietly congratulated each other on a successful mission. Con told Ab he would have Dr. Martin come by in the morning and speak only to him. Ab parked the tow truck in front of his garage and drove his car home. Con climbed in with Jesse, and they sped off down Fremont Street toward Searchlight.

At four o'clock they rolled into the ranch yard at Luis Garza's. The old dog sat near the front porch, and Con glimpsed movement beneath the trees to the right of the house.

"Luis," he said, "it's me."

Luis stepped out from the shadows into the moonlight carrying his shotgun. "Everything has been quiet here. I heard your car and saw the lights so I hid under the trees until you got here. I saw the star on the door, but waited until you called me."

"You did the right thing," Con said, just as Jesse walked around the front of the car. "Luis, this is Jesse Slater, one of my top deputies. Jesse, Luis Garza, my family's oldest and dearest friend."

"Pleased to meet you, sir," Jesse announced, extending his hand.

"Conor is a good judge of people," Luis said. "You must be a good man." And he shook Jesse's hand.

"You lost four more sheep last night," Con told Luis, "but I caught the culprit and he's in jail. You can head back to town, Jesse, but stay close." Con watched as Jesse drove away. "I didn't complete my mission last night, and I have a four-mile hike before daylight to get Paddy's horse. We'll talk more when I get back." Con hurried off up the road behind Luis' barn. The moon was up and he made quick time on the lower road. When it began to climb the hill to meet the upper road, he stayed below the ridge, continuing toward Drago's shooting range. When he thought he was near, Con began watching for the dead sheep. He soon spotted one and confirmed in the predawn light that it was not just sleeping. Knowing he was in the right spot, he turned up the hill.

Just below the crest, he paused to catch his breath. He wanted to be fully alert if someone waited for him. Bob soon caught his scent on the slight breeze and nickered. If someone waited for him that knew much about horses, that would alert them. Con slid the Colt from its holster and cocked it, then crept up the remainder of the hill. On top, he remained crouched for several minutes to avoid sky-lining himself as he carefully scanned the area. Bob nickered again, but was not visible from Con's position. It was almost fully light on top of the ridge. He readied himself, then in a stooped run, dashed some fifty yards to cross the road, where he stopped again, remaining out of sight to steady his breathing. Bob snorted. Staying low, he worked his way to the horse.

Reassured that no one was watching, he stood up and gave the horse another carrot while he loosened the reins from the tree. The day was rapidly dawning. With a quick pat on Bob's neck, Con stepped into the saddle and gazed around from his elevated view. No sign of movement in the direction of the bluffs. Lights in the distance, however, warned of an approaching vehicle from the highway. Probably still three or four miles away, he thought. Con planned earlier to depart the area by a circuitous route to confuse any would-be tracker. The impending danger of being spotted on the ridge required a more expedient exit.

He trotted Bob across the road to the area he thought Drago had shot from. Dismounting, he dropped the reins and ran back to quickly brush out and dust his tracks near the road as well as those he and Drago had left earlier. The hasty work-manship would not deceive an experienced tracker, but might leave a novice scratching his head. As he turned to return to Bob, a dark sedan crested a high spot in the road less than a half mile away. An eyebrow of sun peeked over the horizon as Con raced toward Bob. Three casings glistened in the light as he ran past, but he dared not waste the moment required to collect them as he grabbed Bob's reins and led him over the crest.

They stopped once out of view of the road. Con tried to listen for the sound of the sedan between gasps for breath. Without reasonable rest for just over twenty-four hours, he was far too tired for so many foot-races, he told himself. As the sound of the car came near, he held his breath. It motored on up the road without hesitation as it passed them. He gradually released the air from his lungs and remained where he was for a few minutes before returning for the casings. A heavy cloud of dust followed the car up the road in the distance. That would help camouflage their tracks he considered as he recovered the three casings. They were .30-40 Krag as he was nearly certain they would be. He did not find the fourth. He slipped them into the pocket of his vest, then climbed aboard Bob who trotted down the hill then fell into his familiar lope.

15

At a quarter 'til ten, the bailiff approached Con as he dozed, sitting in the front row of the courtroom. He was still out of uniform with the exception of the badge pinned to his vest. "Excuse me, Sheriff," the bailiff said, startling Con awake. "Judge Tucker would like to speak to you in his chambers."

Con stood and followed. At the door, the bailiff knocked softly, then entered.

"Good morning," Judge Tucker said as he looked up from the sheriff's report in front of him. "My god, Sheriff, you look like hell!" he exclaimed.

"Sorry, Your Honor, it's been a long night."

"I see that," he said, raising the report in his hand. "Do I understand correctly? This man was shooting Luis Garza's sheep while he had thirty-two cases of moonshine in a delivery truck?"

"Yes, sir."

"You apprehended him while he was shooting?"

"Moments afterward, Your Honor. I waited until he put the rifle down in the truck."

"You did not discover the booze until later."

"When I cuffed him to the steering wheel and positioned myself behind him to drive to town."

"Where did the booze come from?"

"Presumably from an alleged moonshine still located up the road he was apprehended on."

"And Mr.," the judge referred to the report, "Drago owns the vehicle?"

"It is registered to Dutch's Oasis."

"Where is it now?"

"Hidden."

"Hidden where?"

Con glanced toward the bailiff.

"Bailiff," Judge Tucker said, "I feel perfectly safe under the protection of Sheriff Armenta. You may step into the courtroom."

"Yes, Your Honor," the bailiff responded as he left the chambers and closed the door behind him.

"Where, Sheriff?"

"It's locked in a warehouse behind the garage at Desert Chevrolet. Until this moment, Ab Collins, Deputy Jesse Slater, Dr. Harold Martin, and me were the only people to know its whereabouts."

"Do you think Dutch is involved in this moonshine business?"

"Probably," Con answered. "At least as a customer."

"What's your plan?"

"Verify that there is a moonshine still and its location. Call Los Angeles."

"Bureau of Prohibition?"

"Yes. It's more than I can handle. Let the big boys take care of it and the booze I have locked up. It's their jurisdiction and keeps us out of court."

"What about the sheep?"

"Luis Garza has already filed the charges."

"We need to get out there," he pointed to the door. "Hang around afterward. We'll talk more."

Con entered the courtroom. Jesse had brought Drago in. He was handcuffed behind his back and seated in front of the bar. Directly behind Drago, sat Jesse. Con took the seat beside him.

"All rise," the bailiff ordered and continued bringing the court into session as Judge Tucker came in and took his seat. "You may be seated."

"I hereby call this court to order," the judge sounded as his gavel struck the block. "Alfonso Drago." Tucker paused as Drago awkwardly came to his feet with his hands bound behind him, then stepped slightly forward.

"Yes, Your Honor," he answered, obviously familiar with the protocol.

"Mr. Drago, you are charged with twelve counts of destruction of livestock. How do you plead?"

"Not guilty, Your Honor."

"Mr. Drago, you are also charged with possession of thirty-two cases of illegal liquor. How do you plead?"

"Not guilty, Your Honor."

"Alfonso Drago, this case is hereby bound over for hearing by a Grand Jury. The time for the hearing will be selected at a later date. You are being held without bond pending the results of that hearing. Do you understand, Mr. Drago?"

"Yes, Your Honor."

"This court is adjourned," Judge Tucker announced as his gavel struck the block.

"All rise," the bailiff commanded as Tucker exited the courtroom.

Jesse escorted Drago back to jail, while Con waited for the courtroom to empty, then knocked on the judge's door.

"Come in Sheriff." His robe and tie hung on the wall behind him. Judge William Tucker sat open-collared behind his desk with his sleeves rolled up above his wrists. In a time when Conor Armenta trusted no one, he trusted Tucker. He admired his insight and frankness. And perhaps most importantly, Con liked him. "What do you make of that plea?"

"He's expecting someone to come to his rescue."

"Dutch Wagner?"

"Possibly."

"I don't trust that kid. Especially not since his mother disappeared."

Con did not reply.

"What's your next move?"

"Hal is…Dr. Martin is taking photographs of the truck and its contents this morning. As soon as he has them developed, he'll drop them at my office. I will select a few and call Stan Olsen at the *Evening-Review*. The judge looked at him questioningly. "He reports honestly." The judge's expression remained unchanged. "And I cut him off at the pockets on the Brice Campbell investigation. I owe him one."

"Okay, I'll go along with that, but what's your objective?"

"If it's Dutch's booze, the photographs in the newspaper will make it less advantageous to steal it back. Kind of hard to claim innocence when everyone has seen the pictures. If Dutch isn't the boss, who is? Maybe smoke the lobo out of his den, before he eats all of the sheep."

"Sort of rattle the can and see what falls out?"

"Yessir."

"Who do you think it is?"

"I don't know, but if they choke on the smoke, I might find out. When do you expect the Grand Jury to convene?"

"Probably next week. The DA will have the paperwork this afternoon. Campbell's funeral is tomorrow. Nothing will move on Friday."

"Thank you, Judge. I've got some loose ends and need some sleep."

"You've been working undercover. I'm no legal eagle, but I've been around the block. If you need advice, don't hesitate to ask."

"Yes, Your Honor," Con answered, reminded of his ride to the Wagner estate.

"When we're alone, my name is Bill, Sheriff."

"And mine is Con."

The judge stood and offered his hand. "Keep me posted, Con."

"Yes, sir," Con answered.

Tucker smiled. Habits are hard to break.

When Con returned to the sheriff's department, Hazel handed him a large envelope from the coroner. He glanced inside. "Call Stanley Olsen at the *Evening-Review*. Tell him I have a scoop," he told her as he stepped into his office. Con laid Hal's photographs out on his desk. There were two copies of each. He had done well to disguise the location of the panel truck in his photographs. He also included mug shots taken last night by the jailers. Within ten minutes, Con heard Stanley addressing Hazel in the outer office.

"Come on in, Stan," he hailed the reporter. As he entered, Con motioned to the chair in front of his desk. Con handed him the mug shot as he sat down. "Alfonso Drago. I arrested him last night on Luis Garza's ranch killing sheep." Stanley scribbled feverishly. "This is the truck he was driving," he said as he handed over a carefully cropped shot of the Graham showing only darkness in the background. "It's owned by the proprietor of an establishment on Block 16."

"Who?" Stan asked, pencil ready to write.

"That's confidential at this point."

Stanley scribbled a note.

"Here's the inside." Con handed over another photograph. Stan let out a long whistle. "Is that all moonshine?"

"Thirty-two cases."

"Holy smoke!" was all he could say as he stared at the photograph. "How much is that worth?"

"I have no idea," Con answered honestly. "When you find out, let me know."

"Where's the truck?"

"Impounded at an undisclosed location."

"Anything else?" Stanley asked.

"Drago pled not guilty on all counts before Judge Tucker in a preliminary hearing about an hour ago. You should be able to get transcripts."

"Great!"

"Stan."

"Yes?"

"Be very careful when you go around asking questions about this. Drago had four deadly weapons hidden on him when I arrested him."

"What were they?"

"A snub-nose .38 special, a Derringer, a switchblade, and a

dagger. He was also carrying a .30-40 Krag rifle, in plain sight."

"Wow! He must have been afraid of somebody."

"He's big enough to rip you in half with his bare hands. I don't think he's afraid of anything. I don't suspect his accomplices are either. Be careful. I don't particularly want to see Dr. Martin performing an autopsy on you anytime soon."

When Stan left the office, Con called the Bureau of Prohibition in Los Angeles. He was connected to Agent Michael O'Sullivan to whom he explained his arrest the previous night and the newspaper story that would appear late this afternoon. Con told O'Sullivan he planned another midnight ride to verify the likely still and its location. O'Sullivan felt that under the circumstances, the moonshiners would probably make every effort to move any alcohol on hand and the still that night. No one could estimate the size of the operation.

They planned for Agent O'Sullivan and three others to travel by train from Los Angeles, arriving at Arden around midnight. Jesse would pick them up there and take them to Luis Garza's ranch. Con and two other deputies would meet them there. All would be heavily armed and in civilian clothing.

Jesse had returned from the jail while Con met with Stanley Olsen. He waited in the outer office. Con called him in after his conversation with O'Sullivan and filled him in on the scheme. Striving to keep Hazel unaware of the plan, Con checked the board and made calls to his chosen deputies personally. He gave directions for each of them to travel separately, after dark, an hour apart, and to drive directly to the Garza Ranch without stopping at the sheriff's department.

"Wear your sidearms and carry shotguns and your

badges," he instructed each of them. "Be wary. We're dealing with some rough men. Be ready for anything. They will be."

"You, too," he told Jesse after hanging up the telephone.

"Got it."

"Go home and get some rest. Don't stop here tonight, head straight out to Arden. Don't be late. Michael O'Sullivan is the agent in charge. When we meet up tonight, this is his show. We're just helping out."

"Got it," Jesse answered with a hint of disappointment in his voice. He rose from his chair and approached the door.

"Be careful," Con added as Jesse's hand met the knob.

"You, too, boss. See you later," he told Hazel as he crossed the room.

Con soon snatched his hat from the hook in his office and followed in Jesse's footsteps. He stopped at Hazel's desk. "I'm going to get some sleep. Jesse is off duty, too. Call me if it's an emergency. Otherwise, I'll see you in the morning."

"Sleep tight, Sheriff" she replied kindly, still unsure of his forgiveness. Dottie told her of the excitement last night and he hadn't seemed the least bit annoyed at her. Hazel had heard from a friend about Con's blowup at the Mesquite Café yesterday and knew her name had been mentioned. Earlier this morning, he had been exhausted, but was cordial as he worked on his arrest report. Right now, he appeared to be a dead man still on his feet. For now, she preferred to tread softly and respect his privacy.

Con climbed in the sheriff's pickup truck. He started toward his parent's café, but changed his mind and turned toward home. It was well past noon when he rinsed his breakfast dishes and left them in the sink. He didn't remember unbelting his gun, pulling off his boots, or climbing into bed.

* * *

The clock showed half-past five when he stumbled into the kitchen and took a Coca-Cola from the icebox. He made his way to the front porch and shuffled through the newspapers accumulated there. "BOOTLEGGER CAUGHT KILLING SHEEP," the bold headline read across the top of the front page of the issue. He sat down in the worn-out chair and began to read Stanley's article. "Sheriff Conor Armenta single-handedly brought in the heavily armed bootlegger last night," it read. *Trying to butter me up*, Con thought to himself. The article went on to describe every detail from Con's arrest report. From the charges filed by Luis Garza to the photographs of the delivery truck, "impounded in a secret location, belonging to a business in Block 16," he missed nothing. The mugshot of Alfonso Drago told of his not-guilty plea and being held without bond pending a Grand Jury hearing. The article estimated the value of the moonshine at $3,200. This amazed Con. He had no idea it would be worth so much.

He went inside, bathed, and shaved. Dressed in a clean gray chambray shirt, he felt refreshed and fairly well-rested. He made himself a sandwich and started on a second Coca-Cola. As he ate, he mentally reviewed the steps of his mission tonight. When he finished his meal, he took the remainder of his Coca-Cola into the living room and slouched into his favorite chair. He stared at the telephone for a moment before picking it up and calling 142.

"Hello," June answered.

"Good evening."

"Con, are you okay?"

"Sure, why?"

"I read the *Evening-Review* when I got home. That was the man we saw in the truck, wasn't it?"

"Yes, it was."

"Were you afraid? He had three guns and two knives."

"I was concerned...and cautious. He is large enough to be pretty dangerous with his bare hands. I didn't discover the knives and third gun until I had him cuffed to the radiator at the sheriff's department."

"He could have killed you anywhere along the way!" she stated disbelievingly.

"If I had given him the opportunity. I didn't."

There was an uncomfortable silence as June calmed herself. "Have you eaten?" she finally asked.

"Yes, I just finished."

"Would you care to come by for dessert? While you were out chasing outlaws last night, I baked cookies."

"I would love to, but while I was catching the outlaw that I hadn't planned to, I didn't accomplish what I set out to. I need to go back out there in a few minutes."

"Oh...okay, I see."

"I wanted to talk to you about something before I left."

"What is it?"

"It seems that while in school, April and my niece, Donna, discussed our picnic Sunday. What Donna told my sister may have been somewhat exaggerated. When my sister confronted me for details, it quickly turned into a rather public display. What I'm trying to say is that...if I embarrassed you in any way, I am very honestly sorry. That was the opposite of my intention."

There was another long pause. "I heard about your argument. Las Vegas is growing rapidly, but it's still a pretty small town. I am not embarrassed. I am honored that you think so highly of me. If anyone thinks there is something indecent or immoral going on between us, they are who should be embarrassed...by their error." June stifled her tears at Con's open integrity.

"Well," Con cleared his throat, "thank you. I wanted to tell you."

"Thank you for being so honest."

"I really need to be going soon."

"Please be careful."

"No one wants me to stay healthy more than me," he replied with a chuckle, hoping to lift her spirits.

"I might be closing in on second place for that title," she said as she giggled.

"I will see you tomorrow."

"Tomorrow."

Con chopped a carrot into four chunks and put them in his vest pocket, then wrapped his gun belt around his waist. Slipping his badge into his shirt pocket, he picked up his hat and stepped out the back door. He climbed into the coupe and headed out Fremont toward Searchlight. When he pulled off the highway the little house and barn already rested in shadow. Luis had seen him coming and he and the dog met him at the gate. Con noticed the shotgun resting against the wall near his chair on the porch.

"Expecting trouble?" Con asked, indicating the gun.

"Are you?"

Con thought briefly. "Yes, I suppose I am. Two deputies will arrive here separately after dark. They will wait until Jesse gets here sometime around one o'clock. He'll have four federal agents with him. Jesse already knows this, but send them up the lower road. If I haven't met them by the time they get to the fork, tell them to shut off their headlights and continue toward the bluff. The moon will be out long before then."

As Con walked over to Bob at the corral, Luis noticed his canteen on the passenger floorboard. He emptied it and went to the springhouse to fill it.

Con gave Bob a friendly pat and rubbed his neck and back before checking each of his feet. Bob then received a carrot reward and followed him to the door of the barn where Con quickly had him bridled and saddled. When Con led Bob over to the coupe, Luis slipped his canteen over the saddle horn. Con returned the two sets of handcuffs and checked the rest of the contents of the saddlebags. He then methodically checked his Winchester and his Colt.

Con stepped into the saddle.

"*Buenas noches, amigo mío,*" Luis said, offering Con his hand.

"*Buenas noches, señor,*" Con replied, leaning over to accept it. "I'll see you in the morning," he added as he rode toward the lower road.

Luis waved to Con's back as he disappeared behind the barn.

An hour and a half later, Con could see the bluffs rising from the desert a mile away. The upper road lay three hundred yards to his left. He could see in the moonlight the cleft Luis had told him the road entered and the smaller one to its right where the good spring was. As he came nearer, he could make out a trail where traffic had been leaving the road heading toward the spring. He turned off to the right in a wide circle reaching the bluffs a quarter-mile from the spring. He worked his way closer for half of the distance before dismounting and proceeding ahead on foot. Perhaps one hundred feet from the mouth of the cleft, he discovered a fissure in the face that might allow a way to access the summit of the cliff. He continued on warily. About thirty feet from the entrance, Con could see the outline of a man standing guard. In the glow from lanterns within the narrow canyon, he appeared to be holding a rifle. *More likely a shotgun*, Con thought to himself.

He retreated back to the fissure and began to scale the cliff. It would be faster in daylight he thought, when a man could better see the finger and toe-holds. Even at that, it was not terribly difficult. About fifty feet in height, he managed to reach the top in less than a half hour. He picked his way across the small plateau to a vantage point above the spring.

Several lanterns lit up the small canyon. It widened considerably at the spring to about fifty feet and appeared to be completely boxed in. A fairly large green tent occupied a space beneath a cottonwood tree on the far side, and Con could make out what appeared to be several cases of moonshine in the doorway. A fire burned beneath a large kettle-looking fixture near the spring with a cone-shaped apparatus atop of it. He assumed it must be the still with its array of tubing connecting a series of oddly shaped vessels and tanks, and he had no idea of their various functions. There were three panel-trucks similar to the Graham and a sedan parked randomly about. He counted six men working around the still and carrying boxes from the tent to the nearest truck. One who loaded boxes he thought was Wesley. He did not recognize anyone else and could not define in particular who might be in charge.

He retraced his way across the top and carefully began his descent back down the fissure. When he reached the bottom, he found no need to reinvestigate the guard and turned along the face to retrieve Bob. Giving him his treat before mounting up, he pointed the gelding cross country toward the fork in the two roads. There, he planned to rendezvous with Jesse, Agent O'Sullivan, and the rest of the raiders. About a mile before reaching the meeting spot, he spied movement along the road. When he brought Bob to a halt, he could hear the faint sounds of the cars idling up the road in the darkness. He thought his reconnaissance must have taken longer than expected.

Not wanting to appear suddenly beside them, he turned Bob around and paralleled the road at a modest gallop until he was well ahead of the cars. He cut over to the road and dismounted, awaiting their arrival. Jesse drove his car in the lead with Agent O'Sullivan riding alongside him. They rolled to a stop twenty feet from the sheriff.

"We're glad to see you," Jesse said. "We're a little early and sure didn't want to miss you. I didn't realize how hard it would be to see out here without any headlights."

"I almost let you slip by," Con replied. "Had to turn around and get out ahead of you. What time is it?"

"One o'clock," the federal man answered. "I'm Mike O'Sullivan, Sheriff," he added, offering his hand.

"Con Armenta. Pleasure."

"What's it look like in there?" O'Sullivan asked.

"One man outside, looks like a shotgun. Six inside. All busy working. Didn't see any guns, but you know they have them. Canyon is narrow, maybe twelve feet at the entrance. Back about a hundred feet, it opens into a sort of meadow, roughly fifty feet wide. Looks boxed in. I couldn't see any way out the back other than up. Three panel-trucks and a car inside. There's a still with a fire under it near the spring and a green tent full of cases under a cottonwood tree against the left wall."

"How could you see all this?" the agent asked.

"I found a fissure in the cliff about a hundred feet to the

right of the entrance. Climbed up it and across the top to look down inside. They have several lanterns lighting up the canyon."

"That's a little beyond the realm of my abilities," O'Sullivan commented.

"I was born out here," Con replied. "Been chasing sheep in these cliffs and canyons since I was a kid." He smiled proudly enough that O'Sullivan could see his teeth in the moonlight. "This road goes into another canyon about a quarter-mile to the left of where our moonshiners are. I'll lead you to where they've been cutting across to the spring. Then I'll circle around and climb back up top."

The caravan followed Con up the road in the darkness for nearly an hour. The bluffs loomed ahead in the moonlight. Con stopped and dismounted. All seven men gathered around now in final preparation as apprehension of the coming invasion filled the night air.

"Here's your road." Con pointed out the path through the desert. "That black line over there in the cliff is the opening to the spring. I'll circle around and climb up over the top. Boys," Con addressed his three deputies, "Agent O'Sullivan here is in charge. Our job is to provide back up to him and his officers." Con indicated the other three agents. "You men do whatever he tells you to."

"Got it," Jesse replied for all.

"Give me a half hour," he told O'Sullivan as he swung his leg over the saddle.

In a matter of seconds, horse and rider had completely disappeared in the darkness. Jesse thought he glimpsed movement in the moonlight a few minutes later, but wasn't certain. In the meantime, Agent O'Sullivan gave each man their assignment. Then, they waited in silence.

Con circled the entrance to the spring, approaching the bluff about where he had ridden before, then guided Bob along the face to within three hundred yards of the fissure. Without a sling, he had no way to carry his Winchester up the cliff, so he left it in the scabbard. He reached in his vest pocket and gave the best horse he had ever ridden his second to last chunk of carrot, then made his way toward the crevice.

He had nearly arrived when a dim movement in the darkness froze him in his tracks. He reached for the Colt in its holster as a spray of bullets suddenly surrounded him and flashes of light exploded before his eyes. The Colt bucked twice in his hand, yet he heard no sound but ringing in his ears. A lantern appeared at the mouth of the canyon. He was on his knees, but lost his balance and fell sideways against the wall of stone beside him.

"Joe! Are you okay?" someone yelled.

Three sets of headlights were racing toward the canyon with spotlights sweeping the bluffs.

"Holy shit!" the same voice yelled just as the Colt bucked again in Con's hand.

Bright headlights and a spotlight stopped in a cloud of dust just a few feet in front of him. Silhouettes of two men raced toward him.

"Are you alright?" It was Jesse's voice, but all he saw was a black outline against the glare of lights.

"No," he finally said. "I think I'm hit."

There was a strange muffled rat-a-tat sound coming from the canyon, and it sounded like a string of firecrackers.

"Thompsons." The voice was Agent O'Sullivan.

Jesse was frantically trying to assess Con's condition. "Hit twice, I think," he told O'Sullivan. "Help me get him in the car."

They sat Con in the passenger seat where Jesse could try to watch him on the way back to town.

"Where's your horse?" O'Sullivan asked.

"You ride?"

"Some."

"Bob, he's a good one," Con slurred in a daze. He pulled the final bite of carrot from his vest pocket and handed it to O'Sullivan. "Three hundred yards." He pointed down the face of the cliff. "That way." Then he lost consciousness.

16

Jesse raced across the ragged road to the gravel highway. When he could see the lights of Las Vegas, his sedan was rolling as fast as the engine could carry it. Con woke up momentarily.

"Am I okay?"

"You're gonna be okay, Con. I'm gonna get you to the hospital." It was the first time he'd ever addressed him by name.

"No," Con's voice was surprisingly firm. "Hal," was all he said before lapsing back into oblivion.

Hal Martin no longer had a medical office. Jesse raced Con on to the hospital. *I'll argue with him later*, Jesse decided. The duty nurse helped get him onto a gurney.

"I'll call Dr. Anderson," she said.

"No. Dr. Martin."

"Are you sure?" she asked.

"He is," Jesse answered.

The nurse left the room and returned a few minutes later. "Hal's on his way," she said.

"You know him well?"

"I should, I was his nurse for twenty years."

"So, why did you question?"

"Dr. Martin hasn't practiced for several years. Doesn't even keep an office anymore."

"I know, but Con insisted that I didn't bring him here. That I take him to Hal. Where? The morgue? He probably has a Band-Aid in case he cuts his finger, but what else? I'll argue with him later."

"You did the right thing."

"Tell *him* that." Jesse nodded toward his boss.

"I will." She began cutting away his bloody shirt. "He seems to have nearly quit bleeding. Maybe ran out of blood," she quipped. Jesse didn't notice. "He'll be alright." She paused. "Deputy?" she asked, not seeing a badge.

"Yes, ma'am," Jesse responded, extracting his badge from a pocket. "We were working undercover," he told her as he pinned the badge on his khaki civilian shirt.

"You didn't shoot him, did you?"

"Oh, no, ma'am. A gangster. Con...Sheriff Armenta killed him."

At that moment, Hal walked in wearing a nightshirt with trousers beneath. "Good morning, Jesse. What happened?"

"Thompson sub-machinegun. Really close. I think he's hit twice. Lots of blood." Jesse was nearly in tears trying to tell him. He had held himself together throughout the ordeal, but suddenly began to unravel.

"Don't worry, Jesse. I'll take care of him. I've been sewing him back together since he was a boy," the aging doctor told him. "Go on outside, call his folks."

"Okay."

"Helen, grab the ether and a mask, please."

Jesse walked out into the entry. He found the telephone on a desk. He didn't feel stable enough to call Juan and Maggie Armenta. He called Dottie. She had not yet fully recovered from her experience the previous night of Con dragging Drago in. That following the turmoil regarding Con and June Sommers, she felt responsible for. This nearly overwhelmed her. She gradually managed to control her crying and attempted to call the home of Mr. and Mrs. Armenta. No answer. It was already past five. They were probably at the café getting ready to open. She hesitated, then picked up the telephone again.

"Operator, this is Dorothy Dickenson with the sheriff's department. Would you connect me with Mrs. June Sommers, please? On 3rd Street, I believe."

June picked up the telephone on the third ring. "Hello?"

"Mrs. Sommers?" Dottie asked. "This is Dorothy Dickenson at the sheriff's department. Most people call me Dottie. I tried to contact Mr. and Mrs. Armenta, but there was no answer." Her voice began to quiver, but she continued. "I don't know who else to call." She started to cry again, but somehow recovered. "Sheriff Armenta has been shot."

"Oh, my God," June blurted out, "Oh, please...please, no."

"He's at the hospital," Dottie finally managed through streams of tears. "I have no idea how bad it is. I am so sorry."

Both women struggled to control their emotions. "Con's sister is Olivia McLeod," June finally managed to tell Dottie. "I don't know what her husband's name is. I will be at the hospital as soon as I can."

June ran next door barefoot and in her nightgown. She banged on the door. The porch light came on as Joyce Wright pulled back the curtain. Seeing June, she quickly opened the door. "My word, deary. What is it?"

June quickly explained. "Can you come sit with April and wake her for school?"

"Certainly. I'll be over as soon as I can dress."

June ran back home and hurried to dress herself. Joyce arrived momentarily. "I will call as soon as I know anything," June told her. "I don't want April to worry all day at school. She adores him."

"And you?"

"I'm very fond of him, too," she replied and ran out the door.

When June Sommers stepped through the door into the waiting room of the hospital, she found a tall, distraught young deputy with blood on his shirt and jeans pacing the floor. He started at the sudden intrusion.

"Where's Con?" she asked urgently.

"He's in...who are you?"

"June Sommers," she answered flatly to a bewildered Jesse Slater. The expression on his face failed to belie his confusion. "His, uh..." June was unsure how to continue. "His girl-friend," she finally answered, suddenly pleased, yet embarrassed by the realization.

"Oh, uh, I heard—"

But June interrupted before he could finish, "—that Con had this big secret he was trying to keep from being the center of Las Vegas gossip."

"Until his sister caused a big ruckus at the Mesquite Café in front of twenty or thirty customers and now everybody knows," a female voice behind her added. "I am so sorry, Mrs. Sommers," Olivia McLeod added as she continued in the door. "I just, I guess I just didn't see why he was being so sneaky."

"I think he was trying to protect me from embarrassment," June answered. "In case I didn't feel the same way about him, as he did about me."

"I take it you know each other?" Jesse asked, somewhat unsure of the circumstances.

"Yes," Olivia answered, "but only as mothers of young classmates at PTA meetings, up until now."

"Con is back there," Jesse began just as Juan and Maggie Armenta came through the door. "Hal Martin and the nurse are working on him right now."

"How bad is it?" June asked, fighting back her tears.

"I don't know," Jesse replied. Suddenly turning pale, he sat down in a chair. Covering his face with his hands and resting his elbows on his knees, he continued. "There was blood everywhere. The gangster shot him with a machine gun. When I got there, I said, 'Are you alright?' and he said, 'No, I think I'm hit.' He was sort of on his knees and leaning his shoulder against the rock wall." Jesse struggled to tell the story. He fought to compose himself.

Maggie Armenta sat down beside him and placed her arm around his shoulders. "It's okay," she consoled him as if she were comforting any of her own children.

"I think he is shot in the chest," he went on slowly, "on the left side, by his heart." June and Maggie gasped in unison. Tears streamed down Olivia's cheeks as she, too, took a seat beside her mother. June wavered unsteadily on her feet, suddenly realizing the blood on Jesse's clothing was Con's. Juan wrapped his arm around her waist and lowered her into a nearby chair. He held her hand and sat down beside her. Jesse took several deep breaths. "And down low on his right side above the hip."

"Oh, Jesus," Maggie wailed, "please help my son."

"Agent O'Sullivan and I loaded him in my car, and I brought him here as fast as I could."

They all sat in silence for several minutes, Maggie with her arm around Jesse and Olivia with hers around her mother.

Across the small room, Juan reassured June. "He'll be okay. He's a good boy. Tough."

Before Juan could continue, Hal nearly roared into the room, "What's with all the sad faces?" Crossing straight to June, he said, "You must be June. These boys can hardly stay quiet about their lady friends when they're under the anesthesia."

"But, how is he?" June exclaimed.

"Excuse me, miss, my name is Hal Martin." He took the seat next to June on the opposite side of Juan and held her other hand. "Con is going to be fine. He should be able to walk out of here in a couple of hours."

"But he was shot," June replied in disbelief, "twice."

"Yes, but both turned out to be fairly superficial wounds."

Jesse was even more shocked than June. "He was shot in the chest, wasn't he?"

"More in the shoulder actually," Hal explained. "Right through the deltoid muscle here." He grabbed the muscle in front of his own armpit in demonstration. "It went deep to the rib behind it and cut an artery, then exited below his armpit. That was the bleeder. And he might be a little bit weak for a few days from the loss of blood. And he'll be sore with that broken rib for a while. Feed him liver." He glanced from June to Maggie to Juan and back to June. "That'll help boost him back from the blood loss."

"What about his side?" Jesse asked.

"Another half inch and it would have missed him completely. Just grazed him. The burn from the bullet nearly cauterized it instantly. Didn't even stitch it up." He turned back to June. "I'm sorry, miss. I've been acquainted with these folks for a long time. Known Juan and Maggie since before they were married. Delivered little Ollie there. Jesse's a good man, too. They're all of pretty good stock so I assume you must be, too."

"June Sommers," she said and somehow managed a slight smile amid the emotional rollercoaster of the morning.

Hal stood, and not letting go of June's hand, pulled her to her feet. "You come on back. He'll be coming out from under the ether pretty soon."

"Shouldn't his parents be back here with him?" June asked.

"He's seen them before," Hal replied with a wink, "and you're prettier."

"I don't feel right about them not being in there with him."

Hal stopped and faced her in the hallway. "He never mentioned any of them in his sleep."

"What did he say?"

"That's between you and him."

Con lay shirtless on the operating table, his upper body slightly elevated. Hal grabbed a chair for June and sat it beside the table. The nurse hung Con's gun belt on a hook beside a bloody leather vest and left the room. The holster was ominously empty.

"You holler if you need us," Hal told her as he followed the nurse out.

June sat on the chair beside him. She carefully lifted his right hand and leaned down to tenderly kiss it before pressing it to her face. Tears again poured and ran down the hand she held so dearly. His face held no expression. Neither the solemn face of duty nor the broad smile she loved. A large bandage covered the wound below his left armpit. Bindings that wrapped all the way around his chest held it in place. A smaller bandage held by adhesive tape covered the wound to his side. "I just found you," she whispered through her tears, "and nearly lost you."

Hal sent Jesse to find a shirt for Con. As he left, a fellow deputy from last night's raid met him in the doorway, bringing with him a handcuffed prisoner with a bloody shirtsleeve.

"Call Joe in for this one, Helen," Hal told the nurse.

"We've got two more out at the Garza Ranch for you, Doc," the deputy told him.

The mention of Garza immediately brought the Armenta family to attention.

"Who?" Hal asked.

"The gangster Sheriff Armenta killed and another one that one of the agents shot last night."

Olivia shared glances with her parents at the remark.

"Con killed someone last night?" Maggie asked.

"These folks are Sheriff Armenta's family, deputy," Hal told him.

"Yes, ma'am," the deputy answered, "the man who shot him." The deputy turned back to Hal. "Is he alright, Doc?"

"Yes, he's going to be fine. His girlfriend is with him now."

"Sheriff Armenta has a girlfriend?" the deputy asked in shock.

"Evidently," Hal answered, raising an eyebrow.

As Jesse drove to the sheriff's department in hopes Con still kept a clean change of clothing there, he failed to recognize Agent O'Sullivan driving Con's new coupe toward the hospital. He walked in to find Hazel already there with Dottie.

"I called her," Dottie explained. "How is the sheriff?"

"He's going to be alright. Not as serious as I thought." Both women stared at Jesse's bloody clothing. "I just came in to get him some clean clothes. He still keeps some here?"

"Yes," Hazel answered. "Bottom drawer of his file cabinet." Jesse returned with a clean uniform shirt and jeans. "You might consider a quick change, yourself," Hazel added, looking at Jesse's shirt and jeans.

"Oh, yeah." Jesse noticed his own appearance for the first time. "I should swing by my house."

As Con began to stir, June quickly wiped her face with the hem of her dress. When he began to open his eyes, she forced a meager smile. "Good morning," she whispered.

"Hi." Con's eyes began to focus on June's face. He smiled. The smile that made the dimples in his cheeks show and accompanied the sparkle in his eyes. "What are you..." he began to ask. "Am I in the hospital?"

"Yes." She started to say more, but Con's smile quickly disappeared.

"Jesse was supposed to take me to Hal's," he interrupted irritably.

"Dr. Martin is here. He operated on your shoulder," June answered, not understanding his annoyance. "Aren't you thankful to be alive? I thought you'd be—"

"So, everybody thought I should be in the hospital?" Con interrupted. "To hell with what I thought and told them. Is that it? Whose idea was this, anyway?" he glared at her accusingly.

"Jesse thought—"

"Jesse thought! Who told him to bring me here? You?"

Seeing his anger, she did not finish the statement. She rose and left the room. She did not stop or look at anyone in the lobby as she rushed out of the hospital.

"What's going on?" Hal scowled as he came into the operating room.

"Why am I here?" Con responded vehemently.

"Because somebody shot you with a machine gun."

"I know that. I told Jesse to take me to your office. Why am I here and not at your office?"

"At the morgue?"

"No, your doctor's office."

"I haven't had an office for three, no four years," Hal responded as forcefully as Con was being.

"Oh," was all he replied.

"Besides, I'd have brought you here anyway. I never had clamps and such to sew that artery back together nor anesthesia, or Helen to assist for that matter. You're lucky to be alive, you fool, and here you are yelling at people. You should be thanking God and Jesse Slater for getting you here before you bled out. I should have stayed in bed, you ungrateful asshole." At that Hal, too, stormed from the room. He stopped long enough to tell the deputy that he was going home to dress appropriately and would be back to visit the crime scene. Then nearly ran over Agent O'Sullivan as they met in the door.

"How old are you, Conor?" Helen asked as she came into the room.

"Thirty-six," he replied.

"Well, you sure don't act it," she scolded. "There's a lot of fine people who love you. They've either been working on or worrying over you for half the night. You lay here throwing a tantrum like a toddler because that young deputy and I decided it was more important to save your life than bend to your way. It's time you grow up, young man."

Helen returned to the lobby. "Any of you are welcome to go in and see him, if you care to."

The door had been open since June left the operating room. All had heard the confrontation with Hal Martin followed by Helen's chastising. Olivia jumped to her feet, but Maggie grabbed her arm.

"You wait!" Maggie said firmly as she stood. Bringing Juan with her, they walked down the hallway. When they entered the room, she closed the door. She did not smile when she came to the side of the operating table. Juan stood near his feet.

"Your color is good," she said calmly. "You must not have lost too much blood." She stood silently, choosing her words carefully.

"Mama," Con started, but she held up her hand to silence him.

"I understand perfectly," she began coolly, "that you want and need your privacy. I know now, since you are the sheriff, that your every move is subject to public scrutiny. I was terrified when I heard you were shot. Do you know how I found out?"

"Did Jesse call you?"

"No, he was so afraid you were going to die, he called Dottie. Papa and I were already at the café getting ready for breakfast. She could not reach us. Not knowing Olivia, in desperation, she called Mrs. Sommers. She told Dottie Olivia's name and Olivia came to the café to tell us. June beat all of us here. For an hour, the five of us cried, and prayed, and comforted each other while Dr. Martin stopped the bleeding and sewed the severed artery back together in your armpit that nearly cost you your life. You cannot imagine what it would have been like for him, or us, if he failed."

"But, Mama," Con began again, but again Maggie silenced him.

"You need to thank Jesse for saving your life. By what Dr. Martin said, you were only minutes from dying when he got you here. We do not know June Sommers well. I remember when she used to come in to eat occasionally a few years ago and Olivia has talked to her at school functions. What I can tell is, she cares a great deal for you. I don't know what you said or did, but you hurt her deeply. We know that you killed a man last night and that must be weighing heavily on you, but you—"

"I what?" Con cut her off mid-sentence. "I did what?"

"We know you killed the man who shot you," she repeated. Con's face went white. Juan started to call the doctor, but remembered he had left. "You didn't know," Maggie suddenly realized.

"I saw movement in the darkness," Con, staring blankly, began. "He was very close. The guard should have been further away. I reached to pull my gun from the holster. I saw the flashes from the man shooting at me. The gun was in my hand. I was on my knees, but fell against the wall. Another man came from the canyon with a lantern. There were bright lights and Jesse was there. And O'Sullivan. I don't remember."

They talked quietly for a few minutes as Con came to comprehend he had killed a man.

"We need to go to work," Maggie finally said. "Do you want to talk to Olivia?"

"Okay."

"Come eat breakfast," Juan told him. "I'll feed you." They

walked out and closed the door behind them. At the lobby, they talked with Helen, Olivia, and Agent O'Sullivan. Dr. Anderson had arrived and was working on the other deputy's prisoner. When Juan and Maggie left to open the café, Olivia came back to see him.

"So," Olivia began, calmly testing the water, "Mama said you didn't know you shot that man last night."

"No, I really don't remember it. Everything happened so fast, it all just sort of blurred together. I don't remember much past the guy shooting at me."

"Maybe it's better that way. Time will tell."

"Yeah, maybe."

"Con," Olivia said, "I'm really sorry about the other day."

"Yeah, okay."

"No, really. It didn't register that you were trying to keep things quiet from Las Vegas. It just felt like you were just trying to keep your family from knowing what was going on. I'm sorry that I probably ended up causing exactly what you were trying to avoid. A whole lot of gossip."

"Well, there will probably be more now."

"It sounds like you didn't want anyone to know you got shot, either."

"Well, I guess I'm not very good at keeping secrets. The more it seems I try to be subtle, the sooner it gets out all over town."

"You need to tell Mrs. Sommers that," Olivia suggested cautiously. "She really likes you and you truly hurt her. She did everything she could to care for you, and you, well, I don't know what you did, but she wouldn't even look at us when she ran out of here."

Con could not look his sister in the eye. He stared away at the wall. He didn't have much experience with women, but one thing he knew was that he liked this one a lot. The other thing he knew was he had totally ignored her feelings in his anger and frustration over getting himself shot. Especially his inability to keep that news secret. "I'm a little green when it comes to women," he finally coaxed himself to share with his sister.

"Rule number one," she began. "Try not to piss them off when they are helping you." She could not help releasing a stifled giggle.

"Well, that's a good place to start," he smiled. "I'll try to remember that."

"Flowers."

"That's rule number two?"

"Especially if you failed on rule number one. But most anytime helps." Olivia moved toward the door. "I need to get to work," she said as she opened the door. "I love you, big brother," she added and rushed down the hall before he could reply.

Moments later, O'Sullivan came in, followed by Jesse carrying a clean change of clothes.

"I heard I shot someone last night," Con said as they came in.

"Yes, you did, Sheriff," Agent O'Sullivan replied. "Two shots in the chest. One dead center and the other, two inches higher and to the right. I couldn't have done better on the pistol range. Let alone under machinegun fire."

"Well, I don't remember it," he said, then repeated the story with only slightly more detail than he told his parents. "What else happened?"

"One of my agents killed another man with a machine gun on the inside and one of your deputies winged another. After it was over, we had the prisoners unload the trucks and the tent, piling the merchandise around the still. Then we had a bonfire. Nearly a thousand gallons of pretty high-grade White Dog. Something around thirty grand over the bar at a speakeasy. Two of my men are escorting all but the wounded prisoner to Carson City. He is in with one of your deputies being patched up by Dr. Anderson right now. He'll be jailed here until we can get him transferred to Carson City. My other agent, who killed the other bootlegger, is out at the canyon with one of your deputies guarding the site until the coroner arrives. He will remain in town until the inquest."

"Sounds like everything came out as well as can be expected, even though our plan had to be aborted."

"Yes, it did. Oh, I almost forgot your horse is back at the ranch and your car is out front."

"One more thing, Agent O'Sullivan. I'd like you to call Stanley Olsen at the *Las Vegas Evening-Review*. Give him the whole story."

"Are you sure?"

"Yes. You don't have to tell him I told you to if you don't want to. He's just the most honest reporter around here. Works hard. Never invents things to make it sound better."

"No problem, Sheriff."

"If you don't mind, I'd like to speak to my deputy in private for a few minutes."

"Sure thing," O'Sullivan answered and closed the door as he left.

"Jesse," Con said, "I want to thank you for saving my life."

"Oh, Sheriff, it wasn't like that at all."

"Well, according to Hal, it was. He said I only had a few minutes left when you got me here. It's a debt I hope to never have to repay, but I want you to know that I will do everything in my power if the circumstances are ever reversed."

"Thank you, Sheriff. I just did the best I know how. I'd do it again in a heartbeat."

"I know you would."

Jesse hurried from the room before he broke down into tears again. It had been a very emotional morning.

Helen entered a moment later and handed Con's clean clothes to him. "You need to put these on," she said.

"Aren't you going to leave?" Con asked.

"No. I've seen you in your drawers before. You've lost enough blood to be lightheaded. I can't have you falling down in here. If you tear those stitches, I'm not sure I could find anyone willing to sew you back up. Now sit up, turn, and hang your feet off the side of that table."

Con did as directed. "Okay?"

"Just sit there for a few minutes." She watched the clock on the wall until three minutes passed. "Are you okay?"

"Yes."

"Not dizzy?"

"No."

"Okay, stand up," she said and moved closer in case he began to totter. "Okay, go ahead."

Con quickly dressed, turning his back while he changed his jeans.

"Okay, sit down right there in the chair," she said and left.

A moment later, Hal walked in and closed the door behind him. "I owe you an apology, Con."

"No, you don't. You didn't say anything I didn't deserve. I'm the one who needs to apologize, and I do. I am sorry for acting that way, Hal. You saved my life. I will be forever indebted to you."

"I remember a young boy about twenty years ago, lived around here. He doctored his father's back, had a severe infection. It must have nearly torn that kid in two to do the best he and his father knew to dig that infection out. Saved his old man's life, though. Did he ever get any special favors for doing that?"

"No, sir, other than to get to grow up with a father."

"Exactly. Now accept my apology so I can go and see what kind of a mess you left out there."

"Yes, sir. Apology accepted. I'll go with you."

"No, you won't. You will go to the Mesquite Café and have the biggest breakfast you can hold. Then you will go home and rest. Sleep, if you can. Understood?"

"Yes, sir."

"That artery I put back together supplies most all the blood to your left arm. If it gets numb, move it around until you get the feeling back. Don't overdo it. You could tear it loose again. If you get a hot burning sensation in your armpit, get your butt right in here and I mean pronto. It's broke loose and me or Joe will have to go in and try to put it back together. Don't play around or you'll lose that arm. Now go do as you're told."

Jesse waited in the lobby. Hal recruited him as an assistant to investigate the scene of last night's raid in the canyon. The two were walking out the door when Con entered the hallway.

"Sheriff," Helen spoke as he neared her desk. "I want to apologize for disrespecting you earlier.

"No apology needed, ma'am. I deserved what you said," he replied and continued out the door. Con felt naked without his hat as he walked to his car. He opened the door awkwardly with his right hand and gingerly climbed in. He made it to the café without great difficulty. His mother served him fried liver and eggs with fried potatoes and coffee. The combination did not seem terribly appealing.

When he started to question his mother, she replied, "Doctor's orders."

It wasn't as bad as it looked. He ate all of it, then drove home and laid down on his couch. A strange sensation for a Thursday morning, he thought. He actually dozed off. The clock read ten-thirty when he woke. Brice Campbell's funeral started in a half hour. He went, keeping his left thumb hooked in his jeans pocket to ease the pressure on his shoulder. Choosing a spot away from the center of things, he leaned against the trunk of a cottonwood tree in the shade. As the service ended, a tall man worked his way through the crowd toward him. It was Newt Campbell.

"Sheriff Armenta?" he asked.

"Yes."

"I am Newton Campbell. You can call me Newt," he said, offering Con his hand.

"What can I do for you, Mr. Campbell?" Con asked as Newt pumped his hand slightly more vigorously than comfortable, considering his injuries.

"My mother would like to speak to you, if she could," Newt answered and led Con through a throng of well-wishers to his mother's side. Midway through the crowd, Con spotted June. She looked away.

"Hello, Sheriff." Leanora Campbell offered her hand. "I hardly recognized you out of uniform and without the hat," she said, pointing toward her head.

"I'm off duty for a few days," Con answered, accepting her handshake. "As for the hat, it's a long story. Please accept my sincere condolences to you and your family, Mrs. Campbell."

"Thank you," she said. "I read in the paper of an arrest you made a couple of nights ago."

"Yes, I did."

"I saw the photograph of Al Drago."

"Yes?" Con questioned.

"He is the man Brice fired for stealing from the company a few years ago."

"Well, now. Isn't that interesting. I will look into it."

17

THURSDAY, APRIL 10, 1930

When Con left the funeral, he drove to the Catholic Church. Father O'Malley met him in the vestibule. "What can I do for you, Sheriff?" he asked.

"I need to confess."

"Cannot wait until Sunday evening?"

"No, Father."

"Come this way." Father O'Malley led Con to the confessional.

Con proceeded to tell the priest of the previous night's operation.

"And you killed the man?"

"Evidently, Father. No one else did and he is dead."

"When did this happen?"

"Around two o'clock."

"And he shot at you?"

"He shot me."

"He shot you?"

"Yes, he hit me twice."

"My word, Sheriff! You were shot twice ten hours ago and you're sitting in my confessional?"

"Yes, Father. I went to the hospital. Then to Brice Campbell's funeral. Then here."

"It's a miracle you're alive, let alone walking around! God was watching over you." The priest concluded the confession. When they came out of the confessional, he escorted Con to the door and shook his hand. "God has blessed you, Conor. May he continue to do so." Then he watched him down the steps and to his car.

When Con drove to the sheriff's department, Hal's sedan delivery sat out front. Hal confronted him as he walked in the door. "I thought I told you to go home and rest."

"I did. Fell asleep on my couch until ten thirty."

"Then went to Brice Campbell's funeral according to your neighbor lady."

"Then to confession with Father O'Malley."

"Okay, I'll give you that one. But you need to stop. You lost a lot of blood. I couldn't tell you what color that shirt was that Helen cut off of you. That stuff doesn't just grow back into your veins in a few hours."

"Duty calls."

"You're off duty until the inquest, Con. That's nine o'clock Monday morning in Judge Tucker's courtroom. Sit on your front porch, watching the birds fly by. Rest. And eat as much liver as you can stand. It helps build your blood back up."

Hazel and Jesse sat back, watching and listening.

"Go in there and open up that safe of yours."

Con did as Hal instructed. "Okay?"

Hal handed him his gun belt. "Your belt and vest were at the hospital. Three shots out of your automatic. I picked up the casings along with your Colt where you fell." He pulled three casings from his shirt pocket and handed them to him. "Put those in an envelope and lock them with the Colt in your safe until after the inquest." Hal crossed Con's office and picked up a Thompson leaning against the wall. "Tag that number one and tie this to it," he said as he handed Con a cotton sack full of casings. "Twenty-six rounds gone from the drum. Twenty-one of them that I found are in the sack. That's the guy that shot you."

Hal walked back across Con's office and retrieved a second Thompson. "All fifty rounds gone from the drum. Forty-four that I found are in there." He handed Con another sack. "That's number two. That's the one the federal agent killed. He didn't hit anybody." Hal crossed the room one more time and retrieved Con's Stetson from the peg. "Sit down in your chair," he ordered as he poked his finger through a hole in the crown of Con's hat. He handed the hat to Con as he examined the top of his head. The furrow of singed hair told the story. "An inch lower and you wouldn't be sitting here right now." Hal walked around to face Con. The bewildered look on his face told Hal that he had finally struck home. "Now go over to your folks' place and have a big plate of liver and onions before they close. Then go home and think about it awhile. Call that pretty lady you pissed off this morning if you've got the guts to."

Con never replied to Hal. He was right. So was Father O'Malley. So was Olivia, for that matter. He was the luckiest man alive and didn't have the brains to see it. He walked past Jesse and Hazel in the outer office without speaking and drove to the café. He saw Olivia walking away from him up the street as he pulled up. He hung his hat on the hook by the door and sat at the counter. Maggie brought him a Coca-Cola.

* * *

Olivia McLeod left work in midafternoon just before the Mesquite Café closed for the day. Out of her ordinary routine, she decided to stop by after school and walk Donna home. When the doors opened to a flood of boisterous children flowing down the steps, Olivia spotted her daughter and April Sommers chattering as they walked among the crowd. They were soon to be met by April's mother, who turned to join them. Olivia calculated her course to intersect their path.

"I'm surprised to see you here," Olivia began. "I thought you would be working."

"Mr. Westcott closed the office today for his father-in-law's funeral."

"Oh," Olivia replied in surprise. "I guess I didn't realize they were related. Well, I'm glad I ran into you anyway. I need to talk to you."

"About what?"

"About Con."

"I'd rather not," June answered, suddenly withdrawn from what began as a pleasant conversation.

"Con hasn't been around very many women," Olivia began anyway. "Except me and Mama. I'm not the best gauge to compare to, when it comes to women. I'm loud and pushy and we butt heads constantly. We always have."

June walked along in silence, looking at the ground ahead of her.

"Con never had time for girlfriends in school. He was too busy working. Always trying to help support the family.

Paddy and I helped, too, as we got older, but...I don't really know because no one ever talked about it, but I think Con gave almost everything he made to Papa. I remember him taking a girl from church to a high school dance once. He bought himself a new shirt and her, a corsage. He was embarrassed when they got there. All of the other boys had jackets and suits with ties. I think he left the girl there and walked home. I was about twelve then."

A tear rolled down June's cheek. "Would you like a glass of tea?" she asked. They were in front of her house.

"Yes, yes I would."

"April, could you and Donna bring Mrs. McLeod and me a glass of tea?"

The girls scampered inside as June and Olivia sat down on the porch swing. The two women talked for an hour. It had been a very stressful day. They did not talk about Con, mostly, they got to know each other. Olivia learned about April's father. June learned about Stuart and what it was like to be married to a rodeo cowboy that dabbled in truck driving, just enough to make the house payments. But she loved him. She really loved him. Loved him more than anything in the world, except her children. Just as June loved April. They talked of their children and what joy they brought into their lives. They searched for all of the things in their pasts that had generated happiness, as they strived to cheer each other up.

Close to five o'clock, a sedan pulled up with Las Vegas Florist painted on the door.

"Mrs. June Sommers?" the young man driving the car asked.

"Yes, that's me."

"These are for you, ma'am," he said as he handed her a

large bouquet of flowers. "I'm sorry for the selection, ma'am, but we're nearly sold out from the funeral today."

"Thank you," she said. "They are lovely."

"Well," Olivia commented. "He listened."

June smiled, but did not comment. She did not want to share feelings she did not fully understand herself.

"I need to be going and figure out what we're having for dinner," Olivia said. "Thank you for the tea and the conversation. Next time...my house."

"Deal," June answered.

As Olivia gathered Donna and walked up the street, June carried her bouquet inside to search for a vase. When she removed them from their wrapping, she found the small card.

I did not mean to hurt you.
I'm sorry, Con.

* * *

When the *Evening-Review* arrived, the headlines created quite a stir around Las Vegas. "G-MEN AND SHERIFF'S DEPARTMENT TEAM-UP ON MOONSHINERS," had top billing, followed by, "SHERIFF ARMENTA KILLS CHICAGO MOB ENFORCER IN RAID," and "SHERIFF ARMENTA HIT TWICE IN GUNBATTLE WITH MOBSTER." Con thought O'Sullivan had probably laid it on a little too thick with Stan Olsen, but honestly could not refute anything he read in the three articles. O'Sullivan made Con out to be the big hero, while Con felt like his contribution had only lasted a few seconds. He would have preferred not to have drawn attention to himself.

Hal was right again, Con thought as he lounged in his

favorite chair. He was exhausted. He picked up the *Zane Grey* that he had begun to read what seemed like a lifetime ago, but soon fell fast asleep. He woke sometime in the darkness and forced his aching body afoot for long enough to climb into bed.

* * *

FRIDAY, APRIL 11, 1930

The telephone ringing woke Con up. The sun had fully risen, filling every room of the small house with light. He was so stiff and sore he could barely move but finally managed to get to the telephone before it quit ringing.

"Hello, this is Con."

"Sheriff, Bill Tucker. I know you're off duty, but I've got some papers—"

"Bill who?" Con interrupted.

"Bill Tucker."

"I don't know a—"

"Judge Tucker," he finally said excitedly. "Look, the clerk just brought in a pile of paperwork that you need to see."

"Okay, I'm half asleep," Con managed. "I'll meet you at the Mesquite Café at nine."

"It's already nine thirty."

"Ten?"

"Okay."

Con washed his face and discovered he was well past needing a shave. It could not wait. Amazingly, he managed a fairly decent shave, barely awake, one-handed, and in a hurry. He quickly brushed his teeth and another glance in the mirror showed a shirt that looked like it had been slept in. It had. His right arm was fine, but his left was stiff and sore. He changed his shirt as quickly as possible, got it tucked into his jeans, and headed out the door.

When he walked into the café at ten after ten, Judge Tucker occupied a table for four in the corner. Con despised being late.

Olivia brought coffee. "Are you having breakfast?"

"Yes. You, Judge?"

"Just coffee," he answered. "You have doughnuts?"

"Fresh peach pie?"

His face lit up. "Perfect."

"So, what's up, Your Honor?"

"Bill is fine. Here," he said, pulling a document from his briefcase to show Con. "Bob Westcott filed these this morning."

The document was for Gary D. Wagner, Jr., filing charges against Alfonso Drago for grand theft of one 1927 Graham Brothers delivery truck.

"Gary D. is Dutch, I take it?"

"Yes," Tucker answered as he handed Con another document.

The second document was for a storage lien on Katherine Wagner's 1929 Auburn Speedster for the sum of $1,860. Stored at the Muleskinner's Rest, Pine Canyon Road, Las Vegas, Nevada.

"I had forgotten that name until recently. Katherine Wagner's place?"

"That's what I thought," the judge agreed and handed Con another document.

The third document was a transfer of title for the entire property to Gary D. Wagner, Jr. for the compensation of one dolar. It was dated three years ago.

"She deeded the place over to Dutch three years ago?"

"So, it seems," Tucker replied. "Smells a bit like a bad can of salmon, wouldn't you say?"

"Yes, I would." Now fully awake, Con mulled over this new situation. "What would bring about this sudden change?"

"Money," Tucker answered. "Somebody burned down thirty-some thousand dollars worth of his moonshine night-before-last."

"And fifty new dump trucks coming beginning in five weeks."

"What?"

"Wagner Trucking ordered fifty brand-new dump trucks. The first five arrive five weeks from now."

"How do you know that?"

"Dutch told me, last week."

"Why would he tell you that?"

"It's amazing what people will tell you sometimes, when they think you're talking about something else."

"You're cagey as a desert fox, Sheriff."

"Smart in some ways maybe, Your Hon—Bill. Dumb as a post in others," he said, reminding himself of his outburst at the hospital.

Olivia brought Con a large serving of liver and eggs and a generous slice of peach pie for the judge. She filled their coffees and left with hardly a word.

"Unusual combination," Judge Tucker noted, staring at Con's breakfast.

"Not my favorite." Noticing Tucker's puzzled expression, he said, "Dr. Martin's orders."

Tucker nodded sympathetically. as he dug into his pie. "This pie is outstanding."

"Papa's a good cook."

"Your folks run this place?" he asked, looking around the room.

"Yes, my sister is our waitress."

"How about that? I've eaten here a few times over the years. Always been good food." He made quick work of his pie and returned the paperwork to his briefcase. "I've got to get going now, but you keep me posted." As he stood, he dropped a five-dollar bill on the table.

"That's not necessary," Con complained.

The judge raised his hand. "No, Sheriff. It's my pleasure," he said and hurried out the door.

When Olivia returned to refill Con's coffee, she eyed the judge's money.

"Nice tip," Con commented.

"Sure is. Who was he?"

"Judge William *call me Bill outside of the courtroom* Tucker. A very wise man."

"I figured he was important." The café was in its lull between breakfast and lunch. She sat the coffeepot down and took the judge's seat. "How's your arm?"

"Sore. Hal says I need to keep moving it for circulation, but not enough to pull the stitches. I'm not sure where I'm supposed to draw the line, but it helps the soreness to move it around some. The broken rib hurts every time I take a breath. So, I'm moving pretty slow."

"You need to. Give it a chance to heal." She waited a minute, trying to decide how to proceed. "I talked to June Sommers yesterday." She saw Con clench his teeth. "Stop that. And don't say anything until I'm done talking." She waited until his jaw relaxed. "Okay. During our conversation, I realized something. I've always been critical of people and bossy. Yesterday I figured out that I don't like that about myself. I need to be nicer to people." Con started to speak. "Shush!" She waited again. "I'm going to start with you, but here's the deal." Olivia studied his expression and could not read it. "You have to be nice to me, too, or it won't work."

Con waited. "Are you finished?"

"I think so."

"I had a long talk with someone yesterday, too. It made me realize that I had no idea how lucky I was to be alive. Or how grateful I should have been to Jesse and Hal for saving my life. And to June and you and Mama and Papa for being there for me. And how much I really needed all of you. So, everyone there was right, except for me. I guess it's a deal."

"So, who did you talk to?"

"Father O'Malley."

When Con grabbed his hat from the hook by the door, the bullet hole in the crown reminded him of his good fortune, but not in a favorable manner. He stepped out the door and turned. Then walked to Beckley's Haberdashery on the corner. It was a pleasant morning, clear and sunny, but cooler than recent days.

"What can I help you with?" the clerk asked as Con came through the door.

"I'm looking for a new hat," Con told him. "Something similar to this one." He handed the man his Stetson.

"Well, sir. It won't have the hole in it, but we should be able to fix you up. You can add your own hole later if you'd like," he joked.

"Nah, it'll be fine without the hole," Con replied in such a serious tone the clerk couldn't be sure if he was joking.

After checking the size tag, he climbed a ladder behind the counter and began shuffling around boxes stacked to the ceiling.

He soon made his way back to the floor with a large box in hand. "I'm sorry, but this is the only one I have in your size, sir." He opened the box and pulled out a light brown hat with a rolled brim. "J. B. Stetson, Four-X Beaver felt. You won't find a finer hat in Las Vegas. Would you like to try it?" he said, handing it to Con.

"Perfect fit," he said when he put it on.

"There is a mirror all the way in the back, if you'd like to take a look."

Con walked to the back of the store. "This will do," he said, returning up the aisle.

"Is there anything else for you today?"

"I could use a new shirt, I suppose."

The clerk quickly sized him up with an experienced eye. "What color, sir?"

"I think the one I ruined was gray."

The clerk quickly rummaged through a stack of folded shirts wrapped in tissue paper. Soon extracting one, he nimbly unwrapped it and handed it to Con. "How do you like this one?" he asked as he handed him a gray shirt with white collar and pinstripes.

"Well, it's a bit fancier than I usually wear, but it will be fine."

The clerk quickly added up the ticket. The seventeen-dollar total caused Con to raise an eyebrow, but he was pleased with his purchase and strolled back to the coupe, wearing his new hat and carrying the rest.

From there, he drove out Charleston Boulevard to Fremont Construction. He removed his hat when he walked in and the same nice girl sat at the first desk.

"Sheriff Armenta, isn't it?" she asked.

"Yes, it is."

"My goodness, how are you feeling? I read in yesterday's paper about you being shot and everything that happened."

"Well, I'm sore," he said, embarrassed by the attention, "but I'll be fine in a few days."

"Mr. Goldstein isn't back yet, but how can I help you?"

"I was hoping you could look up a former employee. At least, I think he might have been. He was one of the men arrested and the name sounded like someone who may have worked here a few years ago. Carl Wesley?"

"Do you know how long ago?"

"Maybe five years, or so."

"Let me see what I can find."

At that moment, Newt Campbell emerged from a private office. "Sheriff Armenta. What are you doing here? I am truly sorry for dragging you through the crowd yesterday. I had no idea that you were injured until I read the newspaper last evening."

"I saw the names of the men arrested and one sounded familiar to me. I thought he may have been one of the men your father discharged in the incident your mother and I were discussing."

"By all means," Newt replied, and turned to the secretary. "Were you checking on that, Amy?"

"Yes, Mr. Campbell. Is it okay?"

"Absolutely. Bring it to my office if you find anything. Come on back, Sheriff. Would you like some lemonade?" he asked as he guided Con to what obviously had been Brice Campbell's office.

"Yes, thank you. I must apologize, Mr. Campbell," Con began. "I had no idea that you would be here today, or I would have brought my question directly to you."

"That's quite alright, Sheriff. I didn't plan to be here until

Monday, but I had business in town, so I thought I would look a few things over."

"So, you'll be working here now?"

"Yes, sir." Newt poured Con a glass of lemonade. "Mother still owns the company, but I will be the general manager. We will maintain a small operation in Wyoming, but everything will be run from here."

"Well then, let me be the first to welcome you to Las Vegas." Con smiled, offering his hand.

Newt accepted the handshake, less vigorously than yesterday. "I thank you, Sheriff, but Dutch Wagner beat you to the honor of being the first, outside of family, of course."

"Dutch?" Con repeated in surprise. "You work quickly, establishing relationships with Fremont's business associates."

"Yes, I suppose that I do. I purchased the Muleskinner's Rest from him this morning. That's why I came into town. It is perfect for me. Adjoining mother's property for convenience, but far enough away for privacy. Sixty-seven grand was perhaps too much, but it's fully furnished, a hundred sixty acres, and when he threw in the car...did you know there is an Auburn Speedster in the garage out there?"

The question caught Con off guard. He could not force himself to lie about the car, nor could he avoid answering completely. "I've heard they are quite an amazing automobile. If I were your sister, I would be jealous. That's a step above her Whiskey Six." Con chuckled.

"We've always held a bit of rivalry when it comes to that sort of thing." Newt grinned. "Dutch said it would take him a few weeks to get the title, but I can start driving it immediately. I will feel more comfortable with it than my father's LaSalle."

Con nodded knowingly between sips of lemonade. He did

not share that Brice Campbell was the last person to drive the Auburn.

At that moment, Amy entered, handing Newt Campbell a file folder. "Here you are, Mr. Campbell."

He glanced through it and handed it to Con. "Your hunch was correct, Sheriff."

There wasn't much there. A simple form giving the employee's name, a rooming house address, and a page from a ledger book containing his payroll record. Below the last entry, it read, "Final Paycheck – Discharged." The date was five years ago.

"Thank you very much, Mr. Campbell. That just about proves my suspicion." He handed the folder back to Newt, but did not return to his seat.

"You're more than welcome. Stop in anytime. I raise a few cattle in Wyoming," he added. "I always loved being around livestock. We may share more common interests than you would think." Newt smiled, again shaking his hand.

Con thanked Amy for her help on his way out and climbed into the coupe. He took a minute before he left, jotting down the date of Carl Wesley's final paycheck and the name of the rooming house. Then, "NC 67k." *Probably cash*, he thought to himself as he motored the coupe down Charleston Boulevard.

Con awoke to near darkness. He had dozed off early in the afternoon again while reading his book. He'd slept more in the last two days than the last two weeks. The din of Friday night crowds drifted faintly across the cool evening air from Block 16. He was hungry and knew without looking, the choices from his kitchen were few. He rose, washed his face and combed his hair. Then stepped out the door and began a four-block stroll toward the ruckus.

The neon sign on the corner lit up the street around

Dutch's Oasis. Two men occupied one of several pool tables on the main floor. A man in a white shirt with sleeve-garters polished the vacant bar. Noise belched from the wide stairwell at the rear of the room.

Descending the stairway brought to Con's mind the entering of an abyss into the bowels of hell. A room the same dimension as that above overflowed with slot machines and gambling tables. Dozens of men and a scattering of women filled the noisy hall. Con crossed to the bar positioned directly below the one on the main floor.

"What'll it be?" the bartender asked.

"Coca-Cola."

The bartender dropped chunks of ice into a tall glass. He adeptly injected two squirts of syrup from a dispenser, then filled it with seltzer water from a tap. Following up with a quick stir from a swizzle stick, he placed it before Con. "That'll be a nickel. Can I get you anything else?"

Con laid a coin on the bar. "Is Janet working tonight?"

"She just went up. Give her a half hour."

"Can I get something to eat?"

"What would you like?"

"Anything but liver."

The bartender looked at him quizzically. "How about a hamburger sandwich?"

"Sure."

The bartender stuck his head through a door behind the bar and hollered to someone. Con watched a half-dozen men at a nearby roulette table while he sipped his Coca-Cola. His sandwich soon arrived, and he watched the crowd in the mirror behind the bar as he ate his meal. He ordered another Coca-Cola and continued to watch the gamblers at the roulette table.

"Good evening, Sheriff. Charlie said the cowboy at the bar was asking for me."

Con hardly recognized the provocatively clad Janet Rae behind her makeup as she stood beside him. "Good evening, Miss Rae."

"I hope this visit is not an indication that my brother is in trouble again."

"No, nothing like that. I have a couple of questions about Dutch Wagner and this place."

"Meet me at the U.P. Park tomorrow at ten."

"Okay," he replied as she quickly turned and crossed the room to a table full of card players.

* * *

SATURDAY, APRIL 12, 1930

Con woke at eight o'clock. He had less stiffness and more mobility in his left arm. The graze on his right side seemed to be mending well, too. He had gotten home from Dutch's by eleven and went straight to bed. He slept nine hours straight after a five or six-hour nap the previous afternoon. "Surely, I'll get rested up pretty soon," he told himself.

He drove to the Mesquite Café for breakfast, then to the park to meet Janet Rae. He arrived at a quarter 'til ten and found her waiting for him beneath a cottonwood tree. She wore the same conservative clothing she had worn to her brother's hearing.

"I'm sorry I couldn't talk to you last night. Too many ears around there and Dutch gets upset if we talk to non-paying customers for very long."

"Not a problem."

"What did you want to ask?"

"How long have you worked for Dutch?"

"Three years."

"Do you know his mother?"

"I have met her, why?"

"I don't suppose you would know of her having a…how should I put this…being friendly with Brice Campbell?"

"Yes, but not from working at the Oasis."

Her answer surprised Con. "Where then?"

"The Hotel Nevada." Understanding the sheriff's confusion, she continued, "I used to work in the restaurant there. Evenings. About five years ago, Mrs. Wagner rented the suite at the hotel for the night. Around eight o'clock she ordered dinner for two, delivered to the room. I carried it up and knocked on the door. Brice Campbell answered. I brought the food in. Mrs. Wagner sat at the table in a lacy nightgown. After I put the food on the table, Mr. Campbell walked me to the door. He handed me a twenty-dollar bill and said, 'You didn't see a thing.' I said 'Yes,' and left. That went on about once a month from then on. Three years ago, when the gypsum mines shut down, business slowed down there and I got laid off… then went to work at the Oasis."

Con was amazed at what Janet had told him. "No way of knowing if the affair continued," Con said, more to himself than Janet.

"It did."

"How do you know that?"

"A month after I left, they met again. Another girl who worked at the hotel told me about delivering their meal and Mr. Campbell's tip. Dutch overheard her and confronted me about it later. I told him I had never heard anything like that before."

So, they were definitely having an affair and Dutch knew it, Con thought to himself. "Does this other girl still work there?"

"Yes. Her name is Susie. We're still friends. We don't see each other often, because...because of my profession. She's a nice girl." Her face became sad. She had lost connection with someone she cared about. Con felt sorry for Janet Rae. He did not know the reason she made the choice she did, but she undeniably understood the consequences of it.

He changed the subject. "Technically, Dutch's Oasis falls under city jurisdiction, so there's little I can do regardless, but how much liquor does Dutch sell there?"

"All that you want. No one really pays much attention except the feds once in a while. You guys really put a burr under his saddle the other night, though. I was there when he heard about it. The veins were sticking out on his head. His face was purple. I thought he would explode. There is something big coming up that he needs a lot of cash for. You guys really hit him hard."

"There was much more liquor there than he could sell at the Oasis."

"Oh, he has deliveries all over. California, Arizona, Utah, you name it."

"What about this guy, Drago?"

"He's worked for Dutch a long time. Way before me, I think. He beats people up, makes deliveries, whatever Dutch wants him to do. He's the one I had in mind when I threatened Nick Logan. I guess I'll have to find somebody else, if it comes to that now." She laughed aloud, smiling. The ironic humor of the situation temporarily overruled her sorrow.

"Dutch pressed charges against him yesterday for stealing his truck."

"What a snake. Drago is as loyal as a puppy dog to Dutch, but he's tossing him out like yesterday's trash, isn't he?"

"So, it seems. I'm going to see Drago later. Anything you want me to tell him?"

"Tell him I'll come see him one morning next week."

"I'll do that. What about Dutch if he finds out you were talking to me?"

"If he says anything, I'll tell him it's about the trouble Harv got into."

"Thank you for your help."

"I'm a good person inside," she said as her eyes began to get glossy. "I don't want to break any laws."

"I knew you were when I saw you in the clerk's office. That's why I wanted to talk to you. Try to enjoy your day," he said as he left the park.

*** * ***

Sheriff Conor Armenta sat across the table in the Clark County Jail from Alonso Drago. The midafternoon sun shone in a window too high to see through. The reinforced concrete building remained reasonably cool but stuffy without adequate ventilation. Drago slouched in his chair with no intention of cooperating with the sheriff. He heard about the raid at the canyon from a fellow prisoner, also an employee of Dutch Wagner. The man who was wounded in the raid awaited a train ride to Carson City to join his associates.

"How are you doing in here, Al? Is your food okay?"

"I'm doin' alright."

"Has anyone sent a lawyer in to talk to you yet, Al? Help figure a way to get you out of here?"

"They will."

"They? Dutch Wagner, maybe?"

"Maybe."

"Doesn't Dutch own that truck you were driving?"

"Maybe."

"Well, Al, Dutch filed charges of grand larceny against you yesterday for stealing that truck."

"Nah, he wouldn't do that. I've been working for him for five years."

"Well, I don't have the paperwork with me, but he did."

Drago did not answer.

"So, you and Carl went to work for Dutch right after Brice Campbell fired the two of you for stealing from him?"

"We never stole nothin'."

"If Mr. Campbell had pressed charges, you and Carl might be getting out of prison right about now. He must have been a little nicer than Dutch, huh?"

"He wasn't nice, he killed Dutch's old man."

"Who told you that, Al? Dutch? The nice guy who is sending you up for stealing his truck? No, Gary Wagner's death was an accident. He and Brice Campbell were best friends. Kind of like you and Carl, huh?"

"Carl's my friend."

"Carl is in Carson City waiting for whatever the feds throw at him."

"I heard that."

"You should be thankful you're down here, Al, and not up there. What happened to Brice Campbell out at the bluffs the other night?"

"I don't know what you're talking about."

"Well, maybe sitting here waiting for your trial, facing twenty years in the penitentiary, considering who your friends really are? Maybe that will help your memory."

"I've got plenty of friends."

"I know one true friend of yours, Al."

"Who do you know? Carl?"

"Janet Rae." The knowledge that the sheriff knew Janet Rae and that they were friends, shocked Drago. "She has a good heart, Al. Honest. Never wants to see anyone hurt." Then Con added, "She said she would stop by to see you one morning next week." He left Drago scratching his head.

* * *

At eight o'clock, Conor Armenta drove to the Hotel Nevada for a late dinner. The crowd had thinned out. A couple at a table across the restaurant were the only occupants. A girl in her midtwenties waited on him. He suspected she was Janet Rae's friend, Susie.

"Have you worked here long?" Con asked casually when she brought his meal.

"Since high school," she answered. "Eight years."

"My parents own the Mesquite Café," he told her. "I recognize a good waitress when I see one."

"Why, thank you." She blushed slightly. "You're Sheriff Armenta, aren't you?"

"Yes, I am."

Halfway through his dinner, she brought Con a second glass of Coca-Cola on ice. "I believe I know a friend of yours," he told her.

"Who would that be?"

"Janet Rae."

Susie suddenly became suspicious. "How do you know Janet?"

"Her brother ran into a little trouble recently," Con answered. "Janet helped him out."

"We don't see each other very often anymore. It's complicated."

"Understandably." By the time Con finished his meal, the couple had left the restaurant leaving Con the only customer. Susie returned to the table.

"Would you like dessert?"

"What do you have?"

"Fresh peach cobbler."

"That and a cup of coffee would be perfect," he replied, then added, "Janet told me I should talk to you."

"What about?"

"Katherine Wagner…and Brice Campbell."

Susie lost most of her cheerfulness and became very serious. She sat down across the table from Con and began to tell a story very similar to the one Janet Rae had shared with him. There was a twist, however. Dutch Wagner had overheard her telling Janet about the first encounter. A few days later, Dutch confronted Susie somewhat forcefully about it. She repeated what she had witnessed, and Dutch paid her five dollars for the information. He gave her a telephone number and told her to call him if she saw them together again. Every time she called, there was an envelope for her at the hotel desk the next day with a five-dollar bill in it. The last time she called, he told her never to tell anyone about it. There was a fifty-dollar bill the next day. A few days later the *Evening-Review* reported Katherine Wagner had disappeared on the night Susie last saw her at the hotel with Brice Campbell.

18

SUNDAY, APRIL 13, 1930

Conor Armenta sat on the pew with his family at Sunday Mass. Unlike recent nights, he had not slept well. Had Brice Campbell murdered Katherine Wagner? Could he have disposed of the body by burying her corpse beneath a mass of fill dirt at one of his construction sites? Then, riddled with guilt, had he truly committed suicide? Or did someone else murder Katherine Wagner? Had Brice Campbell discovered the assassin and himself been murdered before he could reveal the killer? Was Katherine Wagner missing or dead? Why was Dutch Wagner so nonchalant about his own mother's disappearance? The deluge of questions continued to dominate his thoughts through Father O'Malley's sermon which ended almost before Con realized it had begun. He failed to note the message, let alone absorb the meaning it represented.

On departure, Father O'Malley reiterated to Con the

blessing of surviving his recent confrontation. As he shook Con's hand, he pulled him close and whispered a gentle reassurance of forgiveness for the other man's death.

* * *

MONDAY, APRIL 14, 1930

At eight-thirty in the morning, Con sat in Judge Tucker's courtroom awaiting the nine o'clock inquest. Others began to trickle in, as Agent Michael O'Sullivan, Deputy Jesse Slater and Stanley Olsen all sat in the gallery. Three County Commissioners and Dr. Harold Martin took seats behind tables situated several feet apart and facing the judge's bench in front of the bar. These were the coroner's jury. Each of the men had copies of the coroner's report, the sheriff's department's reports, and the Prohibition Department's reports. Con and Prohibition Agent Thomas Walker, who had shot the other suspect, sat before the bar between the tables. At precisely nine o'clock, a robe-less Judge William Tucker entered from his chambers and without formal introduction. He took his seat behind the bench. At the same moment, Olivia McLeod and June Sommers entered the courtroom and took seats in the gallery.

Judge Tucker opened the inquest by announcing that it was an informal proceeding for the purpose of evaluating the evidence in order to determine the necessity of further action.

"Sheriff Conor Armenta, would you tell in your own words what happened last Wednesday night?" Judge Tucker asked. "You may remain where you are seated. Begin with your arrival at the Luis Garza ranch."

Con told the story exactly as he remembered it right up to Agent O'Sullivan asking him about his horse.

"Are there any questions for Sheriff Armenta from the jury?" the judge asked.

"When you left the ranch house, you not only carried your sidearm, but a rifle," one of the commissioners stated. "Were you looking for trouble?"

"I suspected from my experience the previous evening that the men we were dealing with were probably heavily armed and dangerous," Con answered calmly. The question irritated him. "In addition to my rifle, I carried a canteen full of water, extra cartridges, a lariat, a flashlight, lamb jerky, two sets of handcuffs, and carrots for my horse. I wasn't looking for trouble, commissioner. I expected it." Con hesitated, but could not contain his ire. He added in the same calm voice, "I didn't use any of the extra provisions I carried except the carrots. My rifle never left its scabbard."

There were no more questions asked of Con. Agent Walker gave his testimony as well as Michael O'Sullivan and Jesse Slater.

"Dr. Harold Martin, I have read your report," Judge Tucker began at the conclusion of the testimonies. "As coroner of Clark County, what is your opinion as to the cause of death of these two men?"

"It is my professional opinion that victim number one, Joseph Mariano, died from two gunshot wounds to the chest from the .45 caliber pistol of Sheriff Conor Armenta. Based on evidence at the scene and the wounds received by Sheriff Armenta, I believe Joseph Mariano, a man wanted in the State of Illinois and elsewhere for multiple violent crimes, fired not less than twenty-one and not more than twenty-six rounds from his .45 caliber Thompson sub-machine gun at Sheriff

Armenta prior to Sheriff Armenta firing the fatal shots at Mr. Mariano.

"It is also my professional opinion that victim number two died as a result of a twelve-gauge shotgun blast to the upper chest and face from the shotgun carried by Agent Thomas Walker. Based on evidence at the scene, eyewitness accounts in both Bureau of Prohibition reports and sheriff's department reports, and testimonies heard here today, I believe the victim fired not less than forty-four and not more than fifty rounds from his .45 caliber Thompson sub-machine gun at Agent Walker and his fellow officers prior to Agent Walker firing the fatal shot at the victim."

Judge Tucker then polled the coroner's inquest jury. Three called for acquittal of both officers on the grounds of self-defense. The other commissioner, who had questioned Con earlier, called for the charges of second-degree murder to be brought against Agent Walker and first-degree murder against Sheriff Armenta.

"This is not a Grand Jury hearing nor a trial," Judge Tucker began. "A unanimous decision is not mandatory. Had the jury been in a deadlock, I would have cast the deciding vote for acquittal. Since the jury voted by majority for acquittal, that will not be necessary. Agent Walker and Sheriff Armenta, would you stand, please?"

The two men complied.

"It is my honor to preside over a court that two officers such as yourselves serve. I thank you both for your integrity and valor in performing your duty. You are free to go and resume that duty, enforcing the laws of the State of Nevada and the United States of America. This inquest is adjourned." With that, his gavel fell on the block, and he stood and returned to his chambers.

As Con turned around, he glimpsed June leaving the court-room. Olivia stood at the rear in anticipation. Con thanked Hal and the two commissioners who remained.

"Stop by and have Joe Anderson check those wounds." Con rolled his eyes, causing Hal to glare. "Do it. Today! Remember your father? Remember what infection can do?"

Olivia remained at the rear of the gallery with a knowing look on her face. Hal hadn't whispered. She would turn Con's world against him if he failed to comply.

"Yes, sir."

Con then thanked Agents O'Sullivan and Walker.

"On Saturday, we disposed of the liquor from the delivery truck you impounded last week. We'll be collecting our pris-oner from your jail and heading to Carson City on the noon train," O'Sullivan told him. "You were right, by the way."

"About what?"

"That horse of yours. Bob. One heck of a fine animal. If you ever decide to—"

Con interrupted him. "He's not actually my horse. He belongs to my little brother. But before you get any ideas, I've got first dibs on him. If I change my mind, I'll let you know."

"Deal. Thanks for having this all set up for us. We don't get assignments this easy very often. Call us anytime."

"Will do," he replied and moved to meet Jesse.

"Well, boss. It's good to have you back," Jesse said, shaking Con's hand.

"Thank you, Jesse. Thank you for everything. I'll be in the office in the morning."

"Congratulations, big brother," Olivia announced as Con approached her. "I wanted to be here for you."

"Thank you, I appreciate your concern."

"Have you eaten breakfast?"

"No."

"I know this little place not far from here." She grinned. "I'll buy?"

"I'll let you," Con answered, walking her out the door. They strolled to the café chatting along the way. He did not ask about June, and Olivia did not offer nor did she refer to Dr. Martin's orders, but Con knew she would make sure he followed them.

* * *

TUESDAY, APRIL 15, 1930

Con arrived at the sheriff's office at seven o'clock in the morning to a roomful of his subordinates. Hazel and Dottie hosted the festivity with coffee and doughnuts. Jesse and four other deputies joined in congratulations on the result of the inquest and well-wishes for a rapid recovery. Most importantly, all were happy to welcome him back on the job. After a short celebration, Dottie and three of the deputies left for their homes while Jesse and the other deputy departed to their duties.

Con entered his office. With a cup of coffee and doughnut in hand, he sat down at his desk. He stared at the safe for a moment, contemplating his Colt automatic inside. Dr. Anderson was pleased with the healing of his wounds and expected to remove the stitches within a few days. He wore his uniform shirt today for the first time in nearly a week. He did not care to re-arm himself quite yet.

Hazel brought him a stack of his deputies' reports in chronological order and he began to wade through them. The telephone rang and Hazel answered it. "I will tell him," he heard her say to the caller. A minute later, she stood at his door.

"That was the jailer," she said. "Someone named Al wants to talk to you."

Con could not disguise his delight. "Good. Maybe now we'll get somewhere." He did not want to appear over anxious to Drago, so waited until he had finished studying the reports. At nine thirty, he walked to the jail.

The room was cool in the jailhouse. Con stood leaning against the wall in the sun where it crossed the room from the high window. "Good morning, Al," he greeted when the jailer brought Drago in and sat him at the table. "They said you wanted to talk to me."

"Yeah. Janet came to see me yesterday. We had a really long talk. She said it would be better for me if I told the truth, told you what happened." He started to tell of the evening of his arrest.

"Why don't you start when you went to work for Dutch," Con suggested.

"Okay, I guess. A few days after me and Wes...Carl got fired from Fremont, I heard Dutch was looking for a bouncer in the saloon. I went and talked to him and he hired me. A couple of weeks later, he hired Carl to sweep floors and do odd jobs around the Oasis. He heard me and Carl talking about Brice Campbell one day and joined in. He told us how he hated Campbell, how Campbell got his old man killed in the Alps a couple of years before and stuff. Then he tells us that Campbell took his mom there because she wanted to see the mountain where his old man died. This had just happened a few weeks before he hired us. He says that Campbell seduced his mom sometime on the trip. He says he wonders how 'Mr. High and Mighty' would look if all of Las Vegas heard about him stepping out on his wife. It wasn't long after that that Joe showed up from Chicago."

"Joe Mariano?"

"Yeah. He's the one you shot out at the bluffs."

"And who shot me."

The reply startled Drago. "You got shot?"

"Twice. Nearly a third time." Con bent his head forward showing Drago the bald, singed line across his scalp.

"Whew!" Drago responded with a new respect for the sheriff. "That was close."

"So, what happened when Mariano got here?"

"That's when they started bringing in the stuff to build the still and looking for a good place to set it up. For quite a while it was out north by the reservation. They brought in two guys from West Virginia to run it. They kept telling Dutch that the water wasn't good enough. About six months ago we moved it to the bluffs. The Hillbillies were happy, the customers were happy, and everything was good until the old Mexican started moving his sheep up by the road."

"What about Brice Campbell?"

"I never seen or heard nothing about him until he showed up that night out at the bluffs. He was looking for Joe. Heard that he knew something about Dutch's mom. Joe got tired of his questions pretty damned quick and slugged him. Then he told me to put a good scare into him. Carl had climbed all over them cliffs out there and he knew an easy way to the top. We took Campbell up there, and Carl held the lantern out over the edge. Campbell could see that fancy car of his where he parked it by the entrance to the canyon down there. Carl says, 'See that crack there. That's the way back to your car, Mr. Mountain Climber.' He held the lantern and we watched him working his way down. About halfway, he fell. Never heard a peep out of him. Must have hit his head or something. He landed in a pile of sagebrush and never moved. We figured he was dead. We went down the way we came up and scampered right toward the mouth of the canyon just in time to see that fancy car tearing out of there."

"What about Dutch's mother? What happened to Katherine Wagner?"

"I only seen her one time a few years ago. Never heard any mention other than what the papers said about her disappearing. That was about when we moved the still."

Drago went on to talk about shooting the sheep. Dutch thought it would encourage Luis to keep them away from the road. He didn't know whether Dutch or Mariano or someone else owned the still. He knew that Mariano didn't work for Dutch. Drago got along with Mariano okay, but didn't like him.

"Thanks for your help, Al. I'll talk to Judge Tucker and tell him you're cooperating."

"Janet said she would try to find me a lawyer."

"Good, I'll tell the judge that, too."

When Con returned to the sheriff's department, Hazel handed him an envelope. "This arrived while you were out." It was a Western Union telegram.

He sat down at his desk and opened it. It was from the state crime lab in Carson City. It contained a brief summary of their findings. The formal report accompanied the returning evidence which was en route by mail.

"Hazel, would you call Robert Westcott? Tell him I have concluded my investigation of the death of Brice Campbell. Ask him to arrange a meeting with the family and anyone else they feel necessary to attend."

19

Several cars occupied the driveway when Sheriff Conor Armenta pulled up in front of Leanora Campbell's hacienda at seven o'clock in the evening. He recognized the Auburn and Amelia Westcott's Buick. He was not familiar with the sedan.

Newt Campbell answered Con's knock at the door. "Good evening, Sheriff, please come in." He shook Con's hand. "We are all gathered in the sitting room." He led the way. "I believe you know everyone except Elmer, perhaps. He arrived home from Zürich this morning." The rather small, thin man wore a gray pencil mustache that matched the ring of hair that encircled his bald head. He stood and offered his hand. "Elmer, Sheriff Conor Armenta. Sheriff, Elmer Goldstein."

Con took in the room. Robert and Amelia Westcott occupied the sofa with Leanora Campbell. June Sommers sat in the soft leather chair Con had used on his previous visit. She had two pencils and a steno pad in her hands. Elmer sat in the chair next to June. That left two less heavily upholstered armchairs for Newt and himself, which Con preferred.

Robert Westcott stood to shake hands. "I have invited June to take notes, if that is all right with you?"

"Absolutely. Thank you for arranging this meeting. I am sure everyone feels comfortable here."

"Would you like something to drink, Sheriff?" Newt asked. "Iced tea? Lemonade?"

"Tea sounds good. Thank you."

Newt poured a tall glass of iced tea from a pitcher on the coffee table and handed it to Con. "Please begin whenever you are ready," he said, motioning Con to take the chair beside the one he seated himself in.

"Much of what I'm about to tell you, you may already know. Please feel free to ask any questions you may have along the way. I will do my best to answer them. There may also be details that I am unaware of. I would appreciate any additions you might wish to add. Some of what I tell you may be painful to hear. I am sorry for any discomfort I may cause any of you. A long series of events led up to the death of Brice Campbell. Let me begin.

"This all commenced seven years ago with a mountaineering trip to Switzerland when six men decided to take on the north face of the Eiger. There was an accident. Mr. Campbell's close friend, Gary Wagner, was killed, and Mr. Campbell broke his back. When he came home, Brice Campbell was addicted to opium from the pain medications administered to him during his recovery. Dr. Anderson recognized the symptoms and confronted Mr. Campbell, who openly admitted his addiction and expressed the desire to overcome it."

Amelia Westcott's face showed her anger, but she remained quiet.

"Mr. Campbell also suffered from depression and severe nightmares during this time, complicated, Dr. Anderson felt, by the addiction. Withdrawal from this dependency can and did have painful side effects. Some members of this family disagreed with Dr. Anderson's treatment. They furnished opium from other sources to Mr. Campbell to ease the symptoms of the withdrawal. Dr. Anderson felt this prolonged the addiction. Through adjustments in medication and Mr. Campbell's strong will, he overcame the habit over the course of a few months."

Con took a sip of his tea and tried to evaluate his audience without much success.

"About five years ago, Mr. Campbell accompanied Kathrine Wagner to Switzerland. Mrs. Wagner wanted to see the mountain that had so intrigued her husband to travel halfway around the world to climb it. Sometime during that trip, maybe in an attempt to console each other with the loss of a best friend and a husband, they became romantically involved."

"Stop!" Amelia Westcott burst out. "Stop it right now! How could you do this to my mother?" she cried out in tears and tried to rise from her seat, but something held her back. Something, someone, had a hold of her arm in a very firm yet gentle grip. She looked down. It was her mother's hand. She looked at her mother's face. It was calm. A single tear rolled down her cheek.

"It's true, dear. I have known for a very long time. I did not know when it began. I suspected it was just as Sheriff Armenta has described." Amelia sobbed uncontrollably. Her husband had his arm around her shoulders and her mother held her hand. "Please continue, Sheriff."

Con took a long sip of his iced tea and cleared his throat.

"Somehow, Dutch Wagner also found out about the infidelity. He already blamed Brice Campbell's inexperience in mountaineering for his father's death and this flagrant disloyalty by his mother was more than he could stand. He threatened to expose the affair to the public, but—"

"Wait one moment, Sheriff." Leanora Campbell stood and left the room. She returned directly with a medium-sized ledger book in hand. "This is beginning to make sense to me now. Perhaps it will to you, also." It was the ledger book that Con had seen in Brice Campbell's study. The one Leanora had quickly covered when the others had spilled to the floor on the evening Con had visited her. The ledger book with the single word, "Dutch," inscribed on the front of it. Con looked inside. Beginning five years ago were monthly expenditures of one thousand dollars. No income, no check numbers, just dates and expenditures.

"Payments to a blackmailer. A record."

Leanora nodded in agreement. The slightest bit of a smile acknowledged her satisfaction in solving a piece of the puzzle.

Con continued. "A short time later, Mr. Campbell discharged Al Drago and Carl Wesley for stealing from Fremont Construction. Ironically, they both went to work for Dutch Wagner within a few weeks. Soon afterward, Joseph Mariano came to Las Vegas from Chicago, probably to escape warrants there. He began to work with, but not for, Dutch Wagner. They set up a moonshine still north of here somewhere, near the Moapa Indian Reservation.

"Sometime soon after the trip to Switzerland, Mr. Campbell and Mrs. Wagner began meeting about once a month for a discreet dinner in the suite at the Hotel Nevada. The same young waitress always delivered their meal and Mr. Campbell always gave a generous tip, with the understanding that she tell no one. When the gypsum mine cut back three years ago, business also slowed down for the restaurant at the hotel. That young waitress lost her job and ended up going to work at Dutch's Oasis.

"Another waitress, a friend of the first, took over the duty of delivering to the hotel rooms and became the new recipient of Mr. Campbell's regular generosity. Unaware that this had been going on for some time, this second waitress met up with the first at the Oasis and shared the news of her good fortune. Dutch Wagner overheard the conversation and confronted the second waitress a few days later. Dutch gave the girl a stipend for her information and somewhat forcefully convinced her to call and tell him each time they were seen together again. Every time she called, there was an envelope at the front desk for her the next day. Beginning at that time"—Con picked up the ledger book"by what this book tells me, Dutch increased the extortion rate to two-thousand dollars per month. Also, at that same time. Katherine Wagner signed the deed for the Muleskinner's Rest, your new home, Mr. Campbell, over to Dutch. It appears he was not above extorting his own mother."

Con surveyed the room. No one appeared angry. Newt Campbell looked as if he was trying to swallow a golf ball. The look on every other face revealed only anticipation. He continued. "About a year ago, I have not checked the exact date, Mr. Campbell purchased a rather expensive gift for Mrs. Wagner— a brand-new Auburn Speedster." Con looked over at Newt Campbell. He had a completely blank stare, void of facial expression. The latest disclosure had taken him entirely by surprise. The sheriff pressed on. "I only heard of her driving the car one time in public. Whatever Dutch threatened her with, no one ever saw her drive it again. Six months ago, she and Mr. Campbell again dined at the Hotel Nevada. The waitress called Dutch the next day. He told her never to speak of it again. This time, the envelope held ten times the usual amount. A few days later, she read in the *Evening-Review* that Katherine Wagner disappeared the same night that she had delivered their meal to the suite. And the price of blackmail went up to three thousand dollars per month." Con pointed to the ledger. That was also when they moved the still to the bluffs past Luis Garza's ranch.

"Two weeks ago, Brice Campbell heard a rumor that Joseph Mariano knew something about the disappearance of Katherine Wagner."

"Oh, thank God," Leanora Campbell gasped. Everyone turned, staring at her. "I thought...I'm ashamed to say...I thought Brice might have killed her. He was so morose. So depressed. Ever since she disappeared." She burst into tears, only managing a few words between sobs. "I know he still loved me...but he loved her, too...in a different way, I think... maybe more...I was so afraid of losing him...and now he's gone." Newt Campbell moved over, taking a seat on the arm of the sofa, gently consoling his mother while his sister hugged her from the other side.

Con sipped his iced tea. He wondered momentarily why Leanora had told him two weeks ago that Brice had been acting perfectly normal recently. The answer quickly came to him. She had hoped no one would discover her husband's infidelity.

Robert Westcott appeared to be reflecting on the character of his client, Dutch Wagner. "I don't do criminal cases," he unintentionally said aloud, then quickly glanced around to see if anyone had heard him. Con, pretending to be absorbed in his own thoughts, acted as if he had not. Elmer Goldstein sat watching Leanora Campbell compassionately. If he was as closely tied to Brice Campbell's finances as it seemed, he surely would have known of Mr. Campbell's affair and the payments to Dutch Wagner. June continued to write on the steno pad with tears streaming down her face.

Newt returned to his seat as his mother regained her composure. "Please continue, Sheriff," she said calmly.

"Mr. Campbell waited until you, Mrs. Campbell, had gone to bed. He knew the noisy doors of the garage would awaken Lorenzo above in his room. He went out the side gate and walked across the desert to the Wagner's garage. Then he drove the Auburn to the still at the bluffs." Again, Newt Campbell sat nearly unable to believe what he heard. "At the moonshine operation, he confronted Joseph Mariano with a barrage of questions about Katherine Wagner. Joe didn't take much of that and punched Mr. Campbell, then told Al Drago to scare him enough that he wouldn't come back. Drago and Wesley took him up top on the cliff and sent him down, a fissure in the darkness offering his only chance to escape. He fell halfway down and lay motionless in a pile of sagebrush at the bottom. Drago could see him in the light from their lantern. He thought he was dead. He and Wesley rushed back down the easy way just in time to see the Auburn speed away.

"I was on my way back from Luis Garza's ranch when the Auburn passed me. I had been investigating some sheep that had been killed out there. It was after one o'clock in the morning and he had to be going eighty miles per hour or more when he came by me. He had broken his left wrist in the fall and removed his wedding band when the hand began swelling. When he got back to the Wagners' he somehow managed to close and lock the front gate behind him with only his right hand. When I first discovered this, I hadn't realized Mr. Campbell was left-handed. It must have been very difficult. When leaving the Wagner place to come back here, he couldn't get the rear gate closed. He must have gotten home just before Lorenzo began watering.

"Somewhere along the line, he acquired a small vile of opium. He may have had it here. If he was as morose and depressed as you said, Mrs. Campbell, he may have been using it again for a while.

"When I got laid off at the gypsum mine three years ago, Sheriff Baker hired me as a deputy. When I helped him on an investigation a few weeks later, he liked my intuition. He said I had good *gut instinct*. A couple of months later, he sent me to a criminal investigation school for two weeks in Carson City. One of the things we studied was suicide investigation. They said a suicide always involves a combination of most or all of these elements: jealousy, hatred, violence, misery, and depression. I've studied these characteristics through every phase of my investigation. I can easily point out at least three of them with practically no effort and cover the other two with very little imagination. I believe Brice Campbell waited nearly three hours for Lorenzo to finish watering, return to his room, close his windows, and go back to bed. Then he walked out the front door around to the side of the house farthest from the garage, and I suspect, the bedroom Mrs. Campbell slept in. There he tried to put the wedding band back on his swollen finger, but could not. Perhaps he slid it to the first knuckle. Then, at the first light of dawn, Mr. Campbell took his own life, firing the pistol he kept in the desk of his study with his right hand.

"The position Mr. Campbell's body was found in and all

surrounding evidence indicates this was the course of events. The pistol had fingerprints from his left hand beneath prints from his right hand. The wedding band lay under his body adjacent to his left hand. The partial prints on the band were from his right hand.

"The pistol, his wallet, and wedding band are being mailed from the crime lab in Carson City. They will be returned to the family when I receive them. The vile of opium will be disposed of. Do any of you have any questions?"

"What about Dutch Wagner?" Leanora Campbell asked.

"Until tonight, the only evidence I had was circumstantial or hearsay. With that ledger book"—Con indicated the book on the table—"I may have a little better chance of a conviction, but I doubt it. Time may tell otherwise. In the meantime, keep that in a safe place."

"Was Dad the last one to drive the Auburn?" Newt Campbell asked.

"I'm certain of it. If I were to guess, I would bet he really liked that car. I hope knowing that will help you enjoy it even more."

Con turned to June. "I'm sure these folks have things to discuss. Can I offer you a ride home in a half-worn-out county pickup truck?"

"I rode out with Mr. and Mrs. Westcott." She turned to Robert Westcott. "Would it be alright with you if I ride back to town with the sheriff?"

"That will be fine."

"I will bring my notes to work in the morning," she added as she and Con went to the door.

Newt Campbell scrambled to join them. "We can see ourselves out," Con offered.

"Have a good night," Newt said, and waved them goodbye.

* * *

Con walked June to his truck under a star-filled sky and opened the door for her. As he held the door, she turned. Wrapping her arms around his neck, she embraced and kissed him passionately. "I have missed you, Conor Armenta."

Holding her with his arms around her waist, he said, "And I have missed you, June Sommers." Then, pulling her tenderly against his chest, he kissed her again.

20

THURSDAY, APRIL 3, 1930

All of Brice Campbell's misguided plans to rescue Katherine Wagner from whatever evil fate had been bestowed upon her had gone awry. The .32 caliber revolver he planned to threaten the Chicago gangster with never even left his pocket. Now Drago and Wesley, two of his former employees that loathed him, forced him to retreat down the sheer face of a bluff in total darkness, or die trying. Halfway to the bottom, he made his nearly fatal error. One that his old climbing partner and mentor, Gary Wagner, would have chastised him for. He failed to confirm the strength of his fingerhold before lowering his foot in search of the next toehold.

His hand slipped and he fell, now headfirst, toward a massive sagebrush at the bottom. Dimly lit by the lantern held by the two men above, he prepared for the impact. He held his arms ahead of him hoping to roll on impact to lessen the effect. It did not work. His left wrist buckled under the force and he landed in a heap in the bush. He lay motionless, trying to regain his wits.

"Is he dead?" he heard Wesley ask.

"I think so," Drago answered as the two men watched in the lantern light from above. "We need to get down there and see."

Then the light disappeared. Brice knew that he had to act fast. He gained his feet as quickly as possible and half ran, half stumbled toward the car. Being left-handed, he struggled with his right hand to retrieve the pistol from his left jacket pocket before he reached the car. He had to put it back into the other pocket in order to open the door with his good hand, but he made it. To avoid revealing his escape a second too soon, he disengaged the clutch and put the car into gear before starting the engine and did not slam the door closed until he sped from the scene.

It took all of Brice's concentration to maneuver the Auburn down the rolling, twisted road as he hurried to the highway. When he turned toward Las Vegas, he sighed with a slight bit of relief. The big Lycoming engine roared as he accelerated to ninety miles per hour. The pain in his left wrist was excruciating, but he managed to work his wedding band off his swelling left hand as he raced down the straight road. Just as the ring came free, he nearly rear-ended a pickup truck motoring down the road at less than half his speed. He barely caught a glimpse of it as he thundered past, but thought he saw a star on the door through the dust.

* * *

At three a.m. the stocky-built man rolled the sedan past the Muleskinner's Rest. After noting the padlock on the gate, he shut off the headlights and continued slowly along for another quarter-mile. There, he left the car on the side of the road and continued on foot to the estate of Brice and Leanora Campbell. By the time the man slipped through the open gate into the expansive courtyard, his eyes were well-adjusted to the darkness.

Even in the dim moonlight, the man was wary and his dark clothing silhouetted him against the white-washed adobe wall behind him. He crouched as he entered the front garden even though nothing there grew more than knee height. Suddenly, a door closed to his left and he plastered himself to the ground among the shrubbery. Peering that direction, he saw the gardener plod down the steps from his apartment above the garage and veer straight toward him. A second later, he heard the slight complaint from a hinge on the front door of the house as Brice Campbell slipped inside and carefully pulled it closed behind him.

***

Brice leaned his back against the heavy front door and struggled to control his breathing. The last two or three hours had been strenuous, no...exhausting...and very painful. He hoped Lorenzo had not seen or heard him cross that last thirty feet as he rushed into the house. He carefully moved through the dark foyer to the window in time to watch the gardener casually pass. Then Brice entered his study and quietly closed the door behind him. He went to the sideboard and poured several ounces of Canadian whiskey from the decanter into a crystal tumbler. He took a generous swallow, then carried the glass to his desk and slumped into the chair.

Lorenzo could not see the window of the study from where he would be watering. Brice leaned forward and pulled the small chain to illuminate the desk lamp. He saw his injured wrist for the first time. Even though it had swollen to nearly twice its normal size, the visible irregular angle suggested it was broken. He touched his cheek where Mariano had hit him. Swollen also. How would he explain this to Leonora? She had been so faithful through all of his transgressions these past few years. Unaware of his deceit. How could he do this to her? What excuse could he have for tonight's injuries? That he had too much to drink and slipped in the garden when he went out to smoke? Possibly.

He stared at the painting of her that adorned the wall above the sideboard. "She deserves better," he spoke to himself, then downed the rest of the whiskey. Though he began to feel the numbing effect of the alcohol to his face, it did nothing to relieve the pain of his battered wrist. He found the small vial of opium he had hidden in his desk and took the smallest of sips of the revolting liquid. Just a few drops. Then, he crossed to the sideboard and refilled his glass before the opium took effect. He took a large swallow and set the glass on the table by the leather sofa, then laid down on it.

Brice did not know how much time had passed, but his wrist was less painful when he noticed the study brightening as dawn began to break. He rose, took another swallow of whiskey, and found his favorite pipe in his desk. Painstakingly filling it from the humidor with his right hand, he placed it between his teeth. Finding a couple of matches, he went outside to smoke.

* * *

The intruder lay watching and waiting for over two hours as Lorenzo watered the gardens. He felt he had missed his chance as he reassured himself, feeling the little .25 caliber automatic pistol in his pocket. With the first signs of light in the eastern sky, the gardener returned to his room, and the man watched and listened as Lorenzo closed his windows. He waited another twenty minutes and was preparing to stand and leave before it got any lighter out when the front door opened.

Brice Campbell stepped out and closed the door behind him, then clumsily lit his pipe with his right hand. He took a long draw from the pipe and awkwardly shuffled toward the side of the house. Away from the garage and the gardener. The stocky man stood as Campbell ambled away. He donned a thin pair of goatskin gloves, then carefully wiped his fingerprints from his little pistol. Just in case I should accidentally drop it in the scuffle, he thought to himself.

As Brice rounded the corner of the house, the man stalked up behind him. They were out of sight from the garage. Neither left the gravel walkway.

"Good morning, Brice," the man spoke calmly from some ten feet behind him.

"What are you doing here?" Campbell blurted out as he spun to face him.

The man did not reply. As he lunged toward his victim, Campbell fumbled to retrieve the revolver from his pocket. He dropped it as the stocky man tackled him.

"How convenient," the man snarled as Brice struggled beneath him.

The assailant did not let up. He held Campbell down as he scooped up the .32. In less than a second, the attacker cocked the revolver, held it to Campbell's temple, and pulled the trigger.

A LOOK AT BOOK TWO:
SHIFTING SAND

MURDER, LOVE, AND SACRIFICE IN THE NAME OF WESTERN JUSTICE.

In the heart of the Nevada desert, Sheriff Conor Armenta is thrust into a chilling mystery that begins with a grisly discovery: the fragmented remains of a young Moapa Indian found along a lonely stretch of railroad track. The absence of blood raises unsettling questions, hinting at a death more complex than it first appears.

As Conor delves deeper, a peculiar belt buckle becomes a pivotal clue, connecting disparate witnesses with conflicting tales that weave through the social fabric of Las Vegas. One witness claims intimate knowledge of the victim, revealing unexpected ties to Conor himself. Each revelation adds a layer of intrigue and blurs the lines between obsession, hatred, addiction, and love.

Following a trail fraught with desert perils and buried secrets, Conor relies on flashfloods and shifting sands to uncover forbidden secrets. And as the case builds toward a showdown challenging the very meaning of justice, he must navigate the blurred boundaries of guilt and innocence, grappling with the elusive truth of whether justice can ever truly be served.

AVAILABLE OCTOBER 2024

ABOUT THE AUTHOR

Jefferson Glass grew up near the Klamath Indian Reservation in the ranch country of southeastern Oregon. Influenced by the stories found in his grandfather's collection of Zane Grey novels, his young imagination went wild in these rural surroundings. At an early age, he often hiked with his dog over countless miles of public land that bordered his family's property. The only rule was to be home by suppertime. As a teenager, his wanderlust gave way to working the hayfields of a nearby ranch.

In 1981, Jefferson moved to central Wyoming where he began his writing career. He has written numerous articles on Western history for Annals of Wyoming, True West Magazine and WyoHistory.org. His non-fiction books, RESHAW: The Life and Times of John Baptiste Richard and Empire: The Pioneer Legacy of an American Ranch Family, won a Western Writers of America Spur Award and a Will Rogers Medallion Award respectively.

Jefferson began research in 2020 on his Conor Armenta Mystery series, set in 1930s Las Vegas. While exploring Clark

County, Nevada, and surrounding areas, he and his wife stumbled across Kanab, Utah, where they purchased a home and relocated. The magnificent view of The Grand Staircase-Escalante out their back door is certain to inspire years of future writing.

www.ingramcontent.com/pod-product-compliance
Lightning Source LLC
Chambersburg PA
CBHW011423010726
47494CB00011B/2477